The Imaginærium Engine

GREEN BOOK

The Imaginærium Engine

GREEN BOOK

by C. G. Wayne

Otter Track Press

Wetumpka, AL

Otter Track Press

Otter Track Press is a division of MRose Group, LLC. Wetumpka, Alabama. www.ottertrack.mrose.com

First Edition: April 2018

The characters portrayed in these stories are fictitious. Any resemblance to actual persons living or dead is coincidental.

Wayne, Clifford Gordon.

The Imaginærium Engine Green Book/ by C.G. Wayne—1st ed.

Summary: The beginning of a girl and her family's journey in discovering the truth about themselves and their responsibility in preventing the world from being swallowed by darkness.

ISBN: 978-0-9848229-6-6

[1. Fiction—Young Adult. 2. Fiction—Fantasy. 3. Imaginaerum Engine Green Book]

Acknowledgements

This book would not exist if it weren't for Abbey and Danielle. One Saturday, a couple of years ago, Abbey asked me if I had written anything that her parents would allow her to read. I told her that I had started work on something several years ago, and that might be ok. But it wasn't very far along. So, I began work.

Their silent expressions and wrinkled noses provided invaluable critical input. I hope the final version entertains them and you.

Thanks also to Marissa who identified in Saturday workshop the importance of establishing a coherent cosmology when writing about supernatural beings.

Dedication

For my mother, who wanted me to write something nice for a change…

For Bill McAnulty, my mentor who told me stories about growing up in west Texas…

For Hannah, my daughter, who heard the ancestor of this piece as a bedtime story…

And for Rainbow Warrior, my fearless friend.

Front Cover: *Defense of the Imaginærium Engine* by Theresa Wayne

Table of Contents

PROLOGUE I

PART I

1   ONE SATURDAY MORNING IN LATE OCTOBER...........3

2   MR. MUNROE 19

3   DINNER SERVICE 31

4   NIGHT TERRORS 43

5   HIDING IN A LIMESTONE GROTTO............................59

PART II

6   YOU'RE NOT SUPPOSED TO BE HERE! 73

7   VIVIENNE'S FESTIVAL 95

8   CRAZY TALK 119

9   FIRESTORM..127

10   CUP OF CHAMOMILE TEA.....................................137

11   VIEUX CARRIE...143

12   NO JOY...153

13   MRS. SMITH 167

14   THIS TIME TOMORROW.......................................203

15   EGGS BENEDICT...217

16 GET TO THE CARS!..231

17 THEY'RE PROBABLY DEMONS ANYWAY......................247

18 GRAINÉ'S SONG..265

19 HOWL..285

20 NO! THAT'S *MY* JOB!..293

PART III

21 DRAFTY OLD PLACE..299

22 KEEPER OF THE ENGINE..313

23 DARK AND TWISTED 327

24 WE LOOK LIKE A BUNCH OF GANGSTERS 353

25 THIS IS MAGNUS IGNE 361

26 THE ENGINE'S HEART...373

27 DON'T STOP FOR ANYTHING!.....................................387

EPILOGUE 391

NOTES FROM THE CHARACTERS 395

NOTES FROM THE AUTHOR 401

BIBLIOGRAPHY...405

BRIEF BIO OF THE AUTHOR... 407

Prologue

What I did this summer…

My name is Perry. I guess I'm a bad boy, bad in the mean sort of way. Sometimes I try to be nice like everybody wants you to be, but it's just not as much fun.

This summer, my sister and me went to visit my grandmother, at separate times of course. After the first time we went to visit, Grandmother said she couldn't take both of us at the same time anymore. We did that every year, except never together, which makes it boring.

My parents think we need to learn to love her I guess, but she isn't a lovable grandmother. That's my mother's mother. We just call her Grandmother.

My dad's mother is really cool. We call her Gran and she likes it. She lets us do lots of stuff, so naturally we don't get to spend as much time at her place.

Grandmother is strict and makes us do stuff that she says is for our own good. Sometimes, she says it's for our "edification," whatever that means. They say stuff like that to kids to justify almost anything not fun.

She's an old woman. White hair on her head like a mop, old clear plastic rimmed glasses on her nose, and she always wears this old dress like you see in pictures of old women in the country. Kind of long and saggy, almost touching the tops of her shoes, she looks like what you'd think an old woman ought to look like. And something else weird about her are the shoes she wears. She has these old black lace-up clodhoppers. Heels like black blocks of wood about two inches high. If it rained, she could walk across the parking lot and never get her feet wet.

During the mornings, Grandmother makes me go to the Vacation Bible School that they have at the Baptist church down the road from where she lives. I hate it. I'm always the outsider, so every day I just count the minutes until I can get out of there. And every year, I make Mom promise that if I go down there they won't send me. And every year they promise, and every year I have to go.

It's a big con. Don't know why I believe them every year. How stupid is that.

Grandmother lives in an ancient Airstream travel trailer and drives this beat up old Chevy pickup truck. The truck is pretty cool. It's got a two-tone paint job, faded gold and white color, only rusting. And it has a big old 454 cubic inch motor with dual exhaust that makes a lot of noise. The interior is shot, pretty ratted out, except that works for that kind of truck.

It's the kind of truck you could drive through a wall and not worry about messing up 'cause it was already messed up. Like it had already been driven through a wall once or twice before.

Her trailer is dented in a few places, and instead of shiny metal like other Airstreams I've seen it's almost gray. One time I asked her why she didn't live in a normal house like everybody else. She just stared at me from behind those glasses of hers and made me wish I'd never said anything.

Then she said she wanted to be able to take off and go anywhere, anytime if she needed to.

That was weird 'cause who needs to do something like that? Unless you're trying to escape from a hurricane or something bad like that, but they don't have hurricanes in Austin that I know of, so it didn't make any sense.

Another thing about Grandmother was she had this long scar on her throat like she had been cut. Mom said it was from an operation she had when she was young, only nobody could say what it was an operation *for*.

I didn't like her much even if I did have to go visit for a week every summer.

Her trailer isn't very large and when I'm there I have to sleep on the sofa. It isn't that bad really, but I didn't like it. If I was at Gran's house, I'd be sleeping in a real bed.

In the room where Grandmother sleeps, she has this wooden box that she keeps locked. My sister and me have tried to open it every year we visit when Grandmother isn't around, but no luck until this year. For some reason, I was able to open it. I guess all the practice I did finally paid off. I slipped my lock-pick back into its case.

Normally we'd never have been too interested in her things except she made a big deal about us never opening that box. Yeah, right. Like that was going to make us *not* want to see what was inside.

This year though, while she had gone over to the little QuickShop store for some smokes, I was able to open it. She always locked her bedroom door, only it was one of those cheap locks and my sister and me figured out how to open it that first year we stayed there. We didn't even have good tools back then.

Grandmother had a weird room even for being in a trailer. It had more stuff in there than you'd think just by looking at it from the outside. She even had a real full-sized bed in there.

She had these carved sculptures, a glass box with a kind of necklace in it, and a big cabinet in there. The cabinet's where she kept some old clothes. Really crazy looking things like you would wear at Mardi Gras or even Halloween.

I never messed with the necklace. Hey, it was a necklace! One time my sister said she tried it on, but it felt weird, so she took it off and never touched it after that.

The thing that we were after was always the box. I guess because it was locked, and that first year when we were back there with her and asked about it, she said not to ever open it. Naturally, from that point on we tried every year. During the year, we practiced opening locks so we could try again the next next time we went.

So, there I was, with the latch lifted and the lid swung open expecting to see something either really great, like handfuls of diamonds, or really bad, like a dried head or something wicked. Instead it was just some books.

I was really disappointed.

Some of the books were really old, like *Princess of Mars* and *The Gods of Mars*. They had some really wild covers, except the paper crumbled when you touched it, so I didn't mess with those. Wasn't any point really, 'cause you couldn't read them.

There was another book in there that was old, but at least it didn't crumble when you touched it. It had a plain green leather cover. The crazy part was that it was written out by hand. But the worst was, about that time, I felt a hand on my shoulder.

Grandmother was standing behind me.

"I see you finally figured out how to open this lock too."

Busted. I didn't know what to say. All I could do was say, "Yes, Ma'am." We always had to say Ma'am when we talked to her 'cause those were her rules.

"Do you know what this is?" She lifted the big book out of its place in the box.

"A book?"

"Don't be smart with me, boy." She always called me boy when she was angry. Which was usually most of the time she was talking to me.

"No, Ma'am."

"It's the story of how all of this," she motioned through the air around us, "came to be."

"Yes, Ma'am."

She laughed. I had never heard her laugh or anything before, so it scared me. I guess I looked it 'cause she said, "It's alright. If you can open the lock, then you are ready to read the book."

She must have thought the book was what scared me instead of her laughing. It was a weird kind of laugh, kind of squeaky like a rusty lid opening.

"Is this about how you got that scar?"

She smiled. Another first. "That's just a small part of it."

"What are these other books in here?"

"Just some old books someone used to read a long time ago."

"Are they any good?"

"He liked them, but I've never read them."

"They're too old to read now. The paper is just crumbling away."

"Sad isn't it. Something once new and beautiful can one day disintegrate at the touch of a finger. They turn to dust when you try to reach it. You know, often that's how things turn out."

"Yes, Ma'am." I said that 'cause I didn't know what else to say. I don't think she was really talking to me though.

"Your sister was able to open the box this year too."

"What?"

She laughed again. "I made her promise not to tell you. It's something you had to do on your own, not because someone coached you. And you can't read the book unless you have opened the box."

"So, opening the lock was a test."

"All of life is a test, boy. But, yes, it was."

"I don't understand. Why did you tell us not to ever open the box?"

"You wouldn't have tried so hard. Would you? You've been working on this lock for four years. I have to compliment you and your sister on not damaging the lock or the wood."

"Thank you. I think."

"So, now that you've opened the box and have the book, what are you going to do?"

I said, "I don't know. I didn't know what was in it before."

She started to return the book to the box, except I reached out and grabbed her arm.

"Can I read it?"

"If you'd like. It's a bit long. I don't think you'll finish it tonight, but you can get a start and next time you visit

you can read the rest. Provided you can still unlock
the box."

I'd forgotten that I was leaving first thing in the
morning. There was an early flight back to New York that
I was supposed to be on. In fact, I had begged Mom to be
on the earliest flight possible out of Austin. I felt like
kicking myself, if that was physically possible.

"One thing you must know before you begin the read.
Knowing what is in the book places you in danger.
However, it's hard to know with these things to what extent
you might *be* in danger. Knowledge always comes with an
obligation and a risk. You should be aware there is a risk
before you start."

I wasn't so sure I wanted to know what was in it after
she said that. Or she could have been tricking me again,
like telling me not to ever open the box so that I would. I
wasn't sure.

But my sister was already reading it and I wasn't going
to be left behind.

That night I read as much as I could…

GREEN BOOK

Part I

How it began...

many years ago, a boy and a girl lived in a small town in West Texas...

1   One Saturday morning in late October...

Jamison's mother called out, "Jamison. I need for you and Maggie to change the sheets on the bed in room 12. We have guests arriving today."

Jamison sighed and closed his book. "Yes, Ma'am." He had just started Chapter 3 in *The Gods of Mars*. John Carter and Tars Tarkas were trapped in a chamber in the depths of the Golden Cliffs expecting certain death. His mother didn't approve of John Carter, so he put the book back in the drawer of his dresser, slammed the door to their apartment, and stomped down the hall to the stairs.

"I heard that," his mother shouted from the front desk.

"Yes, Ma'am. Sorry." He had been waiting two days to get back to the book. He only got the chance to read it when Mother was working at the front desk.

He wanted to be like John Carter, strong, powerful, and respected by all who saw him. Instead, he was just the tall skinny red headed kid covered in freckles that everyone in school made fun of - he hated school. Next year he would be 16, and, as soon as he could, he was going to quit.

Jamison shouted, "Maggie, get the sheets," and climbed the stairs to room 12.

Maggie's real name was Lorenda Wells, but her mother had always called her Maggie. And so, did everyone else in town. No one really knew why and they never thought of her as Lorenda. Not even her. Lorenda had been her great-grandmother's name.

Maggie had jet-black hair and ice blue eyes. Jamison told everyone that she didn't look like a Maggie, only it didn't change anything. Everyone still called her Maggie, so last year he finally stopped complaining.

No one ever called Jamison by a nickname even though he wanted one. A good one though like Spike or Cowboy. Not a bad one like Stick or Freckle. Sometimes Maggie called him those, but only to tease him.

Once, when he asked his parents if he could have a nickname, his dad said, "Why? Jamison is a *good* name. That's your great uncle's name. *He* never had a nickname. Besides, you can't give yourself a nickname. Somebody else has to do that."

But everyone thought of Jamison as Jamison and never called him anything else. At least anything that he liked.

By the time Maggie arrived with the sheets, Jamison had already stripped the bed down to the mattress and was standing at the window watching the street below.

Fort Richards, the town where they lived, was old, and built at its center in two-story limestone block buildings was the town's square. In the center of the square was the courthouse. It looked like a castle and had a tower with a clock in it. The clock had four faces facing the compass points of north, south, east, and west. You could see the clock from anywhere in town. And, from the room below the clock works, you could see everything for miles around. Sometimes it seemed like you could see as far as the Davis Mountains. A faint blue smudge on the horizon southwest of town, however that was just imagination. No one could really see that far.

Every day, the clock's bell struck on the hour. It wasn't like the bells at the church. The courthouse bell made a single deep sound when it rang, while the church had three bells that would ring in high, middle, and low tones. The church bells rang during holidays, on Sunday morning when it was time to start church, when church was over, and in the evenings at sunset. They rang when someone in town died. The courthouse bell also rang when there was a tornado or a fire or if something unusual happened.

Jamison let the curtain drop back across the window glass. "I hate changing sheets."

Maggie tossed a stack of folded sheets and pillowcases at him. "Me too." He caught them clumsily.

"Do you ever wonder what Dad is doing? I bet he's not changing sheets."

She laughed. "I don't think he ever has to do that."

"Yeah. I wonder where he is now."

"Dunno. Let's get finished, so I can get back downstairs. I have to finish folding clothes."

Saturday was chore day. They had a list of things to do that seemed endless.

"Sure. I guess I'll start cleaning the floors." He grabbed a corner of the sheet and tucked it under the mattress.

They lived in an apartment built onto the back of an old hotel located on the square. Their mother, Judith, ran the hotel for their grandparents.

She was tall and thin with long red blond hair that she wore in a braid coiled into a bun and had a scattering of freckles across her nose. When she smiled, she had dimples in her cheeks, and she laughed so lightly that Maggie would tell her she sounded more like a bird singing than anything.

Judith would always tell Maggie, "You're just teasing me. I laugh like anybody else." And Maggie always replied that she was certain she was not like anybody else.

After they moved into the apartment, their father was gone most of the time. He became a roughneck and travelled around north Texas working on drilling rigs. He was stocky like a south Texas live oak. That's how their mother described him, with fire red hair and beard. Lately he had been working on rigs in north Oklahoma and seldom came home. When he was able to come home, they could hear his voice booming out their names as he climbed out of his truck. It seemed like he enjoyed making a lot of noise. He wore heavy boots and would come stomping in the front door of the hotel, rattling the windows and china when he walked. Their mother didn't like that and would immediately tell him to, "Hush that stomping. This is not the oil patch."

And he would get quiet.

But lately, he didn't come home often, so that was just something that she remembered from the first few years when he went to work on the rigs.

That all happened after one morning, when they were ten and twelve, and their dad had called them into the kitchen of their real home. He told them that he had lost his shop and the bank was going to take their house. "Just like they did to the Millers last year."

They all remembered that. When the Miller's lost their house, Dad had told them, "That's why they're calling it a Depression. Thousands of people are out of work, so we're better off than most."

When she heard her Dad say they were losing their home too, Maggie didn't believe they were better off than most people. She remembered what happened to the Millers.

After the bank took the Millers' house, they had gotten in their car and driven west, to Abilene or maybe Lubbock. No one ever knew what had happened to them. The Millers were just gone and no one knew where.

When her dad said they were going to lose their house, Maggie was terrified. She was certain it was going to be a disaster and that they would disappear just like the Millers.

But Dad told them, "Grams and Old Pa are going to let us live at the hotel while your momma runs it for them. Grams wants to move to Fort Worth, so that works out fine for everyone. Not many people come through town now, so it won't be that bad. And we'll have a place to live until things get better."

They had said, "Yes, sir," only they didn't understand what it meant, to live somewhere else, in a place that wasn't their home.

That's when he told them, "I got on with a crew drilling oil wells for a company out in Lubbock."

They just stood there not saying anything. They heard the words, but it didn't mean anything to them. They didn't know anything about drilling oil wells.

He told them, "I was lucky. A friend got me hired on. While I'm gone, you have to help your mom. Can you do that?"

But it wasn't really a question.

They said, "Yes, sir" and looked around the kitchen wondering what was going to happen to all of their things.

Within the week, they moved to the hotel, then the bank auctioned their house with almost all of their things, and Dad was gone to Lubbock.

Now Jamison was 15 and Maggie was 13. Their dad still worked on drilling rigs and their mother still took care of the hotel.

***

In the early afternoon, a Greyhound bus from Fort Worth stopped at what had been the old stage depot. The October air had suddenly changed overnight the way it does in West Texas, from burning summer to hints of cold. High above their heads, a high-speed wind tore the clouds into wisps of mare's tails. It carried them east, past Fort Worth and the Trinity River toward the Mississippi. The light in the air had also changed, from white summer glare into soft gold autumn hues. It was a day when everything began to change.

A lady and her young son stepped off of the bus. She wore a long black dress with a veil and a wide brimmed black hat. Long black gloves covered her hands. Beneath the veil, large black frame and lensed sunglasses covered her eyes.

The boy was dressed in a fancy black suit that had short pants with matching dress shoes that were polished until they looked like black glass. He wore black-framed sunglasses like his mother. His hair was jet black and combed slick against his skull. His skin was white marble.

They stood on the sidewalk in the shadow of the bus, looking around them, waiting for the driver to unload their bags.

The bus driver placed two small suitcases on the sidewalk, tipped his cap to them, stepped back up into the bus, and pulled back out on the road that would take him up to Lubbock.

The lady and her son picked up their suitcases and walked slowly down the street to the hotel.

The hotel was an old two-story limestone block building that Jamison and Maggie's great-grandfather built on the city square when he was young. It had a front porch and a gloomy central hall that ran from the front to the back with a staircase that went up to the second floor where the rooms for guests were located.

The apartment where Jamison and Maggie lived with their mother was only three small rooms built onto the back of the hotel. Years ago, before Maggie was born, their grandfather had added it onto the hotel for him and their grandmother to live in. Now it was their apartment. It was small but, with the hotel for the rest of their house, it didn't seem that bad.

Jamison and Maggie had finished their chores and were sitting in the lobby playing Crazy Eights when the woman and her son opened the front door and quietly stepped inside.

Maggie nudged Jamison. "Look," she whispered.

"I know. I see them."

No one in town dressed like that. No one they knew even looked like that.

"Who do you think they are?"

"Must be the guests."

"Scary. They look like vampires."

"Yeah. Or dead people."

The mother and her son walked up to the front desk.

Mrs. Wells, Jamison and Maggie's mother, smiled and said, "Welcome to the Fort Richards Hotel. How was your trip?" She slid the register across the counter to the woman so that she could sign her name.

"Uneventful, however it was long." The woman signed the guest register, *Mrs. Penelope Johnson and son, Hiram L. Johnson, New Orleans, LA.* "I'm quite tired. I believe we'll just go up to our room and lie down for a while."

"Of course."

"What time is dinner?"

"That will be 6. Breakfast is served at 8 and of course lunch is noon. I can send one of the children up to fetch you for supper if you want."

"That's quite alright. We will be down at 6." She paused a moment, "But, if we are late, please send one of them to fetch us."

"Certainly. How long do you plan on being with us, Mrs. Johnson?"

"We haven't decided. Possibly a week. We're waiting for my daughter."

"I see. Well, if there's anything I can do while you're here, just let me know."

"I appreciate that. For now, I just need to rest a bit." Mrs. Johnson smiled politely and bent to pick up her suitcase.

"Here's your key. It's room 12. Do you need help with your bags?"

"Oh, no." They held their suitcases close. "We're quite alright. They aren't heavy at all."

"Alright then. Maggie will show you to your room." Mrs. Wells motioned for Maggie to come up to the desk.

Maggie placed her cards on the table, walked across the room to the two strangers, said "If you'll follow me…," and then set off down the dark hall to the stairs.

During the day, the only light that made it into the hall came in from the front and rear doors. The doors had glass panels in them that had etched scenes of pine trees and a single mountain peak. At night, her mother would turn on a couple of sconces mounted along the wall, but they only provided dim light.

"The hallway's always gloomy," she told them.

When they entered the hall, she heard the woman exhale a long slow breath as if she had suddenly relaxed. Maggie turned for a second to look at her. The boy flashed a wide grin at Maggie that made the hairs on her arms stand and goosebumps crawl across her skin. Maggie quickly turned around and climbed the stairs to the second floor where room 12 was located.

She opened a door. "This is it. Do you need anything before I go? There's a bathroom in here with fresh towels and washcloths. Over here is a closet with some blankets in case you need them. It might get cold tonight."

The boy, suitcase still in hand, had walked to the window and was staring across the street in the direction of the old courthouse. The woman placed her suitcase on the bed and waited for Maggie to leave.

The boy looked at Maggie. He still wore his dark glasses. "We noticed the old buildings on the way into town. Do you know anything about them?"

The strange woman interrupted, "Oh, she doesn't have time to talk about that. I'm sure, do you dear. You probably have a number of other errands to perform. Besides that, I would really like to rest a bit before dinner. If you don't mind. And please, I've changed my mind, do come get us when dinner is served."

"Yes, Ma'am." She realized as she left the room that both of them stared at her without moving, still wearing their dark glasses, and the woman was still wearing the veil and wide brimmed hat. Like black tarantulas waiting for a meal. She hurried down the stairs to the lobby.

"Did you get them situated?" Her mother was excited to have guests. Few people came through town anymore and even fewer stayed at the hotel. At night, she talked about it sometimes during supper.

"Yes, Ma'am."

Paying guests for a week. Mrs. Wells smiled at the thought of that. Sometimes they had cattle buyers who came through on the way to Amarillo in one direction or Fort Worth in the other. Other times they might have ranch foremen coming through on their way between jobs. The foremen only stayed the night before moving on in the morning, early morning. The cattle buyers and foremen ate breakfast early, so they could get on their way to wherever it was that they had business.

That meant work in the kitchen before dawn getting the food cooked and the tables set. The kitchen had to open at first light for them.

However, the woman and her son were different guests. They would eat at times when people from the city ate. No pre-dawn cooking or setting tables tomorrow. It would be life like normal people. Or close to it. Mrs. Wells chuckled. It was going to be the best week they'd had in a long time.

Jamison and Maggie sat quietly in the lobby, holding their cards, but no longer playing. Maggie had told him how the woman and her son watched her without moving, shrouded in black, and wearing their creepy black sunglasses.

That killed any feeling or thought of having fun they might have had.

When Maggie got back from showing them to the room, Mother had told them, "Her name is Mrs. Johnson and her son's name is Hiram. Mrs. Johnson is waiting for her daughter, so I imagine that after she gets here they will continue their travels. She said it could be a week. I don't know any more than that."

The grandfather clock in the corner filled the room with its tick-tocking. Before this afternoon, Jamison had never thought much about the sound of it. Now, after hearing Maggie's description of the freaky guests, to him the sound was that of the pendulum in Poe's *The Pit and the Pendulum*. Poe was one of his favorite writers. Next to Edgar Rice Burroughs. For some reason, his mother hated Poe.

"Mother," Jamison called across the lobby. "All of the chores are done. Can we go outside before we have to get supper ready?"

"As long as you're back in time to help."

"Yes, Ma'am. Maggie, let's go over to the courthouse while we still have a chance."

They ran from the hotel before their mother had time to change her mind.

2   Mr. Munroe

"Look, it's that creepy kid from the hotel."

Maggie had been watching the streets below from a window in the clock tower room. That's what she did every time they went up to the tower room. She saw the boy when he stepped out of the hotel and into the town square.

"He's writing in a notebook. Wonder why he's doing that."

Jamison walked over to the window and looked down at the boy. "Maybe he's some kind of history nut."

"He asked me if I knew about the buildings in town."

"Look, he's walking this way." Jamison sounded surprised.

"Do you think he sees us?"

Jamison scoffed, "No, we're too far up. He can't see where we are."

"But he's looking up."

"He's probably looking at the clock. It's about the only thing in town that'd be interesting to somebody from the city."

"Maybe he's checking the time."

"Could be. Look he's stopped. See, he's just looking at the clock."

"I think he knows we're here. He's grinning at us just like he did in the room." It made the hairs on her arms stand and goosebumps crawl across her skin just like back at the hotel.

"Now that's scary." Jamison took a step back from the window.

Maggie whispered, "We should tell Mom."

"She wouldn't understand. Besides, I don't know what we could tell her. And maybe he doesn't know we're up here."

"I hope you're right." Maggie stood by the window with her arms crossed. "But I don't think so."

Jamison pointed, "He's going back. He's probably just out exploring while his mother takes a nap. You said she was tired."

"Yeah. She said she wanted to rest before supper."

"There you go. That's what it is. He was exploring, saw the clock tower, and came over here to investigate."

Maggie dragged one of the chairs over to the window and sat in it while she watched the boy until he was under the awning and out of sight. "He's gone back to the hotel."

"See, I bet he was just out looking around and wanted to get a closer look at the clock."

"I wonder why he didn't come over here. I would have. If I had taken the trouble to walk all the way over here from the hotel, I'd take a closer look at it." She pushed the window open.

In the afternoons, whenever they had the chance, usually after chores and before schoolwork, they would go to the old courthouse in the town square and, when no one was looking, sneak up the stairway to the observation room below the clock works. It had tall windows set in all four walls and, from there they could look out over what seemed like the entire world.

Their friends from school thought the tower was scary, haunted, so they never came with them. They said the same things about their hotel. That it had ghosts.

They wouldn't come over to the hotel after dark. Maggie teased them about being afraid of ghosts, although it didn't change anything. So she stopped teasing them after a while.

Besides it was more fun when it was just her and Jamison anyway.

The tower room was high above the tops of the surrounding buildings and a wind always seemed to blow from some direction. In winter, it was freezing and the wind would storm out of the north from Oklahoma. Even with the windows closed, the cold found its way through the smallest crack. In summer, the wind was a southern blast of heat up from the Chihuahuan Desert that could transform it into a furnace.

They went up to the tower room every day unless something stopped them. Today was a good day and the air was velvet across her skin.

Most days in the tower room, they would look out of the windows that faced west and hunt for signs of soaring hawks and buzzards or imagine Kiowa riding out on the plains to the west of town.

With the creepy kid wandering around their town, today was different.

"How're you chaps today?" It was Mr. Munroe.

He never called them children or kids, always chaps. They didn't know what it meant, but it was always better than being called a kid or a child.

"Hi, Mr. Munroe."

He was a gentle old giant and moved slowly around the building.

When they first met him, he told them he'd been a cowboy before he took on the job at the courthouse.

"I did my cowboying back when I was a young man. Until I couldn't ride out all day long. That's when me and Mrs. Munroe had to move into town. Once I left working for the cattle company, we had to get our own place. Took this here job. They said I was the custodian for the new courthouse, but really, all that means is I'm the handyman and janitor. I clean floors and windows, change burned out light bulbs, repair broken things, and keep the clock running."

And that was what they believed. They couldn't imagine him ever doing anything in a hurry. It just wasn't his way.

Mr. Munroe was the one who showed them the secret door to the stairs that led up to the clock tower. Before he showed them, he made them promise on their ancestors' graves not to tell anyone about the door or that there was a room up there.

He said, "Most folks don't think about things on their own. If they don't get an idea about something, then they'd never think to look for it. That's how the door and room's stayed secret all these years."

C. G. Wayne

He told them that they were the only two people in the entire town he'd ever shown the room to. They liked that. It confirmed that they were special in some way.

One time, Jamison almost blabbed to their friends that he knew about a secret room and they didn't, but Maggie had been able to stomp on his foot before he did, so the secret was saved. He was embarrassed after that and promised her not to tell anybody even if they were taunting him about being skinny and stupid.

Mr. Munroe gave him a dark look that afternoon when they went up to the tower, even though he never said a word to them about it. He didn't need to. Jamison's blood ran cold when he saw Mr. Munroe's face and he never slipped up again after that.

One afternoon when they were looking out to the west of town, Mr. Munroe told them, "The builder of this courthouse was a man named William P Williams. When Texas created the county, Mr. Williams won the contract to build the courthouse. He was from old England and loved castles and wind. So he built it like a small version of a castle near the town where he grew up. Like all magic castles, Mr. Williams added its share of secret passages and secret rooms. The secret passage that leads to the clock tower stairs is only one of 'em."

Mr. Munroe wouldn't tell them where the others were. When they asked him, he always said, "Someday. Maybe."

The passage to the tower stairs was hidden behind a secret door built into a wall in the storage room. The door opened by pushing a decorative stone set at the bottom of the wall. The stone was marked with the design of a horse. Other stones were marked with other animal designs, so you had to know it was the one with the horse.

The door itself was narrow, barely wide enough for Mr. Munroe to fit through when he turned sideways. Sometimes he joked, "I'll have to quit this job if I eat too much barbeque." Somehow, though, he always seemed to be able to go through the narrow door.

"So, what are you chaps up to today?" He eased himself down into one of the chairs that they had put in the room. They were old kitchen chairs from their real house and every time he sat in them, they creaked and Maggie waited for them to collapse.

They never did.

Maggie smiled and told him, "Nothing much. There's a creepy kid and his mom who checked in at the hotel this afternoon." She pointed down at the corner where the boy had stood. "He was standing down there a little while ago looking at the clock tower."

"You don't say. Creepy in what way?"

"He wears black clothes and glasses all the time. Even indoors. And he has a scary grin when he smiles at you."

"Scary, huh."

"Yes, sir. You can see all of his teeth when he grins. And he has perfect white teeth. His mother is creepy too. They look like vampires, only they don't have fangs for teeth."

Mr. Munroe walked over to the window and looked down at the corner where she had pointed.

"Let me guess. She's dressed all in black too and wears dark glasses."

Maggie whirled around and stared at him. "How'd you know?"

"Just guessed." He rubbed the stubble on his chin. Mr. Munroe didn't have a beard, although he always looked like he hadn't shaved.

"Oh." She was disappointed. "I was hoping you knew who they were."

Mr. Munroe looked at Jamison. "What'd you think of them strangers, young man?"

"Maggie's right. They're real creepy, 'cept I didn't see them up close like she did."

"How close up was that?"

"She had to show them to their room."

"You got a good look at them then. Tell me more about what you saw."

So, she told Mr. Munroe about taking them to the room, their holding their suitcases and not taking off their dark glasses even in the dark hall. And he listened.

That's another thing they liked about him. He listened.

"Well, I got to say, you chaps have seen some interesting folks today." He walked over to the window, clasped his giant hands behind him and looked down at the street where the boy had been. "Real interesting."

None of them said anything for several minutes. The sun was dropping closer to the horizon.

Mr. Munroe told them, "Going to be a big moon tonight, but not a full moon, yet. We got a few days before that, only no clouds tonight and it'll be bright."

Mr. Munroe's voice was soft. He wasn't a loud talker anyway, and it seemed to Jamison and Maggie that he was talking more to himself than to them.

"Yes, sir."

"You children should be sure and stay in tonight. When I was a chap, my dad used to call this a killing moon. Predators are out and about when it's bright like it's going to be tonight. Best to be inside where it's safe. OK?"

"Yes, sir." That was the first time he ever called them children.

"Y'all ought to be getting on back to the hotel. It's almost 4. Your mom will be wanting you to help her get things ready for supper."

"Yes, sir."

"I got to start locking up for the day, anyway. Miz Monroe will have six fits if I'm late getting home. She takes it serious if I'm late for supper."

Any other day and they would have laughed thinking about her getting mad at Mr. Munroe. She was as tiny as Mr. Munroe was large.

Maggie always imagined her as an elf, slender and agile. She wore her hair pulled over her ears and fastened in a tight bun at the back of her head, so it was easy to pretend that she was an elf. At least Maggie didn't know for sure that Mrs. Monroe's ears weren't pointed.

The Munroe's were an odd pair. They didn't have any children that Maggie knew of, which was different from everyone else she knew in town. When they walked in town together, they weren't like anyone else either and always seemed a bit alone. Jamison stepped away from the window. "You know something about those people at the hotel that you aren't telling us."

"No." Mr. Munroe rubbed his whiskery cheek. "No. I don't know anything about those folks that you didn't tell me, but they sound pretty strange to *me*. Anyway, you chaps ought to head on back home now. I got to get things locked up."

They looked at each other. He never started locking up at 4. But they said, "Yes, sir," anyway, took one last look through the tower windows at the western sky, and hurried back to the hotel.

3   Dinner Service

Jamison and Maggie slipped into the kitchen just as their mother was turning around.

"Caught you. It's about time you got here. I was getting worried I was going to have to get all this supper done and served by myself."

"We were just at the courthouse."

"I knew where you were, although that was cutting it close. It'll take a couple of hours to get things set. And, we have guests tonight. Hotel guests."

"Yes, Ma'am."

"I have the roast ready to go in the oven. I need Maggie to finish that up and Jamison I need for you to go in the dining room and make sure the tables are set and things are straightened up in there. Once you got that done, come on back in here and help Maggie get the food ready to serve. I've got to get back to the front desk."

"Yes, Ma'am," they said in unison.

"Maggie, the roast needs to cook for an hour. After it's done, it needs to come out and rest for 15 minutes before we serve it. Timing is everything. Set your timers, so you'll know."

Maggie and Jamison smiled at each other. Every evening before preparing supper, their mother told them the same thing, "Timing is everything."

"Then there are the potatoes, beans, and greens. You need to start those cooking in an hour. Don't want to cook those into mush. I have them already in the pots. The bread is already made."

"I know, Momma." Maggie tapped her foot in subtle annoyance.

"Of course, you do." Her mother smiled at her and cupped the palm of her hand to Maggie's cheek. "Yes, you do. I'm just going down the list of things for tonight. You're so grownup now. Call me if you need me. Any questions?"

Maggie and Jamison looked at each other and said, "No, Ma'am."

With that, Mrs. Wells quickly left the kitchen to return to the front desk.

Jamison sighed in relief, "That was close."

Maggie shrugged, "At least she didn't seem to be angry."

"Yeah. I'm glad we weren't any later getting here. I got to go get the dining room ready."

Jamison entered the dining room through a pair of swinging doors that separated it from the kitchen. The dining room was a long narrow room with six small round tables and matching chairs.

Their mother had hung paintings on the walls to make it look more like their home. Paintings of mountains and horses running on the prairie. She painted them herself.

By the wall, between two windows, was a mahogany sideboard with marble top and ornate carvings of forests, hunters, hounds, and stags leaping from riverbanks into space. His mother had it moved from their house before the bank could take it.

Jamison thought he remembered grabbing the vines carved into its edges and pulling up with those when he was learning to walk.

Today he opened its intricate doors and removed a stack of plates.

There were several old people in town that ate supper at the hotel and tonight there would be two guests. After he set the plates, he took the napkins from a drawer and neatly placed them by each plate. From the next drawer he removed the silverware and correctly arranged the forks, knives, and spoons on each napkin.

That was his job each evening and he did it without thinking about the sequence of steps or the order of items. When the food was ready to be served, he would place the serving bowls and plates of vegetables and meat on the sideboard's marble top.

In the kitchen, Maggie stood at the oven a moment before she crossed the room to her mother's pantry. She rummaged through the bundles and jars of herbs before pulling down three cloves of garlic and several anise basil leaves. Mrs. Wells had just picked the basil that morning, so it was fresh and pungent.

Her mother kept a small hothouse at the back of the hotel where she grew her herbs.

"Fresh is best," was what Mother always told them when she brought in a cluster of fresh picked herbs.

Before she left the pantry, Maggie reached down and picked up several clusters of beetroots. Three reds and three yellows, she liked the yellow just because they were different. Everyone expected beets to be red and the yellow contrast was nice. It just seemed like they were needed with the meal. She wasn't sure why.

Quickly Maggie peeled the garlic, topped and quartered the beetroots, opened the oven door, slid out the pan containing the roast, dropped the beet quarters around the edges of the roast, cut three slits in the meat, wrapped the cloves in the basil leaves, and then pressed the small bundles of herbs into the cuts.

Satisfied, she smiled, returned the pan to the oven, set the timer for one hour, and closed the door. After a few minutes, the faint aroma of herbs began to spread from the oven.

***

When the timer went off, Maggie took the roast out of the oven and set it on the counter to cool. It would need to rest before it was sliced.

Time to start the pies and vegetables cooking.

After several minutes had passed, Maggie picked up a large wooden spoon, went to each pot on the stove, and gently stirred the beans and then the greens. The potatoes were covered in their pot, so she peeked at them. They were ok. She gave them a turn anyway just to be safe. Everything was cooking and would be ready on time.

At 5:30, Jamison and Mother came back to the kitchen to plan the dinner service. Every night this was the routine.

"We have the Weston's and the Wagner's tonight as well as our two guests. Might be a couple of others arriving later. The Montour's always seem to straggle in about thirty minutes after we start serving." Mrs. Wells paused in mid breath. "What's that smell?"

"What smell?" Maggie tried to sound innocent.

"Smells like garlic and basil. Did you add beetroots as well?"

Maggie blushed. She hadn't thought out what to say when her mother commented about the change in the roast. So, she said, "Yes, Ma'am."

Her mother thought a moment. "It smells good but ask next time before you start making changes in the food. I just hope everyone likes it. The Montour's aren't very adventurous in what they eat. Well, we will just see how it goes, won't we. Might do to have some ham ready in case they prefer something they're used to eating.

"Anyway," she said as if brushing that to the back of her mind, "Maggie, put the greens in that big blue serving bowl. Jamison, you go ahead and take the bread and the ice tea out to the sideboard. Be sure to ask if anyone wants water to drink.

"After he has that set out, Maggie, put the beans in the red serving bowl. I think that will look nice together. The red bowl and the blue bowl.

"Hand me that knife, Maggie, and I'll slice this roast.

"Wait a minute, Jamison. Before you put the food on the sideboard, take that ham out of the locker, and place it on the table here, so we can have it ready in case we need it."

Dinner service always began a bit frantic while they placed the food in the dining room. As soon as Jamison had the main dishes in place on the sideboard, Mrs. Wells returned to the dining room to welcome guests.

Each evening that was the time when Maggie could relax. The food was served, the guests were dining, and the only thing left that she would have to do was wash the dishes, which she actually didn't mind.

While she was rinsing and drying the dishes, she could let her mind wander far away from the hotel and the town, off to exotic places that only she could imagine.

Tonight, though, after changing the recipe of the roast, she was nervous. Jamison was in the dining room, as usual, filling empty glasses with tea and water, getting fresh napkins, whatever the guests needed.

Maggie was in the kitchen wondering what the creepy woman and her son were doing.

She slipped over to the swinging doors that opened into the dining room and peeked inside to see what was happening. She gasped. Her mother was sitting at the table with the hotel guests, the strange woman and the creepy kid, talking and smiling as if they were friends.

Her mother never sat with guests at dinner. That was one of her rules.

Jamison was standing silently by the sideboard in his usual spot.

Maggie watched her mother expecting to see her move back to her own table at the front of the room. She didn't. Instead, she turned to the swinging doors where Maggie was standing and called, "Maggie, come out here for a minute. Mrs. Johnson would like to thank you for the dinner."

Maggie didn't move. She was riveted to the floor behind the swinging doors.

"Maggie," her mother called again. "Come out here for a minute, please."

Maggie slowly pushed the door open and walked across the room to the table.

"Here she is." Her mother's voice was cheerful. The creepy woman and her son stared at her with their freaky black glasses.

The woman said, "That was a wonderful roast, dear. Just the right amount of garlic and basil. So often people over season with garlic, however you found a nice balance. I also have to compliment you on the use of beet roots in the dish. The yellow beets were a pleasant addition. So many people don't realize that beets don't have to be just the red variety. A very nice combination. I never expected to have something so fine tonight. It was as good as any that I've had."

Maggie stared at the floor, "Thank you, but my momma prepared it."

"She's just being modest," her mother said. "Maggie has a gift."

Mrs. Johnson gave her a tight-lipped smile. "I would have to agree. The dinner was quite spectacular. Thank you, again dear for such a wonderful meal."

Her son said nothing and never took his gaze off her. She couldn't see his eyes behind the dark glasses, even though she imagined they were staring at her.

Maggie murmured, "You're welcome," and looked at her mother. Mrs. Wells smiled at her with eyes that seemed to sparkle. That was confusing. Surely, her mother could see how bizarre these people were. She glanced at Jamison who was standing by the sideboard. He was watching the tables like he always did. *Doesn't seem to be too worried about the freaky people.* "I need to go get the pies out of the oven."

"Pies?" Mrs. Johnson sounded surprised. "What kind?"

Maggie told her, "Peach, apple, and cherry."

"Sounds wonderful," said Mrs. Johnson.

Mrs. Wells leaned forward slightly in her chair. "And ice cream if you would like that too. We have vanilla and chocolate. It's absolutely divine. Made each afternoon by a local epicurean from the choicest ingredients. I believe you will find it most enjoyable."

Immediately, Mrs. Johnson said, "The apple pie sounds absolutely enchanting to me. And with a small scoop of the vanilla ice cream on the side."

Her son said that he wanted a slice of cherry pie with lots of chocolate ice cream.

Maggie glanced at her mother, who was still smiling with twinkling eyes, and then stammered, "Well, let me go serve it." She turned to Jamison, "Would you ask what the others want?"

"Sure." He began to go to each table collecting orders for dessert.

As he did that, the Westons, Wagners, and Montours all called out to Maggie that they thought the dinner was terrific, while she ducked her head in embarrassment and quickly left the dining room.

4 Night Terrors

In the kitchen, Maggie prepared the dishes of pie and ice cream for the strange woman and her son. The warm slices of pie melted the ice cream in dark brown and white rivulets. It smelled delicious.

Mrs. DePrym made the ice cream every evening for the hotel, a half-gallon of vanilla, and a half-gallon of chocolate. She used chocolate from Belgium. She said that was the best. But, her family was from Belgium, so Maggie wasn't sure if that was true or just Mrs. DePrym's opinion. Maggie's favorite was the vanilla. Mrs. DePrym made her own vanilla from vanilla beans that came from Madagascar and soaked them in rum from Jamaica. She knew about that sort of thing. Mrs. DePrym was different from anyone else that Maggie knew.

Jamison stepped through the swinging doors. "I need three peach with vanilla, a cherry with vanilla, and two apple with chocolate."

Maggie held out the dishes of apple and cherry pie. "Here are the pies for the woman and her son." She was going to say *for the two freaks*, but decided that might be a bad idea, just in case they overheard her.

You never know what could happen. Better not to tempt disaster.

That's one of the things her dad used to say.

She wished he were here. A sudden wave of sadness crashed into her. A wave that left her momentarily empty and lost. She brushed that emotion aside and quickly prepared the rest of the orders while Jamison carried them out to the diners.

That was the end of the evening's dinner service.

Maggie and Jamison cleared the dining room tables while Mother made sure that the guests were back in their rooms and the townspeople had left for their homes. After the smiles, laughter, and saying "Good night" had ended, Mother walked into the kitchen where Jamison and Maggie were waiting at the table.

They had already fixed their plates with food left from the guests' supper. Mrs. Wells sat in the chair at the head of the kitchen table and began placing the last remaining slices of roast beef with beets, potatoes, beans, and greens on her plate. "Well, I thought that went well. Maggie, what made you put that garlic and basil in the roast tonight?"

"I don't know," she murmured.

Jamison blurted out, "She thought the guests were vampires."

Maggie swatted Jamison on the arm. "I did not. Well, maybe a little. That's just because they are so peculiar."

"They're not vampires, but everyone liked the roast. Even the Montours. Not too much garlic flavor, just enough really. So it all turned out well."

The table was silent for several minutes with only the sounds of knives and forks clinking on plates as they ate.

Suddenly, her mother glanced up as she cut her roast into delicate bite sized portions. "Why would you think they were vampires, Maggie?" It was one of those hard-eyed looks that always made Maggie feel like she had stolen something or lied about something serious, even though she hadn't. She called it Mother's Inquisition Look.

"Because that's what they look like. Dressed in black and so pale like they never go out in the day."

"I see, but they aren't vampires."

"Yes, Ma'am." Arguing with Mother never worked. Better to just let it go.

"Besides, since they ate the roast, they couldn't be vampires, although that doesn't mean vampires don't exist. Lots of things could exist without you seeing them. Like unicorns." Then her mother added, "At least in this world."

"This world?" Maggie's eyes widened.

"Certainly. Who knows what worlds might be out there." She motioned around them with her fork. "It would be foolish to think that this was the only world that could be."

"Like in John Carter!" Jamison blurted that out before he could stop himself.

"That's science fiction, son. I don't think those books are the kind of reading you should be doing right now."

"But, Mother. It's about Mars. That's a real planet."

"I already told you what I think on that subject. There are no people living on Mars. I know you've been reading those books in spite of what I said." She sighed and looked down at her plate. "I wish your father could be here."

After that, they were silent again while they ate.

Mrs. Wells placed her knife and fork on the edge of her plate. "Maggie, what made you think to use the basil tonight? Garlic I can understand, however bundling basil with garlic was innovative."

Maggie shrugged, "I don't know. It just seemed like the right combination."

Mrs. Wells smiled at her. "I said you had a gift and you do."

Jamison crossed his arms and leaned back in his chair. "Do I have a gift? Why is it just Maggie?"

"Everyone has a gift. They just don't always know what it is. You haven't found yours yet, but you will."

Maggie frowned. "I don't want a gift. I don't even know what that is."

"That's alright. It's just a part of life. We'll talk more about it tomorrow." She took her plate to the sink. "I'm going to the front desk and close the books for the day. Finish cleaning the dishes and, when you're done, it'll be time to get ready for bed."

In unison, Maggie and Jamison said, "Yes, Ma'am."

While Jamison and Maggie washed and dried the dishes, Mrs. Wells began her final rounds for the day. She closed out the ledger, checked the windows, locked the doors, and, when she was satisfied that all was secure, turned off the lights in the lobby and went to the apartment.

"Why do they keep saying I have a gift?" Maggie was washing one of the pots, the one that she had used to cook the greens.

"Maybe because you can cook without having anybody tell you how to."

"That's just talented. I've got a talent for cooking."

"Being talented seems different from having a gift. I think it's like a skill. Being gifted is something like from God."

"All I did was put some garlic and basil in the roast."

"But how did you know to do that."

"Maybe I watched Momma cook and she did it."

"You've never seen her do that. Especially that basil part."

"It just seemed like the thing to do."

"I think that's why it's a gift not a talent. It's not something you know. That's the gift."

"Maybe."

"It's not a knowing thing. It's just something you have inside you. That you feel."

"Yah. Sure." She rolled her eyes in exaggerated frustration. "I'll put the food in the fridge if you finish these last dishes. There's only a couple left to do."

They worked quietly until the kitchen was clean and ready for the morning.

Jamison looked around the room. "I think we have it all done."

"Yeah. No broken dishes tonight!"

"You're never going to forget that are you."

"Never!"

One night, Jamison was trying to put a stack of plates away in only one trip to the sideboard. Naturally, he dropped them and the crash brought Mother running from the apartment. She punished both of them for a week. No activities after school unless it was working at the hotel.

Maggie told her it wasn't fair. Jamison was the one that dropped them, not her. It didn't make any difference. Mother said they were supposed to be working as a team.

Jamison turned the lights off in the kitchen and they went to the apartment.

Mother was sitting in the room that they called their living room. Each night she would sit in her rocking chair and sew, which was usually only repairing their clothes. On the good days, she would hum and sing along with the tunes on the radio. On the bad days, she would be lost in thought and there would be no singing while she patched and mended clothes.

Tonight was a good night. The guests, creepy as they were to Maggie, had brought in enough cash to pay their bills for the month.

"It was a good day today," Mrs. Wells said and then smiled. Her face glowed. "We have a few minutes before bedtime, so after you brush your teeth and get your pajamas on, you can stay up a bit and read. Jamison, you can even read a bit of that John Carter book you have hidden away."

Jamison and Maggie looked at each other. She had never told him he had permission to read any of John Carter before.

"Thanks, Mother." Jamison said.

Maggie fumed, "That's not fair. You told him he wasn't supposed to be reading that book."

"I did, didn't I. Well, tonight we'll make an exception. Just a few pages and, when it's time to turn out the light, I don't want to hear any complaining."

"Yes, Ma'am." Jamison grinned and pulled his copy of John Carter from its hiding place.

"But what about me? I don't have anything like that to read."

"You could read your *Little Women* book. Or maybe *Secret Garden*. You like that one."

"I know, but you always let me read those."

"You can read a book I just got, *To the Lighthouse*. It's by an English writer."

"Sounds boring."

"Try it and see. It's about a family in England who spends their summers at a house on the coast. You'll only have a few minutes though, so you better get going."

The bathroom was only large enough for one person, so they had to take turns brushing their teeth. Tonight, it was Maggie's turn to go first. While she was in the bathroom, Jamison quickly changed into his pajamas, opened his copy of *The Gods of Mars,* and started reading.

Maggie called out from the bathroom, "Momma, that's not fair. Jamison is already reading."

"It's alright, Maggie. You'll get your chance."

"Will I get to read as long as him?"

"Yes, dear. Now brush your teeth, so you can get your pajamas on."

"I'm done."

"No, you aren't. Go back and do a good job."

She grumbled, "Yes, Ma'am."

After a few minutes, Maggie came out. "Your turn, Jamison."

Her mother handed her *To the Lighthouse* and Maggie settled into her chair.

At nine o'clock their mother stood and said the words that they hated hearing, "It's time to go to bed."

Maggie gave the book back to her mother.

"What'd you think?"

"It was alright so far. It was like watching a British movie."

"I imagine the author would be interested to hear you say that. You can read it when you want. I'll leave it out on the end table for you."

"Thank you, Mother."

"Goodnight, Maggie."

"Yes, Ma'am. Goodnight." She went into the small room where her bed was waiting.

The room had been her grandmother's sewing room when she had lived there. Now it held two pieces of furniture, a single bed and a small chest. Maggie used the chest as her dresser, her table, and, when she put a cushion on it, her chair. Tonight, she climbed into bed, pulled the covers over her head, and was asleep in a minute.

In the living room, Jamison pulled out a folded quilt and spread it over the sofa. That was where he slept.

Mrs. Wells cautioned him, "Don't stay up reading. We have to get up early tomorrow to fix the breakfasts."

"Yes, Ma'am."

He pulled the quilt around himself and Mrs. Wells switched off the light in the living room. "Good night, son."

" 'night, Mother."

She went down the short hall leading to her room and closed the door behind her.

***

Maggie's eyes opened. It was still dark. Something had awakened her. She lay very still in her bed listening for unexpected sounds and waiting for her eyes to adjust to the dark. That's when she heard a soft rustle and then a metallic click from something outside her door. Perhaps it was a latch snapping into place.

"Vampires," she whispered to herself. *I knew there was something wrong about that woman and her son.*

Maggie quietly slid out of bed and put her slippers on. The wood floor was cold. She wrapped her flannel robe around her. Grandmother had given her that for Christmas last year. She had said, "Winter gets cold in that old hotel. You'll need this," and handed Maggie the present.

It was a pale blue robe with a crocheted flower, a daisy, sewn onto a pocket positioned over her heart.

Maggie crept into the living room in time to see a hand, her mother's hand, on the edge to the door as she slipped outside into the hallway. Maggie was about to call out to her but stopped. She decided to follow her instead and find out what was going on.

Maggie waited for her mother to move into the hall and then tiptoed to the door. Carefully she opened the door a fraction of an inch and then put her eye to the crack between the door's edge and the frame to see what her mother was doing. Maggie was surprised to see her sneaking out the back door of the hotel.

Maggie stepped quietly into the gloomy hallway. The only light came from a faint nightlight glowing in the lobby. The latch on the back door clicked as it snapped into place.

Her mother had gone outside.

She never goes outside at night. At least not that I know of. Maybe she's gone out before and I just didn't know! I could just scream! but that would wake Jamison. can't do that.

One second it felt as if her heart was going to beat its way out of her chest in panic and in the next second the edges of her ears were burning hot from being angry that Mother could do something like that and they wouldn't know about it.

Maggie quickly tiptoed to the back door and peered through the glass. She saw her mother stand on the back porch a moment and cautiously look around the area before she stepped down into the alley. Once in the alley, she walked briskly toward the courthouse.

Maggie turned the doorknob and eased the door open.

Jamison whispered, "We aren't supposed to go outside tonight."

Maggie jumped, but managed not to scream. "What are you doing out here. You scared me to death."

She didn't wait for him to reply before she started walking down the alley, trying to catch up with her mother. Jamison hurried behind her.

"I heard you sneaking out of the apartment. Does Mother know you're out here?"

"I'm following *her*. She's gone to the courthouse."

"You're joking."

"No, dead serious. Now hush, or she'll hear us."

They slipped into the shadows under a store awning next door to the hotel where they watched their mother stand in the street with her face raised, looking at the clock tower. Blue light streamed from the windows of the clock tower and flowed over her.

Jamison whispered, "What's she doing?"

"I don't know. That light's really scary." Maggie wrapped her arms around herself. She had slipped on her dad's old army trench coat that she picked up on her way out of the apartment. It was cold outside.

"Looks like giant spotlights."

"There aren't any spotlights on the tower," she snapped. *He can be such an idiot.*

"That's what it looks like."

That's when Maggie saw the freaky woman and her son standing in the shadows of the hotel. Maggie pointed at them and whispered, "Look over there. It's the freaky woman and her son. What are they doing out here?"

"Don't know. I wonder if Mother knows they're out here."

"Maybe. Maybe that's why she came outside."

"Could be." He didn't sound very sure about that.

"Maybe they really are vampires and she's lured them out here."

"That's stupid. You got to let go of that vampire stuff."

Maggie shrugged. He didn't have any better explanation.

The light around Mrs. Wells grew brighter until it was blinding and difficult to see her.

The freaky boy tugged on his mother's sleeve and pointed at Jamison and Maggie. He had the same scary grin and was wearing the same dark glasses.

Maggie saw the glasses. *How is he able to see with those things in this dark?*

She nudged Jamison and pointed. "He sees us! The freaky kid sees us!"

The strange woman turned and looked at them and a smile began to spread across her face. She raised her arm and pointed at their mother who was now lost to their view inside the blue light coming from the clock tower.

Suddenly there was an explosion of white light and sound that blanked out everything.

5   Hiding in a Limestone Grotto

When Maggie's eyes recovered from the shock of white light, she saw that she was standing in the center of a limestone grotto. Mr. Munroe was standing beside her holding a glass in his huge hand.

"Here you go," he held it out to her.

She looked at it and asked, "What's this?"

"Water. It's for you. It's from the stream," and he pointed at a stream flowing near where they stood. "It's an artesian spring. A million years ago it cut through the limestone to create this place."

Ignoring him, she demanded, "Where's my mother? What am I doing here?"

"She's still at the courthouse, but she'll be here later. You're safe here."

She emptied the glass on the ground. "I want my mother NOW."

"It's ok, Ma'am."

"It's not ok. I want to go home."

"You can't. It's not safe yet. I told you not to come outside tonight. Not during a killing moon."

"Oh," *that's right.* She had forgotten about that.

"Ma'am, once your Mother gets here..."

"But I want to go now."

"Not until your Mother gets here."

"Why isn't she here now?"

"She had to finish something. Don't you worry though, everything's going to be fine."

"Where's Jamison?"

"Last I saw, he was standing on the sidewalk, but I expect he's back at the hotel by now."

"Why? Why isn't he here? Why just me?"

"You should have sipped some of that water. You'd feel better. It's good for you."

The grotto was large enough for Mr. Munroe to stand without stooping and wide enough for several benches that were placed around the walls. A stream flowed across the center of the floor, entering from a crack in one wall and exiting through a crack in the opposite wall.

In the center of the grotto, the stream formed a shallow pool that gleamed in silver and blue. At several places on the walls, light from stone sconces cast pale patterns across the walls. Light strong enough to see details, yet not so strong that there were no shadows.

Maggie sat on one of the benches and wiped her eyes. She didn't cry. Ever. Except now. She was mad and scared and couldn't do anything about it.

She demanded, "How did I get here?"

"I carried you. We used to hide here during the Indian raids long ago. You sort of fainted back there."

"I see." She tried to sound calm.

She looked around the grotto, imagined families huddled in close groups whispering among themselves trying not to be heard by Kiowa or Comanche raiders. She believed she could feel their fear.

She asked him, "Who put these lights in here?"

"I did. I still come down here sometimes. It's peaceful in here. A good place to think on things." He sighed and looked around the grotto. "These lights are better'n the candles and kerosene lamps we used to use. Those things smoked it up. And the kerosene would stink, especially in this little area."

"The stream is nice." She tried to find something positive that she could say.

"Never had to worry about running out of water. Cool water in the summer too."

"What makes the pool gleam like that?"

"It's the moonlight. It comes down from the clock tower on nights like this and reflects on it. There's a place in the top of the grotto where the light comes in." He pointed up and she looked at the place he pointed out. It was a small silver circle of light high above her head.

Mr. Munroe sat on the bench next to hers. He was so big that he filled the space.

He said, "The light from the moon collects in the tower and gets reflected down here through a bit of a hole in the floor of the basement. Been like that since the time the courthouse was built."

"I didn't know this place existed."

"Nobody talks about it anymore. Most folks have forgotten it. Except the old timers, like me. Most no one in town has been here."

She paused before asking, "What was that light at the clock tower? There was blue light everywhere."

"Some new floodlights. They just installed them last week."

"I don't remember that."

"You were probably in school the day they did that. Didn't take 'em long to get those in."

"I guess. Mrs. Monroe isn't worried about you?"

"No, she knew I was going to be down there at the courthouse tonight testing the lights and I 'spect your Mother's told her where we are."

"Why didn't you just take me back to the hotel? Seems like that would have been the right thing to do."

Silence. "I couldn't get you back there 'cause of a hunter that was out in the street. It was 'tween us and the hotel. So, I brought you here straightaway."

"What kind of a hunter?"

"A panther. Yeah, that was it. It come walking down the street and that was about the time you keeled over. So, I just picked you up quick and brought you in here."

The stream gurgled as it flowed from the crevice in the rock. The gurgling sounds echoed off the walls around them sounding more like a small waterfall than a brook.

"I guess I'd like some water."

"Yes, Ma'am." He reached out, scooped water from the pool, and handed her the glass.

"Thank you." She sipped the water. "It is cool isn't it?"

"Not so cool in August though. The rocks heat up and warm the water pretty good."

"I imagine" She stared at him. "Are you telling the truth about the panther?"

"What makes you ask that?"

"You didn't sound honest."

"I see. Your mother said you had a gift."

"That was for cooking."

"And other things."

"Well. Are you telling the truth?"

"Not exactly, but mostly."

"What was it? Really."

"Kiowa would call it a panther spirit. You seldom see one, but if you do, it's usually going to be during a killing moon."

"Then how do you know that's what it was!"

"When I was a boy, my momma told me about them. They have other spirit animals. You see them sometimes. A panther spirit, though, is one you almost never see."

"But how do you know it wasn't a regular panther."

"I guess I just knew." He shrugged. "They appear in places a normal panther wouldn't be. It was looking at you the whole time it was walking down the street. I was thinking it was coming for you. That's why I brought you in here where it's safe. Panther spirit won't come here." He chuckled, "In the night you can believe almost anything." Then he quickly turned somber, "I wish I was imagining that."

She stood up and walked around the grotto.

"What happened to the weird lady and her son?"

"I don't know. I didn't see them."

"They were standing across the street from me. I remember she smiled at me then pointed at my mother. And the creepy boy was grinning too. With those black glasses on. I don't see how they can see anything with those on. Especially at night."

"I didn't see them. I'd just come out from the courthouse when I saw you and the panther. I was testing the new floodlights. That's what I was doing out there so late."

Second time he said that. He's lying.

She had always trusted Mr. Munroe. Had known him all of her life and now she wasn't sure about him.

"When's my mother going to get here? I want to go home."

"Should be here any minute."

She looked more closely at the walls around them and there was no sign of a way to get into the grotto.

Suddenly, she panicked with a jumble of thoughts running through her. *I'm trapped in a cave somewhere. Underground, I don't know where. It's no place I know of, or ever even heard of.*

Maggie tried to keep her voice steady but couldn't. "How do you get in here?"

"What?"

Her head was spinning. "How do you get in here? There's no opening."

Mr. Munroe rubbed the stubble on his chin.

"It's over there, where the stream runs out. You have to look close to see it. The way the rock is cracked, it looks like its solid, but it's not. There's a set of steps cut in the rock that lead up to the courthouse basement."

It won't help if I'm so afraid I can't think. She tried to calm herself. *After all, this is Mr. Munroe. I've known him all of my life and he was always the nicest man.*

She took a slow breath and then asked, "Is that one of the secret passages?"

"You could say that. People don't remember it's there." He seemed to think a moment before saying, "Guess that makes it like a secret, I suppose. Before they built the courthouse, it was just a narrow gap in the ground that got covered up by bushes. It leads the way down here. That's how folks would come down here to hide. Back then there wasn't no steps. It was just raw rock and slippery. When we cut the steps in, we widened it out a bit. When they built the courthouse, they just made the opening into part of the basement."

She felt her breathing and her heartbeat slow to normal.

I will not imagine things to be afraid of. There are enough real things in life to fear.

That's what her father would tell her at night when she woke up crying after a nightmare and couldn't go back to sleep.

She asked, "What's a panther spirit do? Is it like a demon? They talk about demons in church a lot."

Mr. Munroe sighed, a long, tired sigh, and said, "You'll have to ask your Mother about that. All I know is what little my momma told me. Some of the people think they are dangerous. Others think they are messengers from the underworld. When you fell over, it seemed it was best not to take any chances. The underworld never sounded too inviting to me either. Of course, tomorrow when the sun is up, I expect I'll just feel foolish."

That sounded almost normal. She sipped some water.

Maggie sat on a bench across from him. The pool sat still like a gleaming silver mirror between them.

"Why would mother know about it?"

"She knows all sorts of things. I don't know so much."

After the panic attack, she felt like herself again, but a very tired self. "I'm just going to close my eyes a minute."

"You go ahead, Ma'am. I'll let you know when your Mother arrives."

Maggie's eyes closed and she was asleep while sitting on the bench.

***

The sound of whispering ended her dream of walking on the prairie among sleeping buffalo and her eyes opened to see the strange woman from the hotel standing in the grotto, head bent, and talking softly to Mr. Munroe.

The woman stopped talking and looked at her, a wide smile across her face. "I do believe she is awake."

Mr. Monroe said in his slow way, "She's strong."

Mrs. Johnson replied proudly, "Yes, she is. As she should be."

Maggie quickly sat up. "What are you doing here? Where's my mother?"

Mrs. Johnson stared at her. "I can see this is going to be difficult for you. I was afraid it might be."

"What are you talking about?" Maggie couldn't keep the sound of panic out of her voice.

Mrs. Johnson crossed her arms and stood looking down at Maggie. "Yes, I think this is going to take some time."

Maggie turned to Mr. Munroe and said, "Mr. Monroe, I want to go home *now*."

He looked at Mrs. Johnson and asked, "What do you want me to do, Ma'am?"

Mrs. Johnson sighed and said softly, "Take her Home."

"Now?"

"Yes, it's time."

"Yes, Ma'am. Mr. Munroe stepped around the pool and gently took Maggie's arm. "Miss Maggie, I'm gonna get you Home now. Don't be afraid."

And then he quickly stepped into the pool of water taking her with him.

Part II

What happened next...

stranger and even stranger ...

7   You're Not Supposed to be Here!

"Welcome Home."

The strange woman from the hotel was sitting in an ornate armchair across from Maggie sipping from a teacup. Maggie was sitting in a similar chair with her hands folded in her lap. When she realized where she was, she grabbed onto the arms of the chair. She needed something solid to hold onto.

Maggie looked around her and saw that they were sitting inside an enormous domed space, large enough to fit all of Fort Richards, with rock sconces on the walls around them and giant crystal chandeliers hanging from the ceiling.

The ceiling that arched over their heads was grey rock supported by curved ribs that spanned it. Ribs that made Maggie imagine she was inside the chest of a petrified dragon.

Around them, for as far as she could see, were stacks and mounds of books, chairs, tables, desks, paintings, and things all covered by ancient tapestries and giant drab canvas drop cloths.

"Would you like some tea?" The woman smiled and folded her hands in her lap. "Perhaps some biscuits? You would call those cookies. We have some delightful shortbread that the helpers just took out of the oven."

"How did I get here?"

"Through the Imaginærium Engine. One second you were there in the grotto and now you are sitting here with me."

Maggie was on the verge of tears but refused to cry in front of the woman.

"Where is my mother? What do you want from me? Where's Mr. Munroe? He said he was going to take me home. Why am I here?"

"This *is* your Home."

"No, it's not. I don't even know where this is."

"Your true Home."

"You're lying." Maggie had never told anyone they were lying. Mother wouldn't let them say that. It was one of the bad words, like stupid or dumb that you didn't say to people. This time though it seemed like it was all right.

"And you are my daughter."

"That's a lie." *It was easier to say the second time.*

"In old times, you would be called a changeling. However, in the world today, there is no memory of that.

Have you never felt different from those around you? Your family? As though you didn't quite belong?"

Maggie was silent. *Of course, I have. Everyone does.*

"That's because you are. You are my daughter, placed with the family that has raised you until now. And their daughter has been here, waiting in this place. She has been returned to them now and you are here. She will recall only that she has been a good daughter helping with the hotel. And you will be here, assuming your place in this space." She sipped some tea and then said, "By the way, your true name is Marguerite. I hope you don't mind, but I would prefer to call you Marguerite. Maggie sounds a bit common to my ear."

Maggie shouted at her, "You aren't my mother. You couldn't be!"

"And yet I am. In time, you will understand, but for now that's enough." She stood up. "You've had a traumatic evening and I must take care of final preparations before morning. She motioned across the huge cavern, "Briefly, this space is yours and these are all of your things. You can arrange it and them as you want."

She pointed in the direction of a distant edge of the cavern. "Your bed is over there. You're probably still sleepy. I don't imagine you have had any rest tonight. You'll find that everything you need has been or will be provided for you. And, if you ever need anything that is not here, it will be retrieved for you."

Maggie shouted at her, "What I need is to go home!" and then muttered, "I keep telling you people that, but nobody is paying any attention to me."

"Yes, dear. I understand. Perhaps, it would be best if you rested first. We can talk again in the morning. Please, get some rest. Everything will be fine. Do not worry. Everything will be as it is supposed to be."

And, with those words, in spite of what she was thinking, Maggie felt a calming warm glow spread up from her feet, flowing out through her fingertips and then into her face and the tips of her ears.

The strange woman smiled at her, then turned and walked down an aisle between the rows and mounds of things stacked in the space. Maggie watched her until she was only a speck in the distance.

In a whisper, she asked no one in particular, "Just how big is this room? It's enormous."

Maggie raised her hand to compare it to the size of the chandeliers. Her hand looked so much larger than the chandeliers. They were so far away that their light was dim by the time it reached the floor.

The ceiling must be as high as the clock tower. Or even higher.

In spite of herself, her eyelids drooped. *The woman was right about one thing. I'm tired.*

Maggie headed down an aisle that led in the general direction where the woman said her bed was.

A bed, not mine. My bed is in the apartment at the hotel. She muttered over and over, "The woman is lying. All of this is a lie. I will not forget who I am."

At the end of the aisle between the stacks of things was an open area close to the wall. In it, stood a bed just where the woman said it would be.

It was a giant canopy bed with a floral pattern bedspread and duvet. The canopy over the bed matched the bedspread. She was so sleepy though that she didn't notice or care, as she kicked off her shoes, and crawled under the covers.

The air in the gigantic room was chilly and the down filled bedspread was warm. She was sleeping within seconds of closing her eyes.

***

Maggie opened her eyes. Something had lifted her out of a deep sleep. Now she was awake and confused because this wasn't her tiny room in the hotel apartment or her narrow bed with its sagging cotton stuffed mattress. This was larger and better than anything she had ever seen, even better than the giant bed at her grandmother's house in Fort Worth.

Maggie swung her legs over the edge of the bed, then moved no further. The crazy evening returned to her in a flash.

The freaky woman said this is my home, that this is my room, and she is my mother. Maggie quickly slipped her shoes on. *I have to get away from here now!*

From behind her was a rustling sound, and, as she turned, she glimpsed a flurry of color that disappeared down the trail between the stacks of things that she had walked last night.

When she stood, she saw a teapot and cup with a small plate of scones on a small table placed beside the bed. She sniffed the air.

raisin scones. Butter, real butter not margarine, and cream. Irish butter. That's what woke me, wonderful smells.

She sipped the tea. *Irish Breakfast with a teaspoonful of sugar and a splash of heavy cream.*

She broke off a corner of the scone and ate it. It melted in her mouth, releasing its buttery flavor.

After she finished the tea and scones, she followed the trail back to the center of the cavernous space where she had watched the creepy woman leave the room last night.

There has to be a way to escape.

As she walked, she didn't pay much attention to the stacks of things that lined the path. They were just shapes covered by ornate tapestries, piles of leather bound books on tables with warm glowing lamps, stacks of antiques.

Grandmother would love this place, slipped through her thoughts for a moment.

Back in the center of the space, she found the ornate chairs and table where she and the woman had been sitting last night.

That was when she began to notice details around her.

The rug under the chairs and table was Persian with burgundy and gold threaded designs. The table was an oval rosewood coffee table with ornate carved legs. Shapes of flowers and vines covered the legs and on the top was an inlay of beech, cherry, and mahogany in the shape of a tree. It looked like an apple tree with red fruit hanging in its branches. The carvings reminded her of the sideboard in the dining room.

Last night when she was sitting there with the woman, she hadn't paid any attention to details.

Out of the corner of her eye, she saw the flash of a shape going down the aisle that led to her bed. Maggie whipped around and raced back in time to see a small child, a girl, maybe 6 or 7 years old with curly red hair, hurrying behind a tapestry that covered a gap between some crates.

Without a second thought, Maggie followed, crawling after the little girl through a small opening like a tunnel between the crates and covered objects. It was just large enough for a child, but too small for a grown up. Maggie was almost too large to fit. She wriggled past the tight spots until she emerged in a small open area where the child was brushing crumbs and bits of scones into a bowl while arranging empty teacups and saucers on a small cart.

"Hello," she said.

At the sound of her "Hello," the child gave a start and almost dropped the dishes. The girl whirled around and Maggie saw that she was not a child. She was a tiny person.

The tiny woman exclaimed, "Oh my! What are you doing here?"

"I saw you in the aisle back there and followed. I was hoping you could tell me where I am."

"You're not supposed to be here."

"I know. I think I was kidnapped."

"I mean you aren't supposed to be *here*," she motioned around her. "You should be back in the main areas. This area is for the helpers."

"Sure, but I have to go home. Can you tell me how to get out of here?"

"You can't leave. At least not yet."

"But, I have to go home. My mother will be worried."

The tiny woman looked confused. "But you *are* Home. Your Mother has returned you to us."

"No. This is not my home and she is not my mother. This is all a mistake. I live in Fort Richards in the hotel with my mother and brother. My father works in the oil field and I have no idea what this place is or who that creepy woman is."

"I see." The tiny woman frowned. "But you must go back to the main areas. I cannot help you now. I have work to do and I'm really not supposed to speak to you." The tiny woman paused a moment to think before mumbling, "Of course, I suppose it's ok. You are her daughter." Then she seemed to brighten and said, "Maybe later I can talk with you. How did you find the path?"

"I saw you cross the aisle."

"Yes, that's true. *You* would be able to see me, but go now, please. I have work to do. Much to clean. And you have fresh clothes laid out on your bed. I will clean your old ones later."

"What's your name?"

But the tiny woman had already slipped into a gap between some crates, pushing the cart stacked with dishes from breakfast in front of her, and disappeared without a sound.

Maggie stood in the empty space for a minute. There was nothing distinctive about it. Nothing that she could see made this space different from any of the other open areas between the mounds of things - until she began to notice other gaps around her between the stacks of crates. Some were covered over by tapestries, and she recognized them now as entrances to passages that the tiny woman must use to move unseen around the cavernous space.

"Most curious," she said aloud. However, her attention was on escaping the cavern, not digging into its secrets. So, she returned to the main area in the center as the tiny woman had told her to do.

In the central spot, the freaky woman was sitting in the stuffed armchair.

"Ah, Marguerite."

The name sounded alien to her, but Maggie decided to say nothing and wait.

The minute she makes a mistake, bang, I escape. At least when I can figure out how to get out of here.

The woman was not wearing the dark glasses. She had irises that were scary silver. Not that they were colorless. They were silver moonlight surrounding jet black pupils.

"I'm so pleased to see that you are up." The woman was drinking tea and nibbling on a scone. "I do love these scones. Don't you?"

"Yes. They are delicious."

The woman motioned at her and said, "But you haven't changed into your new clothes. Why don't you do that first and then come back. There's so much I want to show you. I think you're going to enjoy today."

"Of course," Maggie grumbled. However, she went back to her bed and found that the sheets and covers had been straightened and tucked in. Arranged neatly on the bed, were the clothes that the tiny woman had said were set out for her to wear.

Maggie checked the clothes and they all appeared to be the correct size for her. Somehow, she wasn't surprised.

The tiny woman, whatever her name is, must have done all of this.

In the corner of the space that made her bedroom was a partition decorated with forest scenes. She stepped behind it feeling a bit foolish, since she was the only one in the space. Although, after discovering the hidden passages, she wouldn't assume that she was ever entirely alone.

I should be screaming and crying hysterically. Like in the movie when Dracula kidnaps the girl.

She held up her new dress. *At least I should feel like that.*

The dress looked a bit strange, bizarre actually. Made of purple silk with silver flower patterns coiled around themselves, pearl buttons, long poofy sleeves, and giant ruffles.

She slipped the dress on but couldn't reach the buttons that fastened it in the back.

"Hello, Ma'am. Mind if I help?"

Maggie whirled around. It was the tiny woman. She was standing nervously at the edge of the space.

"No, I don't mind. Actually, I can't reach these buttons. Would you mind?"

"Of course, Ma'am." The woman stepped quickly across the space and began buttoning the dress.

"How are you supposed to button this dress anyway?"

"Ma'am, that's why you have a helper."

"Like you?"

"Yes, Ma'am. I am your helper. If you need anything, I will get it for you."

"That's easy, I need to go home."

"I'm sorry, Ma'am. I can't help you with that."

"I didn't think so, but I thought I'd ask anyway."

A pair of slippers made from black suede leather had been placed beside the bed, and she slipped those on. Small emeralds and pearls decorated their edges.

Maggie sighed. *Naturally they fit perfectly too.*

"Ma'am, I placed a table and hair brush for you beside the bed."

The table was small with a gold-framed mirror and an ebony hairbrush resting on it. The back of the hairbrush was mother of pearl and it had soft bristles.

"Thank you. My hair is a mess."

She sat in the chair that was in front of the table and the tiny woman began to brush her hair.

"Mother used to brush my hair like this when I was small." *She stopped doing that several years ago.* "It feels strange now, having someone help me."

85

As she brushed the tangles out of Maggie's hair, the woman said, "Ma'am, you have beautiful hair. So long and dark. It gleams in this light."

"That's kind of you to say so." Then Maggie asked the woman, "What's your name? Do you live here?"

The woman paused a moment before she said, "All of the helpers live here. We wouldn't be able to do our work if we did not."

"What's your name?"

"It's not important, Ma'am." She stopped brushing Maggie's hair. "Well, there you are. Dressed and ready."

"Your name's important to me." Maggie turned to face her, but she had disappeared. Maggie frowned.

I hate it when she does that.

After a moment she stood and began walking back to the center spot where Mrs. Johnson was waiting to take her on "the big tour." She didn't want to be anywhere near the woman, although her best chance to escape was to take the tour.

And that was what it would have to be, an escape. No one knew where she was so that they could come save her. She didn't even know. The way she felt, her only chance to get home was to escape on her own.

As Maggie walked down the aisle to the center of the giant dome, Mrs. Johnson called out, "My dear, that dress suits you. You look delightful."

Yeah. Delightfully hideous, but Maggie smiled and said, "Thank you." *Be polite. Be polite. At least until I find the way out of here.* "Everything fits perfectly."

"Come, let me show you a few things about our home." The freaky woman stood and motioned for Maggie to walk with her. She smiled and pointed to the ceiling that soared above them. "It's roomy don't you think?"

Maggie didn't have to pretend to be awed by the space. "Yes, I've never seen anything like it."

"It's ancient, as you'll find are most things here. I'm sure you've noticed that this space is arranged in the form of a compass, with five points."

Maggie was puzzled. "North, south, east and west are only four points. What is the fifth point?"

"The center. All compasses revolve around their center. Without that, they would be meaningless."

"And this is the center?"

"Yes. It appears simple, just a table and two chairs for us to sit in. However, it is essential for the remainder of the spaces to have reason. This point gives the worlds their orientation. To the west is your sleeping space. You're already familiar with that. This morning I will show you what lies in the eastern point of this compass. Let's be off. We have much to do today."

With that, the strange woman set off walking briskly down the eastern aisle.

Maggie had to hurry to catch up with her. The woman was tall and thin. She moved in fast motions with long legs that covered distance quickly. Her long dress, today it was lavender, swished across the stone floor, which drew Maggie's attention to the floor itself.

Patterns were etched in the smooth grey limestone, geometric whirls and triangles, interlocked in endless ornate patterns. Muted blue, green, red, and yellow shades stained the stone itself.

The woman didn't talk as they walked down the aisle.

In spite of herself, Maggie couldn't resist asking, "What's all of this stuff stacked in here?"

The woman paused in her walk and looked around her.

"They are gifts. People leave them for me and over the years they just accumulate. My helpers collect them and bring them here. It's not the sort of thing you can get rid of, so they remain here. And there are the books. I have an eye for first editions."

"What sort of gifts?"

"It changes with the times. Nevertheless, it's always something that's important to the person."

"Why would they do that?"

"They want something and hope I can help them. Or they don't want something and hope I will stop it. Whatever it is."

"Why you?"

"It's what they believe. That I can change or control the things that happen to them. And I intervene, sometimes, if I am interested. I suppose the gifts make a difference, though not always in the way that people believe. It's not how valuable it is, but how important it is. There is a difference, you know. Not so many people leave gifts now. Although my helpers still find them sometimes, and, when they do, they bring them here."

"Where? Where do they find them?"

"The usual places. Temples, rivers, lakes. Usually there is a small ceremony of some kind before they place the gift. I'm sure you've seen them."

"Are you talking about like at church where they collect the offering."

"Not really, as I understand how that works. That's more about raising money to pay for things. This is much older. It's individual people sacrificing something important to themselves by giving it to me."

"Who are you? Really."

"I'm your mother."

"No, your name. What's your real name? Mrs. Johnson sounds fake."

"I've had many. My favorite was Coventina. Then one time it was Tethys. It is one of my oldest, but no one uses them anymore. Others give names to you, of course. Not something you choose for yourself. Vivienne is what I am called now. I like that one. It has a nice modern sound."

"You told us that you were Mrs. Johnson."

"I invented that to fit in."

"I should have guessed." Maggie looked around them, "Where is your son? I haven't seen him around."

The woman laughed and said, "He's not my son. He's one of my helpers. However, he *is* very talented at getting around when it comes to the world as it is now with its giant structures and steel vehicles. I depend on him when I travel abroad. And he was quite honored to help return you home."

"What is his name?"

"The helpers don't have names."

"How do you call him then?"

"I don't. He knows what I want him to do. I don't have to tell him."

"So, what is your last name? Vivienne what. It's not Johnson."

"We have no last name. We have no custom of last names. We are called the Tuatha Dé, one family. We are not so many that we don't know our brothers and sisters. And you too, my daughter, are also Tuatha Dé."

"What does that mean, anyway?"

"Tribe of the gods. Of course, *we* aren't gods. A frequent misconception. They forget the preposition and article in the translation. Of the gods... not, Of gods. A significant difference, you understand?"

Maggie laughed, but Vivienne did not. "If you are my real mom, who is my father?"

The woman was silent before saying, "In time, you will know. I won't tell you now though." Vivienne resumed walking. "Besides it is not something that you should think about today. Perhaps later we can talk more about that."

"I see." *Crazy talk. I won't get anything real out of her. Better to just change the subject.* "So, where are we?"

"This is one of many spaces in the Otherworlds. You've heard of Avalon. That will suffice for now."

"You mean like in King Arthur?" *This just can't get any crazier.* "Are you the Lady of the Lake?"

"That's what the French named me. But, as I said I've had many names."

Maggie looked at the vaulted ceiling. *Maybe it can get crazier.* "Is this under the lake?"

"You know the story!"

"My brother has that book." Maggie scowled. "King Arthur is make-believe."

"A legend. That's not the same as make-believe. Make-believe would be something that didn't exist and after all," Vivienne motioned around the cavern, "Here you are. Legend is a memory that has been replaced by a story. Most legends are true or, at the least, were memories in their beginnings."

"You said most, but not all."

"True. Some legends have been retold so many times their truth is lost."

"You're saying King Arthur was true?"

"What was called Avalon certainly is, as you now know for yourself."

"But that's somewhere in England and we're in Texas."

"Are you certain you are in Texas?"

"Where else could this be? We couldn't have gone anywhere in just a few hours. We might be in Dallas."

Vivienne laughed and smiled. "You don't believe this is Dallas."

Maggie didn't reply. *I know it isn't Dallas, but I don't have any idea where else we could be. One thing for sure is we aren't in England.*

Vivienne said, "Here we are."

***

They had reached the wall of the cavern and were standing in front of a tall door set in the stone.

The door was made of massive timbers and held on giant hinges by wide iron bands. The wood was dark, almost black, from varnish that had deepened in color with age.

The door swung open for them.

"Follow me," Vivienne said, as she stepped into the darkness on the other side.

Maggie hesitated. She couldn't see what was beyond the open door.

Like everything so far, something horrible is probably waiting for me.

From the other side, Vivienne called, "Come along, dear."

Or it could be the way out. At this point, what have I got to lose?

Maggie stepped across the threshold and into the darkness.

8   Vivienne's Festival

The chattering voices in the garden hushed when Maggie and Vivienne stepped out from the shadow of the doorway. Maggie stopped, stunned to see a crowd of men and women gathered, waiting for her.

She whispered to the woman, "Who are they?"

"Our family. They have come from all points to greet you. It's a day that we have looked forward to for many years."

The people nodded their heads to her.

Maggie whispered, "I don't understand."

"I would be astonished if you did. You might have heard stories of us, although they would only be bits of truth mixed with fantasy."

"What stories?"

"Fairy tales and legends. Most are imaginings and confused stories told on dark nights to entertain or frighten children."

Vivienne turned suddenly and hugged Maggie close to her. "The truth is more terrifying than they can imagine."

After a moment, she released her and said, "However, today we are happy that you are home with us again and that is enough. Let us walk into the orchard and I will present you to the circle."

Vivienne took Maggie's hand and walked with her through the center of the garden, past the fountains, the hawthorn, and beds of roses, until they entered the apple orchard that grew behind it.

The people parted so that they could pass, and then they followed in procession to the orchard where ten from the crowd reformed in a loose circle around Vivienne and Maggie. The rest of the people arrayed themselves outside the inner circle.

Maggie was astounded at the appearance of the crowd. The men were dressed in outrageous costumes unlike anything she had seen before. Certainly not like anything she would ever see in Fort Richards. Most were wearing ornate costumes that looked like the painting of Henry the 8th. They had seen that in history class last month. However, a few of the men were wearing clothes that looked like modern suits, except they were cut in crazy patterns with gold and silver decorations and in wild patterns of bright colors. No one she knew at home wore suits or pants in colors other than charcoal grey, dirt brown, or navy blue. None of the crazy suits were in solid colors much less those drab shades.

The women wore an outlandish variety of dresses and formal gowns. Their dresses and gowns were in wild colors that rivaled those of any of the flowers in the garden. The dresses had wide ruffled collars, so wide that they reached beyond the wearer's shoulders.

Mrs. Hamilton, her history teacher, had shown them paintings of the Renaissance and she recalled seeing Venetian clothes like these in those paintings. Poofy sleeves and ruffles and exotic patterns. The gowns were simpler in their cut, but just as ornately and absurdly patterned as the dresses.

Vivienne folded her hands and faced the circle.

"This is my daughter, Marguerite, who was hidden away many years ago and is now returned to us."

Maggie stood with Vivienne in the center of the circle. The faces were a blur. She wasn't sure what she had been expecting when they went through the door. It certainly, wasn't a garden full of people dressed up in bizarre costumes. Another room maybe. A room with a door that she could use to escape, but a garden was not something on the list.

Maybe they are a cult like the Druids in the newsreels last week. That Druid bunch in the newsreel, was led by a woman, Sister Beverly something. Disappeared for a few days then reappeared. Mother said she scares her. Wears white gowns and acts like she's an angel.

A tall man wearing a bright green cloak stepped forward from the circle. He carried a walking stick with intricate carvings that Maggie thought looked like the carvings on the sideboard at home. When he pulled back the hood on his cloak, she saw that he was old, had long silver hair and a mustache like ones she'd seen in drawings of Vikings. What struck her most was that his hair and moustache were silver, not white. All of the old people she knew had white hair.

"Greetings, Marguerite, daughter of Vivienne. I am the Dagda, first of the circle, and I welcome you to the Tuatha Dé." His voice was deep and mellow. He smiled at her and touched her forehead with his hand. "We gift you with our mind, strength, and skill."

He returned to the circle, and others of the circle stepped forward one by one to introduce themselves and welcome her in the same way.

Those who formed the circle were a mix of women and men.

They're dressed in such ridiculous costumes. They don't look like Druids. It's actually more terrifying than if it was Druids 'cause they don't look like anything I've ever heard of…

Maggie wanted to scream and run out of the orchard, only she kept her panic cornered and her "calm face" in place just as Mother had told her to do when they had difficult guests at the hotel.

Running away screaming won't get me home.

After an old man wearing a somber black and silver trimmed robe had introduced himself as "Dian Cécht, healer for the Tuatha De," a boy, maybe 16 or 17, stepped forward.

She was startled. She hadn't seen anyone in the circle that wasn't old.

The boy wore a wild silk costume of purple and gold patterns that had tiny golden bells sewn onto the ruffles at the cuffs of his sleeves. He had red hair that was a bit longer than most of the boys in Ft. Richards. Although he didn't have freckles which she usually thought of with red hair. Maybe that was because of her mother and Jamison. She quickly searched the other faces in the circle and now saw a few who were as young as he was.

"Greetings, Marguerite. I am Abarta, the trickster of this charming group. More fun than the rest of them." He laughed, and the knot of anxiety in her chest began to unwind.

Vivienne gently reprimanded him, "Abarta, honor the ritual."

"Yes, of course." He gave Maggie a sly smile and continued. "Welcome to the circle of the Tuatha Dé." As the others had done, he stretched out his hand to touch her forehead, except this time a spark of static jumped the gap to shock her.

Maggie gave a start and shouted, "Hey, that hurt!"

He quickly said, "Wow, sorry about that. Didn't mean to zap you."

She wasn't sure if he meant it or not. She suspected he did that on purpose.

Vivienne frowned while Abarta completed the rite and touched Maggie's forehead without shocking her. He grinned and said, "We gift you with our mind, strength, and skill."

Abarta stepped back into the circle, and another came forward to repeat the ceremony. Maggie stood patiently as each of the remaining members of the circle performed the ritual of greeting and gifting.

Abarta was the only one that zapped her.

She muttered to Vivienne, "He really *is* the trickster."

Maggie had never heard names like theirs before, which made them hard to remember. They sounded like words in a foreign song, lilting but never growling.

Vivienne leaned close to her and whispered, "Now, you say to them, I thank you for your welcome and gifts."

Maggie repeated what Vivienne told her to say, and the members of the circle bowed their heads to her.

It was very confusing being in the center of the group.

They act as if everything is normal. Except they are as bizarre as anything I could have ever imagined.

She wished that she were home, standing in the kitchen or working in the hotel doing normal boring chores. Or back in the clock tower looking down on the streets below, safe from things happening that don't make sense.

I want to go home! I want things to make sense again; just like they did yesterday before Vivienne and her so-called helper arrived. Where is Mother? What is Jamison doing? Are they going to rescue me?

The same questions without answers ran around in an endless loop inside her brain every time she let them.

Vivienne smiled and raised her arms, fingers outstretched to the circle, sleeves falling back on her arms.

Her voice rang across the orchard, "Let us begin the festival. My helpers have prepared the pavilions and tables. Please join us on this day of celebration. My daughter is now home and safe among us."

With that, she led them back from the orchard to the fountain where the helpers had raised pavilion tents around the hawthorn tree.

There were so many tents that Maggie imagined it was a city, a city that sprang up while they were in the orchard.

"Unbelievable," she whispered as she walked with Vivienne. "The helpers placed all of these tents just now."

Vivienne smiled at her and whispered, "My helpers are the best."

The sound of violins drifted through the area, however she couldn't locate the source. They seemed to come from every direction.

Maggie asked Vivienne, "Are the musicians in a different area? I don't see them anywhere."

"Yes, they are. The acoustics in the garden are perfect, so it sounds as though their music is coming from all around us. I have a preference for stringed instruments. Harps and lutes. What music do you like, dear?"

"Piano. Blues especially. I have some Jelly Roll Morton records that I listen to at home."

"New Orleans, yes, I can understand your interest in that music. There's so much I don't know about you, yet.

All these years," Vivienne snapped her fingers, "gone like that. It was my greatest sorrow to have to hide you away," her voice softened, "for so many years." She sighed and then brightened, "But here you are at last."

Maggie stared at her and asked, "How do I know that you really are my mother?"

"I don't expect you to believe today. With time, as you learn who you are, there will be a moment in your heart when you will, but not your head. That is how you will believe it. Now take my arm and walk with me. We must mingle with our guests as they celebrate your return. Just follow my lead, and we will have a wonderful time."

Maggie walked with Vivienne among the guests and smiled as they complimented her on her dress, hair, or smile. She returned their compliments, copying Vivienne's remarks to the guests, and she appeared to have fun even though she felt alone.

As they were walking past a mime who was making her way through the circle of pavilions, a group of teenagers rushed up and took Maggie by the arm.

A girl in a light blue formal gown asked, "Vivienne, you don't mind if we show her around a bit, do you?"

Vivienne didn't look enthusiastic about the idea. "Well …"

"We'll take care of her. Please…She needs to get to know us, not just the older crowd."

Vivienne reluctantly smiled, "You're right, Áine. It's selfish of me to keep her so close today."

"So, she can come with us?"

"Certainly. While you are exploring the festival, I will talk with Clíodhna. You can find me in the main pavilion later." And with that, Vivienne left Maggie with them.

"Let's go, Marguerite!" Áine tugged her arm. "Let's see this festival. By the way, in case you don't remember from the ceremony, I'm Áine. You pronounce it Annah, but you spell it Á·i·n·e." She was tall and thin with jet black hair and pale skin. Áine motioned at the others walking with them, "This is Abarta. You remember him of course."

Abarta laughed. "Sure, she does! I'm unforgettable."

Maggie frowned at him and told the group, "Yes, I found him to be quite shocking."

Áine shoved him, and they all laughed. It was a happy group, which made Maggie feel more relaxed. At least in comparison to being completely terrified, which is mostly how she had been feeling ever since she had been taken.

The blond-haired guy walking on her left said "I'm Goibniu. You can call me Gee, though. Everybody does since it's shorter. These other two characters," he pointed to the two boys walking behind her, "are my brothers. This is Luchtaine and that is Credne." Gee was stocky with hands that were huge.

Luchtaine, who had dark brown curly hair said, "You can just call me Luke. I'm a carpenter. Not as fancy as being smiths like my two brothers here, but I do all of the woodcraft work for the Tuatha. I used to make the bows, arrows, and shields. Only no one uses those anymore unless it's for a festival. We should go over to the archery exhibition. You can see some of my bows over there. Do you shoot? I can make you a bow if you want."

Maggie smiled at him. "No, I don't. But, I think I'd like to learn. I might be good at it." Unlike Gee, he was skinny. Her mother would have said he was thin as a reed.

Credne, who was also walking behind Maggie, said enthusiastically, "Hi, I'm Credne. Most just call me CR. If you want, you can call me CR, too. I don't mind. That's chromium on the periodic table you know. I like that."

Maggie laughed. "That seems to fit you!"

CR was built like Gee and had short blond hair. He said, "Yeah, I'm a smith like Gee. One time I helped make a silver hand for King Nuada. It worked just like that real thing!"

Maggie was puzzled and asked him, "Why did you do that?"

"He lost it in a battle. Got it cut off that is, not lost it like he accidentally dropped his hand or something."

"Oh, I see." *More bizarre stuff.* "That's interesting. And gruesome."

"But, now I mainly work in gold."

"Like a jeweler?"

"Lately that's what I've been doing. This is one of mine." He held up his hand to show off a gold ring that looked like a chunk of rock.

"Oh, that's very nice." *It's awful. I wonder if anyone has told him.* Maggie turned to the girl walking beside Áine. "I remember you from the circle."

"Right, I was there. My name is pronounced Nee-af. Since you don't know Irish, it's spelled N·i·a·m·h." Niamh was tall and thin with golden hair. She was wearing a formal gown covered in interwoven patterns of pale blue flowers and had on white gloves that went up to her elbows.

She looks like a movie star. Maggie said, "Do you make things, too?"

"I'm not a crafts person like the brothers. I'm an equestrian. I like horses and riding. That's my biggest interest, I suppose."

"Do you work in a stable or do training?"

"Not really. I'm one of the queens of Tir na nÓg."

Maggie blushed and stammered, "I'm sorry. I didn't know. I've never met a queen before. We don't have queens in the US. The only ones I've seen are in pictures at school, and all of those were old ladies. You seem normal."

"What do you mean, I seem normal?"

"You laugh, and everyone seems to like you. That's not how I imagined a queen."

"I'm glad then that I surprised you."

"Where is your country? I'm not familiar with it."

"It's near here. It's another space in the Otherworlds, like Avalon. Our spaces are linked, but not the same. Avalon is your Mother's. And yours too, of course."

Áine tugged on Maggie's arm, "Let's go see the jugglers. Your Mother's helpers get the best jugglers."

"Sure. That sounds like fun." Which was really the last thing that Maggie thought of as fun.

Watching people throw things in the air and then catch them. Over and over again, how boring was that. How could that be called fun? But, if these kids want to see jugglers, I'm not going to be the odd one in the group.

But the group itself was odd. A girl who looked like a movie star and said she was a queen of someplace called Tir na nÓg, wherever that was, and one guy who was a jeweler or something. She wasn't quite sure what he was talking about. None of that was normal. Áine hadn't said what she was or did, and so far, she seemed normal.

And then there was Abarta.

She thought he was cute, and his jokes and stories were funny. Plus, she liked being around him, even if he had shocked her at the ceremony and then laughed at her like it was a big joke.

As far as she could tell, the others were fun to be with too, so she decided to go along with the flow, unless they got too crazy.

They seem like regular kids, though, in spite of some weirdness. At least no one is trying to kill me.

As long as they believe I'm part of the group, maybe I'll be ok.

Áine said, "The jugglers are in the central circle." She guided them down a path between the pavilions while

Abarta and the three brothers kept up a constant banter back and forth.

Each pavilion contained something special, exotic food and drinks, games, racks of clothes presented by different designers, collections of blades and shields from different armorers. It was all new stuff, except none of it looked modern.

In the center, there were five groups of jugglers surrounded by small crowds of admirers.

Niamh pointed at a group of spectators, "Look, there's Michaelson. Let's watch him."

Abarta said, "Sure, we can start with him, but I'd like to watch Flinniana after that."

Maggie had never seen anyone get excited about watching jugglers. Of course, the only jugglers she'd seen were at the county fair one year. They tossed apples and baseballs in the air. Not much to get excited about.

As they walked up to Michaelson, the crowd around him moved aside so that they could approach the performer. That was when she caught a glimpse of something flashing around his wrists and arms. There was a whirling group of daggers spinning in the air around him, with flashes of light bouncing off the blades like small bolts of lightning.

Áine whispered to Maggie, "He's doing the Arms of Steel. Oh, look, he's shifting to the axes. He calls this The Halo."

As Maggie watched, the blur of daggers shifted into a slower moving arc of axes with electric fire moving around the juggler's head. The crowd made oooooing and ahhhing sounds.

Gee discreetly told them, "I made his daggers and axes."

Maggie whispered to Áine, "Is he really juggling? I don't see him throwing anything into the air."

Áine giggled. "That's the best kind of juggler."

Abarta said, "Wait until you see Flinniana."

Maggie asked, "What does he do?"

Abarta grinned. "*She* juggles dishes."

As it turned out, Flinniana didn't juggle dishes, another of Abarta's jokes. Maggie whacked him on the shoulder when she saw a whorl of oranges, apples, and pears around the woman. She couldn't help laughing. The scene was absurd until she realized that the juggler was changing the order of the objects as they flew through the air without touching them. The juggler was also adding groups of objects from somewhere to the circle until it became a rainbow of alternating colors. She wasn't sure where the objects were coming from though.

Flinniana's hands were moving so little that it seemed to Maggie that the objects were just flying through the air on their own. There was a beauty in the moment that she hadn't recognized before.

Maggie whispered, "Abarta, you are right. It's beautiful."

He smiled. "I knew you'd like this one."

When Flinniana ended her routine, and as the crowd applauded, Maggie made her way to the juggler. "I really enjoyed your juggling. It's not like anything I've ever seen before."

"I'm honored," she said and bowed her head.

"How do you do it? Your hands hardly moved."

"That's true. It's not my hands moving the objects. It's my changing the direction in which they are falling."

"But, if they are falling, how do you get them to go up?"

Flinniana smiled and leaned close to Maggie to whisper, "I can get them to fall up. Each object has its own character. You find it and influence it." She looked at the others in the group to see if they had overheard. "That's our secret. I'm certain you will respect it."

"Of course." Maggie frowned a bit because the explanation was more gibberish than information. It didn't really explain anything, but it was a secret, so she wouldn't tell anyone. Maybe she could figure out what it meant.

Flinniana curtsied. "I'm pleased, Ma'am, to know that you enjoyed my display of skill."

"I did. Very much."

And at that point Niamh and Áine began pulling on her to go. Maggie waved goodbye to the juggler and the small group resumed wandering through the festival.

The other jugglers were also good and seemed to move their objects in arcs about them without effort. Maggie watched them more carefully now that Flinniana had shared her secret.

There must be some technique they're using to move the objects. Or to make the objects move. Perhaps that's the key.

There was one, a short stocky man, who juggled plates and, when they saw him, Maggie laughed and whacked

Abarta on the arm again. The plates spun so fast in front of him that they looked like a single disk of porcelain.

Áine said, "Fergus calls this his Shield of Glass. Technically, it's not really glass. Sounds better than Shield of Fired Clays though." And they all laughed.

The morning passed, and as they walked from pavilion to pavilion, a growing group of kids Maggie's age gathered around them. Maggie didn't recall seeing any at the ceremony who were her age and was surprised.

Maybe the crowd hid them. Or maybe they didn't go into the orchard with everyone else. I wouldn't have either if I had a choice.

All morning, Abarta was never far from her, telling outrageous stories and laughing. Niamh laughed at all of them. She was pleasant, and Maggie enjoyed her laughter. She was someone Maggie thought might be a friend, and it was impossible to imagine her as a queen. All of them seemed like friends not kidnappers.

Maggie turned to Gee, who was standing behind her, and said, "You've been very quiet." *He has freckles that must cover him from head to toe. If he wasn't wearing shoes, I bet I'd see he has freckles on his feet.*

113

Which was funny to her, because after she thought that, he looked at his feet and turned deep red, before mumbling, "Not much to say really."

"Do you do anything else, or do you just do smith work?"

He looked up with a big grin on his face. "I also help with the feasts."

"Really. What kind of help? Did you help with this feast?"

"Sure. I always help. It's preparing the food where I pitch in. The helpers always use my kitchen to do the cooking. I have the best ovens in all the universes and a complete pantry."

"That sounds wonderful. I like to cook too. Do you have a house?"

"Yeah. That's where I do my work. Smithing. Cooking. You have to try the roast beef when it's time to eat. That's one of my specialties."

"Mine too!"

"Although, I like fixing a good lamb rack."

"I've never fixed lamb. They don't raise many sheep around home. Just cows. And chickens. Everybody has chickens at home."

"I don't work with chicken much. This crowd," he motioned to those around them, "Likes beef. Lots of stews and roasts. That sort of thing."

She and Gee talked about cooking and recipes until a group of minstrels skipped past them followed by a growing crowd. All of them were singing something in a language she didn't understand. At first it sounded familiar, however when she focused on the words she realized she didn't know them at all.

That's creepy. Maggie asked, "Where is everyone going?"

Gee said, "That's the signal. It's time for the feast!"

Niamh and Áine took Maggie by each arm and fell in behind the minstrels singing and dancing with the rest of the crowd. Maggie stumbled a bit at first, but quickly found the rhythm. Even though she didn't know the words, she was able to hum the tune.

She was surprised that it was really feeling like a festival. In spite of herself, she was having fun.

***

At the feast, Vivienne wouldn't let Maggie choose a goblet of mead.

"You're a little too young for that."

Maggie pointed at her friends, "Abarta and the others got some. Besides, Gee says he crafted it."

"Gee? You mean Goibniu. They're a bit older than you. When you are a little older, you can too, but not just yet. There is some wonderful cider here made from the apples of our orchard. For now, you should drink that."

Maggie sighed and took the cider. It was the best that she'd ever tasted, so she didn't mind as much. She loaded her plate with roast beef and told Gee that he was right. It was perfect.

By the afternoon, the conversations were lagging and the excitement of the morning had settled back into the normal flow of events. The minstrels, jugglers, and other entertainers walked among the tables performing. They were a pleasant break from conversation.

The words of the songs that they were singing still sounded familiar, only their meanings were hiding from her. She was beginning to feel tired, and for the first time, she began to wish that the festival would end.

No one asked Maggie about Fort Richards and her family, so she didn't offer any stories to match those she heard being told around her. She suspected that most of the stories had been told before, however the groups of listeners always enjoyed them. It was as though they re-experienced the events each time the story was told.

Jamison would enjoy hearing them. He likes listening to Mr. Munroe tell about the Kiowa and these stories are like that. Narrow escapes, hunting, and playing tricks on other people. I bet Abarta has a million of those!

She would have enjoyed it more if she weren't also thinking about escaping. Thinking about that while smiling at everybody around her and enjoying the entertainment made her feel like a liar.

Everyone is happy that I'm here. Niamh, Áine, Abarta, Gee, Luke, and CR are my friends now. Better friends in a couple of hours than any of the kids in Fort Richards.

And they really believe I've returned home. It's all very confusing.

The sun was beginning its slide behind the trees.

Soon, Vivienne stood and addressed the group. Her voice carried across the pavilion city, "The day has ended and I want to thank each of you for joining us in our celebration of Marguerite's return home. Now at the closing of day and beginning of night, it is time for us to take our leave of you. We wish you safe travel on your journeys. On Samhain, we will join you again."

The members of the circle stood and in one voice thanked Vivienne for her hospitality. They then wished Marguerite happiness and peace. While the minstrels played their sweet songs, Vivienne and Marguerite walked through the door into the side of the hill and were gone.

9   Crazy Talk

Vivienne paused in the doorway. "I hope you enjoyed today. It was truly special. Other than the usual holiday feasts, we don't gather together as often as we used to do."

"I don't really understand who everyone was. They were so different."

"From those you have known?"

"Yes. Who is the boy named Abarta? He was very funny. Kind of cute. I thought so anyway."

"Abarta. Yes, he is something isn't he?" She smiled at Maggie. "Seemed to spend a lot of time with us today." She paused a moment before saying, "Let's walk back to the compass center, and I'll tell you more about him."

Vivienne walked briskly down the corridor between the stacks of gifts. Maggie followed her, half running to keep up.

As they walked, Vivienne said, "I think I'd like some tea, English Breakfast, with some shortbread biscuits. Would you like anything, dear?"

"I don't think so," Maggie replied between breaths. "I ate so much today I don't feel hungry."

"It *was* wonderful wasn't it. The helpers did marvelous work getting all in place. I always appreciate them. The circle enjoys visiting me because they know I have the best helpers."

"How did they get everything set up so quickly?"

"Helper magic, of course. Mine are quite adept at it."

"I see." *More crazy talk. Maybe I won't learn anything real after all.* Her excitement began to ebb.

As they approached the center of the cavern, Maggie saw that waiting for them on the table was a silver-serving tray with a teapot, a cup with saucer, and a platter of shortbread cookies.

"Just in time." Vivienne sighed, settled into one of the armchairs, picked up the cup of tea that had apparently been poured for her, and daintily sipped. "I have to have my afternoon tea even if it is late. It's just a habit I have acquired over the years. However, I don't feel that my day is complete until I've had my tea. And a bit of shortbread."

Maggie sat in the chair next to her and waited for her to tell her about Abarta. She tried not to fidget while Vivienne sipped her tea and nibbled at the edges of a cookie. Her mother was always telling her to "Stop that fidgeting." Patience wasn't one of her virtues, although today she forced herself to remain calm and quiet.

After several minutes, Vivienne settled her cup in its saucer. "Abarta is a bit wild. He attends all of our festivals. I don't think he's ever missed any. Always laughing and telling jokes, he adds a light touch to every festival. However, he has a dark side as well. Like all of us. There are more sides to us than the one that's seen. He is a fighter and can be hard to deal with when he is focused and on task. He can be selfish sometimes. However, he is one of us and would never betray us. We can trust him. You can trust him."

"That's good to know." She smiled politely at Vivienne, but she didn't trust any of them. Why would she trust them anyway? "So, who was the older one? The man named Dagda? I've never heard these names before."

"I'm not surprised. Our names are old. The Dagda is the first of the Tuatha De, and we are his children."

Great, it is a cult. Maggie held her breath and squeezed her elbows into her sides. *I want my mother. My real mother. AND I WANT TO GO HOME.*

"But not children in the way that you know the word. Children because he has empowered us." Vivienne spread out her hands, palms up, as though she were catching an invisible cascade of water. "And you are one of us not just by my blood as your mother, but also by our spirit as your family. It's what we shared with you today."

"I have power?"

121

"Of course, although you already had power. It's just beginning to find focus now."

"What kind of power?"

"I don't know yet. It is just awakening, so we'll see as you grow."

"That's not very helpful. It could be anything. What powers do you have? And, if you have powers and I was really your child, why would you leave me with somebody else to raise? It doesn't make sense."

"You couldn't grow here surrounded by all of this. You needed to be outside, but in a safe place to become you. As for my powers, my primary realm is water, fresh water. Lakes, streams, and rivers that is where my power rests." Vivienne smiled. "But not oceans. I never cared for salt water and have no influence there. Your power could also be in some other realm."

Maggie clenched her jaws while Vivienne was talking about powers. *More crazy talk.* Except, instead of saying that, she tried to smile. "You said that we would see them again on Samhain. What's that?"

"Samhain? It is the Fall festival. We gather to celebrate the end of harvest before the beginning of winter. There are bonfires and feasts. We travel from feast to feast to share and protect."

"Protect. Protect what?"

"The world. It has enemies, and we have enemies."

Maggie folded her hands in her lap and sat quietly. *Finally, this is the crazy talk I was expecting to hear from a bunch of cult kidnappers. There's always an enemy somewhere.*

"They use the seam between summer and winter to enter this space. The wards holding them back are weakest then." Vivienne placed her teacup and saucer on the table beside her with a sharp clink of porcelain. "They thrive on fear and pain while destroying what's good and beautiful. *We* protect existence from the Fomoire wolves."

"They're wolves?"

"That's just an expression."

"I see. Sounds strange."

"Yes. It would. Samhain is a bit of a paradox. Feasting and celebration while at the same time a period of high risk." Vivienne sighed and her voice trailed off. She seemed to forget that Maggie was sitting in the chair beside her.

They sat together in silence, until Vivienne suddenly glanced at Maggie and said, "Don't worry about this now. It's strange to you and you've had more than enough for one day. You are back home. That's enough. It's a day for you to be happy not burdened."

Vivienne stood. "It's time for me to retire. Is there anything that you need? I haven't thought to ask you."

Maggie stood quietly with her for a moment before saying, "I'd like a notebook and some pens and my record player and records. Those are at the hotel, though."

"Of course. I believe my helpers can take care of that for you. If you need anything else, just ask. What kind of pens?"

"I have a fountain pen that I like. A Schaffer. My father bought it for me last year, for my birthday."

"Of course." With that, Vivienne briefly hugged Maggie, her perfume filled Maggie's head with the warm smells of vanilla and allspice before she turned to walk down the aisle in the direction of the garden. She called over her shoulder, "Have a pleasant sleep, dear one. I'll see you tomorrow."

"Thank you," Maggie called. "You too."

This is so unreal.

Maggie walked down the aisle to the space where her bed was.

Vivienne seems nice even when she's talking about Fomoire wolves, whatever that is. Doesn't act like she's bonkers even if she talks like it.

She laughed. *Jamison likes to say that about people he doesn't like. Oh, he's bonkers. That teacher is bonkers.*

He started saying that about everybody after he read it in a book. Jeeves the butler and Bertie the worthless rich kid.

Those were funny stories. I wish this were funny like that.

I wish I was home.

10   Firestorm

On Maggie's bed, rested a bound leather notebook and her fountain pen. She wasn't surprised about the notebook. She actually expected Vivienne to give her one because she had asked for it.

But the pen was a shock.

It was her pen from her bedroom in the hotel.

She cautiously touched the pen as if it was an illusion. It was real. She uncapped it, and no ink was leaking from it. It always leaked ink if she dropped it, made a mess on her fingers, but it was perfect.

She opened the notebook and smoothed the paper with her fingers. The paper was smooth and soft. Perfect for writing. The green leather cover was soft and flexible.

She took them to her new writing table that was standing beside her bed. That was when she saw her record player and a stack of records. They were hers from the hotel.

Hurriedly she flipped through the records. They were all there, even her Jelly Roll Morton. Her father had given her those for Christmas.

Maggie picked up the electric plug for the player and searched for an outlet. She wanted to play Jelly as loud as the volume knob would go.

Vivienne said this place and all of the stuff in it is mine. Time to test that!

Except there were no outlets.

Of course, there really were no walls, just stacks of crates covered by draped tapestries. On the side where there was something like a wall, it was the solid stone of the cavern's side.

She dropped the plug and stood by the player. It wasn't any good without an electric outlet.

The turntable sat there with its green felt surface waiting for the drop of a record.

Absent-mindedly she turned the knob that turned on the record player. To her surprise, the turntable began to spin. She looked at the back of the player. It wasn't plugged in. She shrugged.

Just more strange stuff that happened today. Strange is becoming normal.

Maggie put on her Jelly Roll record and cranked the volume up as high as it would go. The sound of his band echoed through the cavern, and she was happy for a minute before becoming sad. It reminded her of home, her real home, and her mother, her real mother, and Jamison and doing chores, and standing in the top of the clock tower looking out across west Texas.

She didn't know where she was anymore. She didn't even know what day or time it was. The light in the cavern seemed to come from everywhere, rising and falling when she needed or didn't need it, not because of the time of day.

After a minute, she turned the volume down to something that was normal, sat at the desk, and began writing in her new notebook.

Yesterday a cult kidnapped me. At least I think they are a cult.

I'm not sure where I am.

Today they had a ceremony where they welcomed me in their "circle," and they were all nice. It was also scary because they are so bizarre. Everything here is crazy.

The people, the place where they have me staying, everything about this is weird. Sometimes I think I'm having a nightmare. I hope I'll wake up in the morning in my bed and have to go fix breakfast for the guests.

I met some kids today that were about my age, actually a little older, but they were nice, and I did have fun. One of them, a girl named Niamh – it's pronounced something like Nee-f - said she was the queen of someplace I never heard of...

None of the names here are anything I ever heard of, except Vivienne. Niamh might have been lying though. She was about my age. How can somebody get to be a queen when they are my age?

Vivienne, the woman that kidnapped me, says she is my real mother. She said when I was born she swapped me with my mother's real daughter. That makes me a changeling. Not sure what that means except that I got replaced, but I don't believe her. Why would she do that?

As soon as I figure out how, I'm getting out of here and going home. For now, I'm waiting until I get my chance.

At least they are nice to me.

I wonder if anybody is looking for me? And Mr. Munroe turned out to be evil. He's the one that took me. I hate him now.

She closed the notebook.

Jelly Roll's band had stopped playing, and the record spun making the small snick-snick sound as the needle traced the final groove.

Maggie lifted the needle from the record and turned the power off. For a minute, she left the record on the turntable.

Why bother doing anything anymore.

But her father always insisted she put them back in their jackets, so she slipped the record back in its sleeve and placed it on the stack.

She was ready to go to bed. *Mother would be proud of me going to bed without being told.*

But after the festival all day, she needed to get a bath and brush her teeth.

Provided I can find the bathroom. It has to be around here somewhere.

She grumbled out loud, "The way things work around here, that gap in the tapestries probably leads to the bathroom."

Maggie pulled the tapestry aside and laughed because it *was* the bathroom — although not like any bathroom she had ever seen. Typical of her experience so far, all of the fixtures of a normal bathroom were present, only they were formed from the stone of the cavern.

In the center, was a pool of water filled by a stream flowing from the wall. She felt the water expecting it to be ice cold, except it wasn't. It was warm, almost hot, and just right. The pool wasn't overflowing, so she assumed there must be a drain somewhere.

Set in the wall was an alcove that contained a basin formed from stone with water trickling into it from the cavern wall and a silver framed mirror set above it.

Beside the pool was a stool carved from stone and folded neatly on the stool were her pajamas, her own pajamas from her room at the hotel.

On a hunch, she hurried to the stone basin in the wall and, of course, there were her own toothbrush and toothpaste from the hotel. All of the things from her life were appearing in this place.

Before long, there won't be any of my things left at the hotel. All of them will be here in the cavern.

At first the thought was alarming until she told herself, "At least for now, I have my own things here. That makes it a little better."

After finishing her bath, putting on her pajamas, and brushing her teeth, she sat in the center of the bed with her notebook and wrote about the celebration. She was reluctant to write much about Abarta at first, She wasn't sure what she wanted to say about him. In the end, she just wrote…

At the ceremony today, there was a boy named Abarta. Everyone here has strange names like that. Dagda was the name of another one. Except, he is an old man.

At least the three brothers have nicknames that I can say - even if they are a bit odd.

One of the boys is called Gee. His real name is Goibniu. That's how it's spelled, except it's actually pronounced something like Guv-noo. That's strange, only not too bad. Gee is better, though.

And then there is boy called CR because, he says, it's a symbol of chromium in the periodic table. That's a strange one. I'll have to look it up when I get home. The school might have one of those tables. His real name is spelled Credne but pronounced something like Cray-en-ya. I'm glad it's ok to call him CR.

But Abarta was funny and handsome. In the ceremony, they say something about gifting you, and then they touch you on the forehead. It was all kind of stupid, except when he reached out to touch my head there was a giant spark that jumped across and shocked me.

He warned me that he was the prankster of the group. I guess I found out.

Vivienne frowned when it happened. Everyone else seemed to take that ceremony like it was serious, but he's cute, so I didn't get too angry about him shocking me.

She set the notebook down. In a minute, she fell asleep as the cavern light around her dimmed to twilight.

***

An explosion rolled across the floor of the cavern scattering the stacks of crates and tapestries. Gouts of flame tore through the air incinerating everything before it.

Maggie was instantly awake, sat up in her bed, but froze a fraction of a second before vaulting to the floor and racing to the compass center. It was the only way she knew to navigate in the cavern. She ducked as a fireball flew over her head, flames flicking out to touch her hair.

She shrieked, not something that she ever did, except this was something she had never had happen before. She climbed over fallen crates that blocked the aisle until she reached the center where the chairs and table had been. There was only a smoking hole in the ground now to mark that spot. The lights in the cavern were flickering.

Flames burned around her, and the air in the cavern was filling with smoke. She began coughing and knew she had to get out, or she would die in there.

Maggie started to run down the aisle that went to the garden until she realized that it was the source of the fireballs and occasional explosions that tore through the cavern. Quickly she turned and began running toward the northern aisle. If there was a door on the east side and her bed was on the west, there might be a door on the other aisles.

As she raced, climbed, and jumped her way in the direction of what she hoped would be another door, she kept looking over her shoulder to make sure that one of the blasts of flame coming from the garden door didn't roast her. She had no idea how far away it was. She thought that it should be about the same distance from the center as the other door. Hopefully she could make it before she collapsed.

The smoke made her cough, and ashes began to fall from the cavern's ceiling where they were collecting in a swirling cloud of orange embers. The heat was increasing rapidly. She remembered her father telling a story several years before of his being caught in a forest fire over in east Texas when the fire began to swirl like a tornado.

An inferno. That's what this is going to become.

She began to panic as she ran and would have started screaming except for the ashes filling the air. She buried her nose and mouth in her elbow to filter the air through the cloth of her pajama sleeve.

She tripped over a dark lump on the floor and fell. It was the tiny woman.

She was finished. She couldn't breathe and was gasping for breath. The cavern was growing dim with only the burning flames from the opposite door spewing out over her head and the storm of fire rising around her giving light to see. She put her head in the crook of her elbow and waited to die.

"Ma'am. Wake up Ma'am."

11 Cup of Chamomile Tea

Maggie lifted her head and opened her eyes. She was lying on the floor in the aisle, except there was no fire or smoke. The lights in the cavern weren't dim or flickering.

She sat up and looked around. The stacks of things around her were intact, and none were scattered across the floor or broken into pieces.

"Are you ok, Ma'am?" The tiny woman was standing in front of her, wringing her hands, with a concerned frown on her face.

"Yes." Maggie touched the crates next to her. "I suppose I am. I guess I dreamed that everything was on fire. But it's not, so I guess I'm alright."

"You saw the hall on fire?"

"Yes, only it was a dream." Maggie motioned around her. "See, everything is fine."

"Ma'am, you must come with me at once." The tiny woman hurried Maggie back down the aisle to the compass center where Vivienne was sitting with her constant cup of tea.

"Ma'am," the little woman said as they approached, "she has had a vision."

Maggie corrected her, "A dream. I had a dream. And how did you get here so quickly?"

Vivienne replied, "I was called, so I came. Please have a seat." She motioned to the chair beside her. "Tell me what you saw."

Maggie sat in the chair that was quickly becoming hers and began to tell Vivienne what she had seen.

"It was a dream. I dreamed that there was an explosion that ripped through the cavern and blew up all of the crates and stuff. Then there were these giant balls of flame that came tearing across the room setting everything on fire. Then there was this firestorm that started filling the air with smoke and ashes, and I was running trying to get out, but the fire was coming from the door where the garden is, so I didn't know where to go. The only thing I could think of doing was running in another direction. Then the air was so thick with smoke that I couldn't go any farther, and I just collapsed on the ground not able to breathe. I thought I was dying. Then," Maggie pointed to the tiny woman who was still standing beside her, "she woke me."

Vivienne cradled her teacup in her hands without saying anything.

The tiny woman handed Maggie a cup of tea, and Maggie told her, "Thank you." It wasn't something she wanted so late at night, only she didn't have the heart to refuse.

"Don't worry, Ma'am. It's chamomile," the little woman whispered and then smiled. "It will help you sleep."

Maggie returned her smile. "Thank you again."

Vivienne sighed and set her cup in its saucer. "Did you see anyone in your vision?"

"It was a dream. And there was no one other than me. Oh, I forgot. She...," Maggie pointed to the little woman, "...was lying in the aisle. The compass center here was completely destroyed. It was just a deep hole in the ground."

"Was it like any dream you have ever had?"

"Not really."

"Have you ever run somewhere in the waking world while having one of your dreams? Been bruised from jumping and falling?" She pointed to a purple bruise forming on Maggie's arm.

"No."

"That was not a dream. It was a vision. There is a difference, as you will learn. This is just the first."

"What do you mean, the first?"

"There will be more. It is one of your abilities now. I suspected it might be a possibility, although one never knows what abilities will find you after gifting."

"Ability?"

"We are all different. One never knows what abilities we will manifest. For you, as a perceptive, it is only natural that you would have foresight. The task for us now is to understand the vision."

"The abilities come from the gifting."

"Yes, this is one, and there will be others. Clíodhna is strong in this area, and it is probably one of her gifts to you that have taken hold. We must speak with her. For now, though, you have seen a great threat, and I thank you. You should return to bed."

"How can I sleep after something like that?"

"Finish the chamomile tea. Sleep will find you. And thank you again, for sharing your vision."

Maggie walked back to her bed with the little woman following closely, and the heavy weight of sleep closed her eyes as she crawled under the comforter.

The little woman tenderly tucked the covers in around her and sat in a small chair set in the corner of the room keeping watch while she slept.

"Peace keep you, Marguerite."

*****

Vivienne sat in her chair long after Maggie had gone back to sleep.

12   Vieux Carrie

In the morning, Vivienne was waiting when Maggie walked into the compass center.

"Did you have a good breakfast?"

"Yes, it was wonderful."

"That's good. We have a full day ahead, so it's best to begin without hunger. Last night I didn't have a chance to ask you if those were the music recordings that you wanted. Were they?"

"Yes, those were mine. Thank you for getting them."

"They are yours, so you should have them. Let me know if there is anything else that you want. Or need." Vivienne smiled. "All you have to do is ask. Now about your vision, I have been dwelling on it, and I have a few questions to ask. Please have a seat." She motioned at the empty chair beside her. "If you would like it, there is a cup of tea for you. But not chamomile this morning!" Vivienne discretely smiled at her own attempt at humor.

Maggie sat in the chair and picked up the teacup. The porcelain was so thin she could see the shadow of the tea through its walls. She took a sip – *Irish Breakfast*.

"Please, tell me again what you saw in your vision. I would like to know every detail."

Maggie retold what she had seen and answered Vivienne's questions, each question more specific than the last.

At last, Vivienne sighed and said, "That's enough. There aren't any details left to uncover." She stood and said, "Come with me, and I'll show you what lies at the end of the aisle you were running down when you fell."

Vivienne walked briskly down the northern aisle.

"This is the north point." She was motioning around the room as they walked, pointing to crates stacked in different areas. "This might look disorganized to you, but there is a system to how these items are stored. In time you will come to understand it, so I won't bother trying to describe it now. Besides, we have more critical things to concentrate on. Let me show you something that I believe you will enjoy."

They had reached the door in the far wall. The door itself was made of six-inch thick apple wood beams held together by ornate hammered iron straps. Vivienne pushed them open, and they stepped into swirling fog.

"It's usually foggy when I come here. I like fog as you might guess. It will take a second to clear." As she was speaking, the fog thinned and then disappeared. "Fog is in my realm, you know."

Vivienne and Maggie were standing in a courtyard surrounded by walls with balconies and windows. In the center of the courtyard, a fountain trickled water from its top into a series of increasingly larger basins below that spilled into each other.

Growing around the fountain's basin were tropical plants. Except for some tall banana trees and giant ferns in the corners of the space, Maggie didn't recognize any of them.

Vivienne motioned around the courtyard and said, "This is one of my favorite places. It is surrounded by fresh water."

"Where are we?"

"This is New Orleans, in the Vieux Carrie."

"How did we get here?"

"It's linked to our space. I've had this house for ages. We're in the center of the city, and yet, with the galleries around us," she motioned at the balconies surrounding them, "it feels very private and also quiet. Most of the time, that is." As an afterthought, she added, "Except at Mardi Gras!"

"Oh." Maggie looked around the courtyard. *It's real. That's for sure, but it, none of it, makes sense.* "Can you take me to Fort Richards?"

"My dear, why would you want to go back there? Besides it's not connected to Avalon."

"If it's not connected, how did we get to Avalon from there in the first place?"

"The Imaginærium Engine. Remember? I told you."

"I just didn't understand. Don't understand."

"That's quite alright, dear. One of the things the Imaginærium Engine can do is take you anywhere. However, that's only going in one direction. Going in the other direction is a different story. Now, we have other things to do." Vivienne set out across the courtyard to an open door. "We have guests waiting."

***

She led Maggie through a set of French doors and into a long dining room. Abarta, Niamh, Áine, Clíodhna, and the three brothers were sitting at a long conference table laughing.

Vivienne whispered, "Abarta must have told another joke."

At first, Maggie didn't recognize them. Niamh, Áine, and Clíodhna were in dresses that might have come from a boutique dress shop in Dallas or Fort Worth. Nothing extravagant though like the bizarre costumes they were wearing at the welcome celebration.

Abarta and the three brothers were wearing business suits with white shirts and ties. Nice clothes and yet clothes that anyone might wear.

They look almost normal today.

Abarta jumped to his feet. "Our host!"

Vivienne smiled, "Always a flare for the dramatic. Please be seated Abarta. I thank you for coming."

"It's always a pleasure, Vivienne. And it's good to see you again, Marguerite. You're as pretty as always."

Maggie blushed. "I've only known you for one day."

"A day can last forever."

Vivienne frowned. "Abarta, don't annoy my daughter. She's just come home and doesn't know you yet as I do. Besides, we have important work ahead. Marguerite has had a vision. One in which she has seen the destruction of my space."

Clíodhna turned to stare at Maggie. "So soon after gifting. That is most unusual."

Vivienne straightened her shoulders and tilted her chin up. "She's my daughter. We should expect nothing less of her."

A smile flickered over Clíodhna's lips. "Of course. She is unique. That is apparent. What is it that you need from us?"

Vivienne sat at the table and motioned for Maggie to sit beside her. "How should we understand it?"

Clíodhna sighed and leaned back in her chair. "It's a vision not a prediction. It can be a warning of the future or a reflection from the past. What was it you saw, Marguerite?"

Maggie told Clíodhna what she had seen while Clíodhna sat quietly with her eyes closed. At the end of Maggie's story, she asked, "So what do *you* believe it means?"

"I don't know. It was so real I thought that I was going to die."

"Was anyone with you?"

"No, I was alone."

"Can you recall seeing anyone else in the great hall? Close your eyes and relive each moment, except this time tell me what you see."

With her eyes closed, she saw the explosion and flames that incinerated the hall.

"You saw no helpers?"

She opened her eyes in surprise. "Only one, the tiny woman who has been helping me. I didn't see any others."

"You are able to see the helpers, aren't you?"

"Yes. The tiny woman who has been helping me said she wasn't surprised considering who I was."

"Of course. There is a reason then, that other than your helper, they were not present. Perhaps they were warned and left, but I believe they would not have left you alone if there was a threat that they recognized. So perhaps they were lured away from the hall for a moment. Just long enough for the invaders to strike."

Vivienne spoke up, "We can surmise that it is the Fomoire. They must have found the Imaginærium Engine. It's the only way that they could enter Avalon."

Abarta drummed his fingers on the table. "Fomoire. The root of evil in the universe."

His three companions pounded the table and shouted, "Death to Fomoire."

It was so sudden and loud, Maggie looked at Vivienne to see what her reaction was. The others didn't seem surprised, so she tried to ignore their shouting. Fomoire sounded like characters from one of Jamison's science fiction books. However, she had experienced the vision, and it literally felt real. If they were the ones that wanted to destroy Avalon, then she believed Abarta was probably right. They must be evil.

After a minute, Clíodhna raised her hand, "Please, Abarta. Allow us to speak."

Abarta motioned to his companions, and they gradually stopped chanting and pounding the table.

Vivienne said, "If the Fomoire have found the Imaginæruim, they will attack on Samhain. The moon will be full, and that is when the Imaginæruim is strongest."

Clíodhna looked at the faces in the group, "That will be in three days."

Maggie asked, "Why would they want it?"

Clíodhna said, "If they seize it, they can use it to take them anywhere. Forces of destruction, moving effortlessly through all of existence."

Abarta told the three brothers, "We must protect it."

Vivienne said, "Of course. The threat is to all of us. I have helpers watching the Imaginæruim, but they will not be able to stop a full attack by Fomoire."

Abarta asked, "Where is it? Where do we go?"

Vivienne looked at Maggie and reached out to grasp her hand. "Fort Richards. Where we hid my daughter so long ago."

C. G. Wayne

152

13 No Joy

It took an hour of arguing and pounding fists on tables before it was agreed that the group would travel to Fort Richards to defend the Imaginærium Engine.

Vivienne was hesitant about Maggie joining the group, and only agreed after Clíodhna insisted that she go.

"It is her vision that guides us."

"But she's only arrived. She's just been home *one* day!"

"In three days, Vivienne, Fomoire will run rampant. She must go."

"If she must." Vivienne didn't sound convinced.

Maggie sat at the table listening to the arguments flying around her and said nothing.

More and more bizarre. They are actually going to take me back home!

Earlier she had thought about running out in the courtyard to find a cop and beg to go home. Now, suddenly she was going to be going home without having to do anything.

Her head spun.

Her heart raced.

This was her break, but it didn't make sense.

Why would they take me back home after kidnapping me?

Maybe this is some strange game they're playing with me, and I don't understand the rules yet.

Vivienne abruptly stood and said, "We must leave at once. We only have three days."

With that, there was a polite knock on the door. When the door opened, the strange boy who had been with Vivienne in Fort Richards stepped into the room. He was dressed in the same dark clothes and wearing the same dark glasses.

"Ma'am, I have the cars waiting outside. If you and the others will follow me...."

The strange boy handed Vivienne her dark glasses as she left the room.

Maggie whispered to her, "Why do you wear those?"

Vivienne whispered back, "The sunlight hurts my eyes."

"Oh. That makes sense." *Now I feel stupid.* "I was just wondering. They make you look so sinister."

"But, I'm not." Vivienne hugged her tightly for a moment and then hurried from the room.

They followed the boy down the hall and through a heavy wooden door out to the street where four cars were parked. They were long black Rolls Royce's parked bumper to bumper. 1929 Rolls Royce Phantoms with tall chrome grills and large round headlights perched between the grills and the front fenders.

Jamison was a car nut, and Maggie recognized them from one of his car books.

He would just die to be here and see these.

Unbelievable. In a couple of days, I will be able to tell him all about them.

The strange boy opened the door of the first Phantom for Vivienne and Maggie. Other helpers opened the doors of the other cars. All of them were dressed in black suits. Some helpers, though, were short like the strange boy while others were as tall as Mr. Munroe.

Clíodhna and Abarta entered the next Phantom, the one with the giant-sized helper holding the door. To Maggie, Clíodhna was really the queen. Everyone, including Vivienne, listened to what she said and did what she told them to do, even Abarta, which surprised her. Abarta didn't impress her as doing what anyone told him to do, much less listening to them.

Niamh and Áine entered the third car while the three brothers entered the final car. They were so large that Maggie wasn't sure at first how they could fit, and yet, they managed to squeeze inside.

Maggie sat next to Vivienne. The seat was plush and covered in soft cashmere, softer than any piece of furniture. The windows had polished wood trim around them with walnut and mother of pearl inlays. A glass separated them from the driver in the front. It was as though they were riding inside a room not a car.

The peculiar boy opened the front door and sat beside the driver, who slowly pulled away from the curb and drove them down the street. The engine made a gentle whirring sound that could hardly be heard inside the car.

It was nothing like the noisy Ford pickup truck her dad drove or her grandfather's old Buick sedan.

She couldn't see the other cars but imagined them dropping in line behind them. Four black limos moving through the streets of New Orleans just like they were the mob. Maybe they were. That would explain why they were so strange. After all, they did kidnap her.

She looked at Vivienne and quickly dropped the idea that they were mobsters.

None of them look like criminals. Not even Abarta and his three friends. They were all strange, but not criminals. Maybe the Fomoire are the mob.

Vivienne was staring at the passing façades of wrought iron balconied buildings.

"What are Fomoire? Is that some kind of a gang?"

"A gang? I don't understand. They are our mortal enemies. Have always been. Broken spirits, they thrive on fear and hate. All of the dark thoughts that fill the night and poison the day. With the Imaginærium, they could cross from here to any place, all homes and all spaces in existence.

"We work to restrain them. Yet, war, disease, and evil still enter this world in spite of our efforts."

Vivienne turned back to the window. "When I first came to this town, the buildings were new, springing up from the marsh, yet vibrant and hopeful. Now they are old and crumbling. It makes me sad. And yet, that is the way of cities. Its people are afraid and tired, both their minds and hearts. Being here today makes me appreciate my Avalon."

Maggie listened without speaking. She had never been to New Orleans, but she had seen photographs in magazines of the buildings.

It was odd to think that only two days ago she had been in Fort Richards working in the kitchen helping get dinner ready for guests.

And today she was riding in a limousine with a woman who said that she was her real mother.

And she was dressed in expensive clothes, silk not cotton.

Which was the dream? Life in Fort Richards or Avalon?

"Have you ever been to New Orleans?" Vivienne was asking as though she had read her thoughts.

"No. I've never been anywhere before. Except to Fort Worth to see my grandparents. And a couple of times to Dallas on the Interurban. That's like a train, but that's about it."

"When we have stopped this threat, we should spend some time here. It's an interesting city. Full of restless spirits with many interesting stories to tell. If that is one of your abilities, and I expect that it will be."

"Are we going to drive all the way to Fort Richards?"

"No. You will take the train instead. I have a private car for you to use."

"I don't understand."

"A private rail car. They connect it to the train that will take you to Fort Worth. It's more comfortable on a long trip like this."

"You have your own private rail car? When you came to Fort Richards, why were you riding on a bus? You could afford something really nice."

"At the time, arriving any other way would have drawn too much attention to you. Fomoire have agents watching in unexpected places. They are always on the watch. And your safety was always my greatest concern."

Vivienne sighed and absentmindedly tapped the window glass with her fingernails. She had long fingernails, perfectly shaped and painted to match her dress. "Now, of course, discretion doesn't matter. We must save the Imaginærium. Speed is more important than discretion."

The car stopped at Canal Street. It was the widest street Maggie had ever seen with six lanes of cars and a wide median running down its center that had streetcars going back and forth.

Vivienne told her, "They call this center strip the neutral ground because it used to mark the boundary between the American sector and the French Quarter. When the Americans arrived, they had to settle on the west side where it was swamp. Of course, the French Quarter was the city before the Americans came. Naturally the Americans and the French hated each other. The American district was originally named Lafayette. Now, it's known as the Garden District, and the city contains both the Quarter and the District...."

Maggie only half listened to her. None of it was interesting. She thought Fort Worth was nicer. It was newer and had big houses too.

Maggie sat up suddenly and asked, "You said that I would take the train and use your private car."

"Yes, that's correct."

"Aren't you coming too?"

"I'm sorry, but I can't."

Elated, Maggie sat back in her seat but put on her disappointed face. "I see."

"I know, it's terrible to have to leave you again." Vivienne hid her face by turning to look out the window at the passing crowds and traffic. "I have to return with Clíodhna to Avalon. We will prepare for the worst. Abarta and the others will accompany you. They have fought the Fomoire before and will be good companions."

Vivienne turned to face Maggie. "And when you return, we will have the greatest victory celebration that the Otherworlds have ever known." With that she tried to smile as she wiped away faint traces of tears from her cheeks. Maggie's heart lurched in her chest with confused feelings of joy and sadness.

The woman is nuts. Why does this make me sad! That's what's nuts.

The traffic light changed to green, and they crossed Canal Street.

"On this side of Canal, we're in the Garden District." Vivienne pointed to a few houses and talked cheerfully about architectural styles. She told Maggie, "This is St Charles Avenue." The rest of Vivienne's history of the Garden District was a blur, although it helped time pass while they slowly worked their way down a street electrified for streetcars. Maggie hid a yawn. She was too preoccupied with the thought of going home to pay much attention to Vivienne's stories about New Orleans.

Finally, their driver turned left. In a few blocks, they pulled up beside the curb at a train station. The station was a blocky looking building with concrete columns and tall arched windows. It looked more like a bank than a train terminal.

The car doors opened, and they began walking as a group to the station. Abarta and his three friends walked in front, while their helpers followed, pushing carts piled with trunks.

Maggie wasn't surprised that somehow, they had assembled luggage in a matter of minutes for all members of the group. After the last two days she would have been more surprised to find that the helpers had *not* managed somehow to pack luggage for them.

As they approached the building, a crippled beggar held out a cup and begged for coins. A pasteboard sign propped up by him on the ground said...

Army War Veteran

Please help

Maggie frowned. He was wearing a heavy army trench coat like her dad's, too heavy for a hot and humid New Orleans morning. October and it was still hot. He looked out of place among the others at the station.

They were quickly moving around him to the front doors when Maggie suddenly reached out to grab Vivienne's sleeve. But she was too late.

Before Abarta could react, the beggar stepped past him into their midst. He pulled a large Army pistol from his ragged coat and fired it at Vivienne, who then collapsed to the ground in a spreading pool of dark red blood.

In the chaos that happened immediately after, Abarta and the three brothers jumped on the beggar before he could fire a second shot, Maggie dropped to her knees beside Vivienne and grabbed her arm. Vivienne was gasping frantically, unable to catch her breath.

Clíodhna motioned to her helper, the giant standing beside her. "Take Vivienne to our car."

Maggie looked up at her and demanded, "Where are you taking her?"

"Avalon." Clíodhna gave her a warming smile and whispered, "Please, release her, Marguerite. We must go now, while there is time."

Maggie insisted, "She needs to go to a hospital!" Maggie's grip was locked on Vivienne's arm.

"Not here. Avalon. You *know* that."

Vivienne's hands were clenched into blood covered fists and pressed hard on her chest in the place where blood pulsed from the wound. Maggie slowly released her grip and the giant helper gently lifted Vivienne from the ground and, in long strides, took her back to the car.

Maggie asked Clíodhna, "Will she be ok?"

"If there is time to return…." With that, Clíodhna turned and hurried back to the car. The moment that she stepped inside, the car pulled away from the curb and raced back in the direction of the house in the French Quarter.

The assassin was kneeling, gagged and with hands bound behind his back.

"What should we do with this guy." CR and Gee each had a locked grip on the assassin's upper arms. Their massive hands completely encircled his arms.

Abarta kicked him in the back and said, "Take him to the train."

People moving to the train station ignored them.

Maggie, covered with Vivienne's blood, stood at the edge of the blood pool, staring at the crowd. She waved her arms frantically at the bloody scene and the kneeling beggar. "Why don't they say something about all of this?"

Áine was standing beside her with hands held out, palms flat and facing the people walking past. "I've bent the light around us. We are masked from them, but the light will not hold its bend for long. We must be on the train *now*."

Maggie stared at people walking around them, and none seemed to realize that they were standing there. "What will we do when the cops get here?"

Niamh said, "We will be gone before that. The helpers will clean this."

Abarta told the group, "Be vigilant. This may not be the only assassin."

Gee lifted the beggar from the floor as though he were nothing more than a bundle of ragged clothes and carried him into the train station.

Maggie stumbled behind them, reluctant to leave the scene. Her head was spinning from the speed of events around her. She was going back to Fort Richards and her home, but Vivienne was either dead or dying.

There was no joy now. Not after this.

14 Mrs. Smith

They walked straight through the train station and onto the tracks where the rail car was parked on its siding.

Gee slung the assassin over his shoulder like a big sack of feed and climbed the steps into the railcar.

The inside of the railcar was huge with bedrooms along the right side and, on the left, a narrow hall running from one end to the other. At either end of it were open areas with sofas, chairs, and tables.

Gee dropped the assassin on the floor while Abarta, CR, and Luke crowded around him.

Maggie asked them, "What are you going to do?"

Abarta glanced at her and then turned back to the assassin. "We have to find out why he was here. Why, out of everyone, he tried to kill Vivienne."

"What if he won't say?"

"He will, but we won't begin asking until we are away from the city."

With that, the railcar lurched forward, and Luke said, "They are loading the car now."

Gee looked out of the windows as the car began moving. "Stay alert. There might be others."

Abarta fumed, "Guns are hard to guard against. A killer could strike from anywhere."

"A coward's weapon," Gee agreed. "But deadly."

Maggie, Niamh, and Áine sat on the sofas that ran around the wall.

Maggie's hands were trembling. "That was horrible. Is Vivienne going to be ok? There was blood everywhere."

Niamh turned and stared out the window. "I'm not sure. It just depends on how quickly Clíodhna and the helpers can return her to the Otherworlds."

Áine gave the assassin a kick in the small of his back. "I'd like to know how they found out we were going to be at the station. And why did this pig shoot her and not one of us. Clíodhna would have been an easier target."

Abarta sighed and said, "Patience, Áine. We can't ask until the train is rolling."

There was a lurch and the sense of motion stopped. Gee glanced at them, "We're on the ferry. It won't be long now."

Maggie looked puzzled and asked, "Ferry?"

Gee said, "That's how they get the rail cars across the river. Once we get on the other side, they hook us up to the engine and away we go. This time tomorrow we'll be in Fort Worth."

"How do you know all of that?" Maggie looked out the window trying to see what was happening.

Gee muttered, "I've been up this way before."

In a moment, Maggie heard the sound of the ferry engines and felt their vibration travel through the floor of the railcar as they began to shove them across the river.

The group was quiet. It was the first time that Maggie had been with them that they were not telling jokes and laughing. The change made her feel gloomy. Vivienne may have kidnapped her, but the sight of her lying in a pool of blood was horrible. Maybe she was sad. Perhaps they were all sad. Not knowing if Vivienne was alive or dead was a dark cloud hanging over all of them.

Maggie stood up and told the group, "I'm going to take one of the rooms. Did you have any preferences?"

At that, Niamh and Áine stood too. "We'll go with you. We don't have any preferences, but it would be better than sitting here watching Abarta and the brothers question the assassin."

As they left the room, Áine told Abarta, "Personally, I'd like to be here when you ask your questions. Be sure and let us know what you find out."

Niamh called over her shoulder, "Try not to make too much noise when you talk to him. Even if others can't hear, I will."

***

When they entered the rooms, they found that the helpers had already unpacked their luggage and were waiting for them, so there was no need to decide whose room was whose.

Maggie's room was in the middle, between Áine and Niamh. Abarta and the brothers had the rooms at the ends of the car. No one would be able to enter without having to get past them. Maggie felt a bit safer, even if she also felt trapped.

No way I can escape with everyone around me.

Duh. Except, I don't need to escape now. They're actually taking me home.

Before the others went to their rooms, Maggie said, "I've never been in a private car before. What do we do when it's time to eat?"

Niamh laughed. "The helpers will take care of that. Don't worry."

"Oh, right." Maggie was so embarrassed she blushed. "Usually I have to fix my own food."

Áine told her, "There is other work for you to do. We have to preserve the Engine. That is not going to be an easy task. Best to rest and prepare."

Niamh leaned out from her doorway and said, "See if you can have another vision. Or control water or something. Vivienne rules water. Since she's your mom, maybe that's something you can control. If you try, who knows what you can do."

"Sure," Maggie laughed a short, mirthless laugh as she went inside her new room. *I haven't worked for it, so why would I have it. Besides, Vivienne is not my mother.* She didn't believe all the talk about gifts.

The tiny woman was standing in a corner of the room waiting for her.

"Why are you standing over there?"

"Waiting for you, Ma'am. Are you hurt in any way?

"No, I'm fine. What about Vivienne? Is she alright?"

"Yes, Ma'am. She is recovering."

"That's a relief. I thought she was dead."

"Your mother is strong, Ma'am. It would take more than a simple bullet to end her."

Maggie looked at the tiny woman, placed her hands on her hips, and frowned. "I don't know your name."

"I don't have a name, Ma'am."

"But I have to know who you are, so I can talk to you."

"We don't have names."

"That's what Vivienne said, but I have to be able to talk to you. So, I'm going to give you a name and, if you don't like it, then we can change it."

"Yes, Ma'am."

"I'm Maggie."

"Yes, Ma'am."

"Maggie."

"As you wish, Ma'am."

"So, I'm going to call you Mrs. Smith."

"Yes, Ma'am."

Maggie sighed. She could tell this was not going to work. *What is it with this name stuff?* "Unless you would prefer something else."

Even though the tiny woman looked a bit puzzled, she politely said, "No Ma'am. That will be fine. My name is Mrs. Smith."

"Right." Maggie didn't have any hope that this was going to stick, but she couldn't just say Hey you. That would be awful. "Where is the boy that was with Vivienne?"

"He is gone with Vivienne back to Avalon. That is his role. I'm here to help you on the journey north. It is good that we start on water."

"The Mississippi is almost half a mile wide at New Orleans and almost 200 feet deep. My father told me that."

"Yes, Ma'am."

Through the window she could see the riverbank at New Orleans slowly moving away. The water glittered where it reflected sunlight and swirled in brown tints where it did not. "My father said they call it the Big

Muddy because it carries 500 million tons of sediment into the Gulf of Mexico each year."

"Yes, Ma'am. I understand."

Maggie was surprised that she remembered those details. She was even more surprised that she had told them to Mrs. Smith. *How boring! They make me sound like a bookworm.*

"Look, that's unusual." Maggie pointed out the window to the river. "There's a group of small fishing boats on the water. Looks like they are following us."

"Yes, Ma'am. Those are helpers. They know that you are here and are easing the path of the ferry on the river. Your mother has sent them to watch over us as far as the bank of the river."

"I see." But she didn't really. "What do you mean that they are easing the path?"

"They are easing the flow of the river against this boat. There is no force from the river to slow us reaching the other side."

"Of course." Maggie tried to sound sincere but she didn't believe any of it.

In minutes, the ferry docked and the railcars were moved into line on the tracks that would take them north along the west bank of the river.

The train lurched and the rumbling sound of rolling steel wheels on steel rails traveled up from the floor.

After she had cleaned the blood from her hands and changed her clothes, Maggie sat on the edge of the bed. "I believe I'll lie down for a bit. I feel tired now."

"Of course, Ma'am. It has been an upsetting morning for you. I'll keep watch as always and wake you if anything unexpected occurs."

"Thank you." Maggie lay down on the covers and was asleep in seconds.

Mrs. Smith resumed standing quietly in the corner of the room and waited. There was a moment when the flicker of a smile passed across her face - but only for a moment until the stoic expression that all helpers wore resumed its place.

***

Maggie opened her eyes. She wasn't confused at all about where she was. She remembered everything.

"Ma'am, would you care for a cup of tea?" Mrs. Smith was standing beside the bed holding a cup and saucer. "It will help you get a good start to the rest of your day."

"What time is it?"

"That would be about noon. You've only been asleep for an hour."

"That's good. I hate to lose my day to sleep." Maggie took the cup and saucer and sipped the tea. Irish Breakfast with a teaspoon of cane sugar. "Do you know how the jugglers make objects move? It's not the way that I thought."

"I'm not sure I could say, Ma'am."

"I'd like to learn."

"Ma'am, then you should try with something small. Something of water."

"Not steel?"

Maggie said that as a joke, but Mrs. Smith quickly said, "Oh, no. Certainly not. Water is in your mother's realm and you should start with that."

"But, how do they force the objects to move without touching them?"

"There is no forcing involved, Ma'am. Coax perhaps, or permit might be another way of seeing it. Guide would be another. Everything that makes up everything is in constant motion. Only, the scale is so small, it can't be seen by the eye. What you must do to properly juggle is first find the element within the entity you seek to influence and then guide it in the direction that you wish."

Maggie listened to the tiny woman, for the first time considering what was being said as something that might be real. The question was how she could influence something like an orange to suddenly begin, on its own, to whirl through the air.

Mrs. Smith reached into a pocket and pulled out a small orange. "Here, Ma'am. It will not be easy, although you are your mother's daughter. I expect you will soon master this."

Maggie took the orange from her and asked, "Do you always carry oranges around with you?"

"No, Ma'am. Only when you have need of them. You might want to go to the lounge area at the end of the car now. A nice lunch is set there for you and the others."

"Good. I could eat a horse."

Mrs. Smith frowned. "Ma'am! I don't believe you would do that!"

"You're right. It's just an expression. I wouldn't really."

"Good, Ma'am." She looked relieved. "I wouldn't use it around Niamh and Áine. Horses are in their realm."

"Of course." Maggie hurried out of the room and down the corridor to the lounge area, muttering, "What is a realm anyway and how am I supposed to know whose what is."

Outside the window, she glimpsed endless fields as they flew by. Flat stretches of land broken by swaths of trees. In the distance she could see singular houses and groupings of buildings. There was the smell of burning grass in the air and in the distance, she could see blue smoke drifting across the fields. Louisiana was nothing like west Texas.

She wondered what they were burning. She knew fire was not in her realm. *Rain might be.*

When she reached the lounge area, she found that it had been transformed into a small lunch buffet. Arranged along the walls, the sofas had been replaced by small bistro tables and chairs. The buffet table was circular and positioned in the center of the space.

The rest of the group was already seated and eating lunch when she walked in holding the orange.

Abarta stood and bowed. "Welcome, Princess."

Maggie smiled. *Abarta made the gloomiest day brighter.* "I'm sorry to be late. I was more tired than I realized."

The three brothers hurriedly stood too. They had changed from their suits into casual clothes but they didn't look comfortable in them.

Niamh called out, "Fix a plate and come sit with us."

Áine said, "Everything is perfect as usual. Burgers and fries. I love these things."

Gee blurted, "We finished questioning the assassin."

Áine scowled at him but said nothing.

Niamh quickly said, "Please. Not before we have eaten. I want to enjoy lunch."

Gee apologized, "Of course. I wasn't thinking."

Luke interrupted him, "I'm partial to the milk shakes. I get them whenever we come here. Do you have a favorite?"

Maggie smiled at him. She hadn't heard him say more than a dozen words before this. *He is trying to cheer me up. That's sweet.* "I usually get chocolate."

Luke said, "I like the vanilla. As long as it's real vanilla. These are the best, but of course they would be. Vivienne only has the best."

Abarta said, "We've heard that she is recovering."

Maggie confirmed, "That's what Mrs. Smith said."

They all looked puzzled, glancing from one person to the other. Finally Niamh asked, "Who is Mrs. Smith?"

"Oh, she's my helper. I had to call her something, so I gave her a name. She said she didn't have one." Maggie created a cheeseburger from the trays of food on the buffet table, picked up a handful of French fries and put them on her plate, poured out a dollop of catsup, and picked up a glass containing chocolate milkshake that was sitting inside a small icebox on the table.

Áine and Niamh looked at one another then back at Maggie. They said in unison, "Helpers don't have names."

"That's what Vivienne said. Mrs. Smith too, but it felt odd not being able to talk to her without her having a name. So, I made up one for her."

Áine scowled. "You talk to your helper?"

"Sure. How else would I find out stuff?" Maggie was dipping the end of a french-fry into the catsup and didn't notice the expressions on their faces.

Niamh gasped and almost shouted, "What would you want to know that *they* can answer?"

"How things work here. It's quite different from where I grew up. So, I asked her things like that. And she is helpful, so it all works out. Do any of you know how to juggle? I'm going to learn, but the instructions are really vague."

Abarta grinned and asked, "Do you mean like the entertainers at the festival?

"Sure. It looked like it would be fun to send things whirling around in the air. Obviously, it's not so easy to do."

Abarta had to admit, "That's not a skill I know. What about you, Gee? You're always whirling hammers and tongs around." He laughed at his own joke.

Gee looked at Maggie with a perplexed expression, "I'm afraid I cannot help you. I shape metal, but I don't move it through the air." He paused a minute to think then said, "Unless, of course, I've thrown an ax or a knife. However, that is not the delicate work that you want to master."

Abarta laughed and slapped him on the back. "Always serious! You are a good friend, Gee."

Áine asked, "Have you tried to make it move? Without throwing it that is."

Maggie looked at the orange in her hand, "Not yet. Mrs. Smith said it's not a matter of forcing it to move. It's more like convincing it to move in the direction that you want it to go."

Áine snapped out. "Helper magic. That's not in my area."

Maggie didn't notice her tone and replied, "She said that I should try water first."

Niamh smirked. "Well, let's see what happens. Do you feel anything about the object?"

Maggie turned it over in her hand. "Not really. It's just an orange."

Gee looked over at her. "Perhaps it's not the object itself, but the essence of the object."

"What's that mean?" Maggie was frustrated and it came through in her voice. "Everybody uses these abstract words that don't mean anything."

Gee apologized, "It's alright. It's just our way of talking about the things that can't be seen with your eyes or touched with your hands."

Luke joined them. "The essence of an object is what gives it the shape that you see or smell."

Áine rejoined the discussion. "Or hear. If it's not an orange. Like my horses, what they say to me is not something that one hears with their ears."

Maggie's eyes widened. "Are you talking about their thoughts?"

Áine shrugged. "Possibly. I've never tried to describe it before. It's not verbal words like human speech." She was quiet a moment as she thought. "It might be more like a vibration within the space that separates us."

Maggie stared at the orange. "Mrs. Smith said that everything was in motion even though you couldn't see it. Perhaps it's something like that."

Gee asked her, "Can you sense a movement in the orange as you hold it?"

"I don't know. I wouldn't know what I was feeling."

Áine said, "I think you should try to feel the vibration with your entire self, not just your fingertips." She frowned. "That's another abstract idea that you complained about. Let's try this, close your eyes and wait to see if there is some faint feeling nibbling there that you never felt before. Once you know what it is, you may be able to find it again."

Maggie closed her eyes and sat at the bistro table with the orange in her hand. *I feel ridiculous. I bet they're laughing at me.* She opened her eyes, but no one was laughing. Instead they were all looking at her intently as if they expected her to say she felt something. "No, nothing. That's ok. I didn't mean to ask all of you questions about juggling. It sounds so trivial."

Luke smiled at her and said, "That's part of learning. You should try this at a time when you don't have such a demanding audience." He pretended to whisper, "Áine is so demanding!" Everyone laughed when he said that, because he was right. "I learn best when I have time for quiet and reflection. Influencing such small forces is one of those skills." He tapped his forehead, "The learning and skill is here, not in your arms or hands." He grinned at her. "Me and my brothers are more arms and hands."

"Thank you, Luke." Maggie was beginning to believe that he might be the smartest one in the group.

Outside the window, the countryside began to change from wide flat fields of cut over sugar cane stubble to stretches of wetlands and segments of piney woods.

Suddenly Maggie asked, "What did you find out from the assassin?"

The lighthearted banter around her stopped, and Abarta cleared his throat before saying, "He did not want to speak, although we were able to uncover that the Fomoire know of Vivienne's house in New Orleans. They had agents stationed in each train station as well as along each road and on each ferry leaving the city."

Niamh asked in an acidic tone, "But, how did they know we would be there? And why her?"

Abarta replied, "They know she controls the Engine. Naturally her place in New Orleans would be our logical entry point."

Gee added, "And, if Vivienne was killed, the role of protecting the Engine becomes Marguerite's. Their belief was that with Vivienne gone, the protection of the Engine would easily fail."

Maggie felt a wave of ice spread through her, and her heart raced. The idea that she might be the Imaginærium Engine's protector was frightening. She knew nothing about protecting it.

Abarta told them, "It's really not that bad. Marguerite's vision was correct. They are trying to force their way through the Engine into all spaces. However, their seer's vision isn't as strong as Marguerite's. They only glimpsed shadows of our travel to the Engine and don't know where it is. Yet. They are still searching for it."

Áine let out a sarcastic laugh and said, "Great. So, they know we're traveling to the Engine, *and* they don't know exactly where it is. This couldn't get any worse. They are probably following us."

Luke, who had been silent until then, said in a sardonic voice, "So, that settles it. We are on a grand venture to save the Imaginærium Engine from the control of the Fomoire. And we must not fail.

"If we do, it will bring about the destruction of the Otherworlds and plunge all into darkness!"

Abarta grumbled, "Reminds me of the beginning of the Dark Ages. It took a thousand years to undo that disaster."

The group was silent. Maggie could hear the rhythmic two-beat clunk of iron wheels rolling over the seams between the rails.

Like a heartbeat, ta dump, ta dump, over and over, taking us to Fort Worth and me back home, but not how I wanted to go home.

Maggie complained, "Seems stupid to build something like the Engine that could be used to destroy the Otherworlds."

There was an embarrassed silence in the group. Áine touched Maggie's arm to get her attention. "It is one of Vivienne's abilities, to empower movement between spaces. She is the Engine's creator and protector."

Maggie protested, "I thought she just influenced fresh water."

Áine reminded her, "We all have more than one ability, you know. She also has movement between spaces."

"But why did she pick Fort Richards? Why not someplace nice, like New York City. Or even New Orleans where her house is?"

Why did I say that? There's nothing wrong with Fort Richards. It's just as good a place as any other. Plus, I've never even been to New York.

Gee spoke up before anyone else could respond, "It remains hidden because Fort Richards was and still is relatively remote. The location also has a special feature necessary for the engine."

The underground pool in the grotto, I knew there was something odd about that.

Abarta leaned back, stretched, and then folded his hands behind his head.

He looks so calm. In control. I wonder what he thinks about me. If he thinks about me.

Abarta said, "She has other houses. Her place in Seattle is much nicer. I think New Orleans must be something sentimental. To her at least. I prefer New York myself."

Niamh cut him off, "But with the railroad, she could easily travel to the Engine."

Maggie said, "Dallas would be closer."

Áine responded, "True, but you know there's not as much water surrounding Dallas as New Orleans. The Mississippi is her power."

Maggie looked around the group at their faces, their eyes. She thought they looked anxious. Only Abarta seemed to be enjoying the trip.

Maggie hesitated before asking, "But why even build this Engine thing? That just doesn't make sense..."

CR interrupted her, "It is the hub, the nexus if you will, of the power for all connections with the Otherworlds. Without it we would be unable to travel between spaces."

Maggie thought a minute and then told them, "Vivienne said the Fomoire could only come here on Samhain."

Abarta frowned. "Actually, Fomoire always linger here. We prevent their hordes from crossing, however, there are always those who escape each year and work undiscovered.

"With the Engine, they would be able to move massive numbers across the spaces. That is the great threat."

Maggie tried to imagine what it would be like to have masses of criminals running loose in town. Vivienne described them as wolves, but that seemed too romantic. Criminals were something that Maggie could understand. "Why can't you just get your own hordes to stop them?"

For the first time during the trip, Abarta looked uncomfortable. "There are not as many of us as there are of them. They have numerous converts who act for them, so their numbers are overwhelming. For some reason, dark power draws more agents than that of light."

For the first time in several minutes, Niamh spoke, "Maybe the weak are more easily drawn than the strong."

Maggie decided to agree with her. *Better to build some bridges right now than burn them down.* "That's probably true.

"So where is the assassin now?"

Abarta looked at his friends before answering, "He is gone. The helpers have taken him to Clíodhna."

Maggie was surprised. *Sounds like there's more that he isn't saying. How'd they get him off of the train anyway?* But she only asked, "Who was he?"

Abarta looked confused by the question. "He was a Fomoire agent."

"Duh. Did he tell you what his name was? How is his family supposed to know what happened to him? We don't even know who his family is."

Luke quickly responded, "We didn't ask him. I'll have my helpers find out and inform his family."

"Thank you." Maggie dipped a French fry into some ketchup and drew a circle on her plate with it while she thought. She looked up at Luke and asked, "How does someone become a Fomoire?"

He looked her directly in the eyes and said, "Actually, agents aren't Fomoire. Agents are those who have allied with them. One doesn't become a Fomoire."

"So, the assassin really was a veteran, not a Fomoire."

Luke sighed. "If his sign was truthful, then, yes he was a veteran."

"I just don't understand. Why would he do that?"

"There are many reasons. Despair. Fear. Hate. All of these emotions make people vulnerable to doing the work of destruction." Luke abruptly stood and walked to a window on the other side of the car.

He stood at the window with his back to her and watched the pine woods stream past them. "I read some news article not long ago about unemployed veterans marching to Washington asking for aid. It called them the Bonus Army. I suspect that he was part of that group. When they reached Washington, the government attacked them. The Army moved in with tanks and troops. Killed two of the veterans and injured over a thousand including their family members who were with them.

"Being attacked by your brothers when you're asking for help could change you. Damage your spirit, break it, if you will. Sometimes in this space it's hard to know who the Fomoire are and who they are not."

Maggie was afraid she had upset him. She liked talking to him, so she didn't push him further. Instead, she said, "Yes, there's always some news story about some crazy person doing something evil. They usually call it the work of the Devil at church. The preacher is always going on about that. I never thought of the Devil as real."

Niamh said, "Devils and demons are names used for the dark spirits, the twisted and broken of us. If it helps you to understand them in that way, then you can call them demons."

Maggie nodded. "Makes sense to me."

Abarta said, "Then we shall simply call them demons."

Maggie's eyes suddenly opened wide. "You mean demons are getting ready to attack my home?"

Niamh quietly said, "Yes, that is what you have foreseen. And we are traveling to this Fort Richards to stop them."

CR added, "That is our purpose, the reason for our being."

That was when Áine said with a smirk, "If you call them demons of darkness, then you might as well describe us as warriors of light."

Maggie frowned and said, "It sounds like one of Jamison's books. Good versus evil." *They aren't a cult. They're just insane. I've been kidnapped by a bunch of crazy people who are taking me **home** to help them fight some other crazy people.*

Niamh replied, "I don't know about these books, but this is an eternal war. To outsiders, it seems to have a beginning and an end. But that's only in their own memories. There is no end."

Áine added, "We do not always succeed and the outcome is not always what we want."

Maggie wasn't able to hide her surprise. "You mean demons can win?"

Gee rejoined the conversation. "Bluntly? Yes. Often, they do. And when they do, they drive us from this space and into the Otherworlds, while the world descends into the chaos and darkness that they create."

Áine softly said, "There is never certainty that good will triumph. History is as full of our defeat as it is of our triumph."

Abby was feeling a flutter in her chest. "You mean we might fail?" Somehow, in the stories that Jameson read, the heroes always won. Evil was always defeated. That was what they learned in church. After a struggle, and some close calls, good always defeated evil in the end.

Gee said, "Of course, we might fail. Your vision indicates that we will be defeated and Avalon destroyed. And yet we still must do what is expected of us. We must work to prevent the victory of the broken spirits. The ones you call demons."

Maggie was quiet and stared out of the window at the land rushing past them. *Wonder what Pastor Wilson would say about good losing to evil? He wouldn't accept it. That's not how it's supposed to work.*

All traces of the marshes were gone and the piney woods and rolling hills took their place. No one spoke now. The conversation had taken a gloomy turn that no one wanted to resume.

The train hurried them on to Fort Worth.

She had been to Fort Worth several times to see her grandparents. There was a large terminal south of downtown, and she expected that was their destination for this segment of the trip.

To break the silent gloom, Maggie finally asked the group, "What time will we arrive?"

Abarta replied, "Tomorrow morning. Private transportation will be waiting. We can't afford to encounter any more assassins."

Niamh added, "It was fortunate that Vivienne was near her home in the French Quarter. If any of us are wounded, there may not be an opportunity to return to the Otherworlds."

Maggie asked them, "You could die?"

Luke returned from the window with a sad expression and told her, "We might all die."

Maggie gasped, "What?"

Áine hurriedly added, "But we will be at the Engine. Those of us who are injured can return to the Otherworlds."

Abarta leaned forward and gently touched Maggie on the arm. "Don't worry. We will protect you."

Maggie couldn't help feeling a bit flustered and blushed. *He's really cute.*

Áine muttered, "Hopefully you can do a better job of it than you did at the train station."

Gee immediately apologized to Maggie, "It's true. We failed to stop the assassin in New Orleans. There are no excuses."

CR said to the group, "It will not happen again. It is our responsibility to return Marguerite safely to Vivienne."

Maggie complained, "But I don't know why I'm even here. I don't know how to fight." She was turning the orange in her hand, while thinking of Vivienne lying in the pool of blood at the train station.

Niamh pointed at her and shouted, "Look, you're doing it!"

"What?" Maggie looked down and saw the orange spinning in her palm. She jerked her hand away, but it hovered and continued spinning in the air.

Áine said, "I've never seen a juggler do that!"

Niamh asked, "How are you controlling it?"

"I don't think I am. It's just spinning by itself."

Abarta pulled his hand back from Abby's arm. "Can you move it?"

"I'm not sure."

Áine told her, "Try to sense it. Anything that doesn't seem familiar."

Abby snapped back, "That makes no sense at all!"

Áine insisted, "Just try."

"So, what is it I'm trying to do?"

Áine told her, "Can you feel anything different? Something new? If it's like my horses, it might be a soft whispering. Not words, something sounding more like a silk dress moving across the floor."

Maggie closed her eyes and held her breath, trying to hear something strange, but there was nothing. She opened her eyes and told them, "Nope. I don't think that's it."

Gee looked at her as though she had suddenly changed into an unknown creature. "Well, what were you doing then, before we saw that the orange was spinning?"

"I was thinking about Vivienne lying in the blood."

He looked puzzled, "Was that all?"

"I was imagining what the world would be like if we fail."

Luke stepped closer to her, "The world?"

"Right. The world would be…"

Luke looked at the others before he said, "So you were imagining the world."

She snapped at him, "That's what I said!"

Luke grinned and said, "A spinning world. And the orange began spinning in the palm of your hand."

Abarta asked, "Can you imagine the world moving through space?"

Maggie asked him, "Like in an orbit?"

Abarta thought a minute and then said, "Sure, only please don't imagine it orbiting the sun. Better just to work with this for now."

Niamh added, "True. We don't know yet what that might do."

Maggie anxiously asked, "Should I close my eyes? Or do I just look at the orange?"

Áine said, "I don't think that matters. It started spinning while you were talking to us. Just try imagining the world moving in a circle."

Mrs. Wilson at school gave a science lesson one time about the earth moving around the sun, but Niamh said not to imagine the sun. Mrs. Wilson was mean. Sometimes she would frown and look like her head was going to explode.

A shower of orange juice, peel, and pulp covered everyone.

Abarta and the three brothers cheered while Áine and Niamh shrieked. The railcar was a scene of pandemonium.

Abarta shouted, "It just exploded! Fantastic!"

Gee, CR, and Luke grinned. Talking over each other at once they immediately asked, "How did you do that?"

Niamh was not as happy as the brothers were to be covered in orange pulp and juice, and yet, she still laughed at the surprise and said, "I've never seen anything like that before! The jugglers can only make objects move."

Áine was more reserved and annoyed. She did not like the mess it made of her clothes and hair. She only asked, "What did you do?"

Maggie picked bits of orange peel out of her hair and said, "I was thinking of my science class at school, and then I remembered how my teacher would frown sometimes so much it looked like her head was going to explode." Maggie looked concerned. "And then it did. The orange that is. You don't think that Mrs. Wilson's head exploded, do you?"

Niamh reassured her, "No, just this orange."

Abarta rubbed his chin and thoughtfully said, "I suppose you might be able to…"

Niamh quickly interrupted him. "Don't even say it, Abarta. That's not how the abilities work. We influence. We do not force." Turning back to Maggie, she said, "Holding the object established a link between you and the water within it. The water moved in response to your thought."

Áine told her, "It's more like listening and cooperation. The object is listening to you. For my horses and me, it is a form of visual dialog. In this case, the water is elemental, so it is only responding to you. You speak to it through your imagination and, if there is a link, it responds.

Maggie picked up an apple from the buffet table.

Immediately Abarta told her, "Make it explode like you did with the orange!"

Maggie looked at the apple she was holding in the palm of her hand and frowned. "No, this apple is from the orchard on Avalon."

"How do you know?" Gee scratched his head, "It looks like any other apple to me."

"It feels different. Like it has a glow in it. I can't describe it, but I can tell. It's like the apples that were in the orchard. At the time, I didn't notice that there was warmth from them and a delicate scent in the air."

She put the apple to her nose and breathed in. "They smell like cinnamon and roses."

Áine scowled, "You really are a food nut aren't you."

Maggie smiled, "It's one of my gifts."

Gee grinned at them and said, "And a special gift too."

"Thank you, Gee." Maggie flashed him a smile. He was becoming one of her favorites.

He nodded to her. "It's true."

"The apples of Avalon are precious." Maggie placed the apple back in the bowl of fruit. "So, what do we do when we get to Fort Worth?"

Abarta said, "Let's move to the other end of the car, so the helpers can clean, and we will have more room to talk."

Áine agreed, "Yes, it's time to plan our strategy."

At that, the group stood and moved down the hall to the other lounge.

15 This Time Tomorrow

Every time the train lurched and jolted, Maggie couldn't help but believe that assassins were attacking them. She glanced out the windows even though Abarta had told her not to worry. He said they were safe as long as they were in Vivienne's private car.

The only thing was that after New Orleans, Maggie didn't believe that any place was safe.

In the lounge area, there was no indication that the assassin had even been there. If she hadn't been walking next to Vivienne when she was shot, it would be difficult to believe that there ever was an assassin.

Life in Fort Richards seems like a dream now.

Maggie watched the countryside pass by the window. The low lands were gone, and the vast plantation fields had been replaced by small farms and dark stretches of piney woods. She began to notice that whenever they crossed a river, for a brief moment, she felt the air turn peaceful and cool around her. It was a small thing, but she was paying attention to small things now. Like the glow of the apple from Avalon, small details seemed to indicate larger things.

Abarta, Áine, Gee, and CR were playing a card game, Niamh was reading, and Luke dozed in one of the lounge chairs.

The four who were playing cards kept up a constant banter about who was the best at cards, throwing knives, throwing axes, eating, or riding horses. It didn't seem to matter what it was they talked about doing or being, each one declared that they were the best at it, and even though they were laughing and knew better, Maggie believed that they could *become* the best if they really wanted to be.

Maggie enjoyed listening to them. She didn't know any kids in Fort Richards who were like them.

It feels like I've known them longer than just a few days. Two days? And here I am on a train, with them taking me back home! How stupid is that.

Who are they anyway?

The sun slipped low behind the trees and the shadows in the rail car spread.

Mrs. Smith appeared in the doorway and announced, "The evening meal is served." And, just as quickly as she had appeared, she turned and disappeared down the passageway.

Luke stood and stretched. "About time, I'm famished."

Abarta and the others laughed. "How could you be famished! All you've done today is sleep."

"I'm a growing boy and I need lots of both."

Gee said, "I'll have to take my brother's side in this case. I'm starving too."

With that the group stood and made its way down the passageway to the other lounge.

The helpers had reconfigured it for the evening meal. The buffet table, bistro tables, and chairs were gone. In their place was a single round formal table with ornate Louis XIV chairs. Maggie had seen those once in a history text at school.

Mrs. Smith appeared at Maggie's elbow. "Ma'am, please sit here." She pulled out a chair from the table. "I'll bring your plate in a moment. What would you care to eat this evening?"

"Thanks, but I'm not very hungry."

"I understand, Ma'am. It's a very confusing time. So much is happening too soon after your coming home. I shall bring you a small bowl of soup to begin, and you can decide what you would like when you have finished."

"Thank you. Is there anything I can do to help?"

"No, Ma'am. It is mine to do."

And Mrs. Smith was gone as silently and quickly as she had appeared.

Maggie looked around the table, and each of her companions also had their helpers with them. She had already noted that none of the helpers were the same size, age, or gender. The brothers' helpers looked like they could be giants. She wasn't sure how they managed to move around in the small space without breaking something. They were dressed in bizarre clothes, wild looking Hawaiian shirts in crazy colors with khaki Bermuda shorts, which didn't surprise her. Few things did anymore. *It's probably their idea of dressing casual.*

Abarta's helper was a dapper little man dressed in an outfit that looked like he'd come straight from a foxhunt. He had a scarlet jacket, white jodhpurs, and black riding boots. Unlike the brother's giant helpers whose heads were shaved bald, he had long white hair that was tied back in a queue by a black ribbon. He seemed to match Abarta's personality like the giant helpers matched the three brothers.

Áine's helper was a small slender boy dressed in a child's black three-piece suit. His hair was straight black and cut in straight bangs across his forehead and at his shoulders. He looked like a pageboy from the middle ages.

Niamh's helper was an older girl, a teenager, maybe sixteen. She had flaming red hair done up in braids coiled into a bun. She was wearing a green velvet dress that had white lace trim around the collar and cuffs of her sleeves. For the work that most helpers did, her dress seemed too fragile.

Mrs. Smith always wore the same plain plaid dress covered by her apron. *Nothing fancy and quite functional, with many pockets for storing things, like oranges!* Maggie smiled when she thought about that.

When the helpers began serving the meal, all conversations stopped. Each member of the group was served something different. The three brothers had a heavy meal of roast beef with parsnips and potatoes.

Mother would have told them, "You need something green on your plate." The memory of her voice just popped out of nowhere and Maggie paused while sipping her soup. She would be home tomorrow. *What am I going to do?*

Mrs. Smith appeared beside her. "Ma'am, is the asparagus soup acceptable?"

"Yes, it's going to be on my favorite list now."

"I'm pleased that you like it. After soup, would you care for chilled roast beef or perhaps a lamb chop?"

"I've never had lamb before."

"I'll bring you the lamb then. You should try something new whenever the chance arises." And with that, Mrs. Smith left the lounge area.

Maggie asked the group at the table, "Does anyone know where we are?"

Abarta said, "We are near a city named Shreveport. It's on the edge of Louisiana. After that we will cross into Texas. There is a stop there, for an hour or so, before we resume travel."

Maggie asked, "Do we have to get off?" She was concerned now about leaving the refuge of Vivienne's car until they reached For Worth.

Abarta smiled and told her, "It's just a delay for traffic, to clear the line ahead of us. We'll stay in the car."

Maggie returned his smile. *He has nice eyes when he smiles. They light up with mischief, but I guess I trust him anyway. Vivienne said I could. I think mischief is his way of stirring things up.*

Poking the ant mound to see what happens.

That was what her mother called it, when someone was being mischievous. They weren't trying to hurt anyone, just break the boredom of routine.

And Abarta is anything, but routine.

Áine said, "We should all get a good rest tonight. Tomorrow we reach the Engine."

Mrs. Smith suddenly arrived beside Maggie holding a tray.

"Ma'am, are you ready for me to serve the main course?"

"Yes, please. I'm actually hungry now. What kind of dish is it?"

"Ma'am, it's rosemary braised lamb shanks with mashed potatoes. I have a side dish of fresh green beans and yellow crook necked squash for you."

"That's good. I was just thinking that there should be something green on the plate."

"Yes, Ma'am, of course."

Mrs. Smith moved the dishes from her tray to the table in front of Maggie and waited for her to sample the food.

Maggie cut a small piece of the lamb and swirled it in the sauce. "Rosemary, also thyme and some onions with carrots. A touch of garlic, it's nice that it's not overpowering. And there's something else here that I'm not familiar with."

"Yes, Ma'am. That would be a touch of burgundy. The alcohol in the wine cooks off yet leaves its deep flavoring."

Maggie tasted the lamb and then told Mrs. Smith, "It's delicious."

"Thank you, Ma'am." And then Mrs. Smith was gone.

Maggie realized that the others of the group were watching her.

"What is it?" Maggie used her napkin to dab at the corners of her mouth in case she might have some food, sauce, or something else on her face that made her look ridiculous.

Niamh said, "You were talking to your helper."

"Sure. That's Mrs. Smith. I was telling you about her earlier."

Áine asked, "Why were you talking to her?"

"It was the polite thing to do. She was telling me about the food that she prepared. At least I think she made it. Do the helpers actually make the food or does someone else do that and then they just bring it out?"

Niamh said, "I wouldn't know how they do that. It just happens. That's all I want to know!"

They all laughed when she said that, except for Maggie. Maggie looked surprised. "You've never asked?"

Abarta said, "We never talk to them. They just know what we need or want, and it happens. No need to talk to them."

Maggie persisted, "But how do you know anything about them?"

The group was silent until Áine finally answered her, "They're helpers. It's what they do. Why would we need to know anything else about them?"

Maggie didn't say anything else after that. They wouldn't understand, so she decided to let it go. She felt like Mrs. Smith was her friend as much as her helper. Maybe the others didn't think that way. Yet.

When Maggie finished the main course, Mrs. Smith returned to collect the dishes, and Maggie told her, "The lamb was so tender it seemed to melt. And the sauce was wonderful."

Mrs. Smith nodded in response but said nothing. Instead, she simply placed a bowl of apple pie and vanilla ice cream on the table. Then she dipped her head and left the room, silent as a shadow.

How did she know they didn't want her to talk? **Might be best to let that issue rest for now. It is obviously making the others in the group angry.**

The apple pie was wonderful, as she expected it would be. Made with apples from Avalon and the ice cream was made using Madagascar vanilla.

Conversations around the table had dimmed and then stopped. The sparring conversation about the helpers hung over them like a heavy cloud.

Some among the Tuatha shared Maggie's view, and occasionally there were arguments among themselves about how much interaction there should be between the Tuatha and the helpers. Old school insisted that the helpers were to serve and not to be heard, so in the end, the old ways held and the Tuatha didn't speak to helpers in front of others - much less address them by a name. Giving helpers names was unbelievable.

After Maggie finished her dessert, she stood and told the group, "I'm going to turn in now. I'm exhausted."

Abarta smiled at her as he always did. "Of course. Tomorrow will be a hard day for all of us. When you wake, we should be pulling into the terminal in Fort Worth."

Gee and his brothers stood. "Rest well, Marguerite. There will be no troubles for you tonight."

However, Niamh and Áine remained seated. They gave her slight frowns and Áine said, "Yeah, get some sleep, Princess. Tomorrow we take on the Fomoire. Won't be any time to rest when the action starts."

Maggie put on her *I don't care* face and replied, "I'll be ready. Don't worry about me." And with that, she left the lounge for her compartment in the rail car.

When she opened the door, Mrs. Smith was waiting by her bed, holding out a cup of tea.

"Thank you." Maggie took the tea. It was chamomile.

"That will help you to relax, Ma'am."

"I'm glad you're still talking to me."

"Ma'am, I must apologize. I had forgotten how the others would react to your talking to me. I should have warned you."

"That's alright. It doesn't make sense to me."

"It's an old custom, Ma'am. I doubt that they recall now how it began."

"How did it?"

"It's not my place to say, Ma'am."

"Is there a reason for it, or is it just stupid?"

"There was a reason, at first, Ma'am. Perhaps, now it is not remembered and not important. For now, though, I will be more traditional when the others are present. That will save us from unnecessary complications."

"How will you know what I'm going to say if I don't say it?"

"It is a helper's gift to know."

"So, you can read my mind! That's crazy."

"I can't read minds as you describe it, Ma'am. It's more that I know what your need is. It's not the same as reading minds." Mrs. Smith motioned to a door in the corner of the room. "If you would like to wash before going to bed, you will find all of your personal items in the bathroom."

Maggie opened it and looked inside. Inside was a sink and a washstand with her toothbrush and toothpaste placed in perfect parallel alignment on its top. On the left of the room was a small shower with soft cotton towels and washcloths hanging from silver loops set on the wall. The shower curtain was soft silken cloth that had a forest scene printed on it.

When she turned around, she realized that Mrs. Smith had already left the room. She smiled and imagined a billboard sign out on the highway from Fort Richards to Fort Worth that said Thank You in big red letters.

Maybe tomorrow I'll ask her if she got my message.

Her pajamas were neatly folded on the bed and her pen and notebook were on a small writing desk located in the corner of the room.

Mrs. Smith thought of everything.

Maggie got her shower, put on her pajamas, brushed her teeth, and climbed into bed. Before she turned off the light, she pulled her notebook and pen from the table and wrote in her journal about her day.

Each day feels longer and more confusing than the day before. Ever since Vivienne kidnapped me that's how it's been.

What is tomorrow going to be like when I get back to Fort Richards? Are they going to let me just walk around like I'm not going to get rescued? How stupid is that!

But it sounds like that's what they are going to do! All they talk about are stopping some people called Fomoire from attacking the "Engine," whatever that is. And they think I'm going to help them.

Of course, the assassin in New Orleans makes things complicated.

There's more happening now than just this bunch of crazy people kidnapping me. There's also some other crazy people trying to kill THEM. I know that was real. There was blood everywhere.

After I get home, what's to stop the assassins from coming after me? Or my family? I haven't figured that part out yet, but at least I'll be back home.

Maggie closed her notebook and slipped it back on the top of the desk.

Softly she whispered, "This time tomorrow, I'll be sleeping in my own bed."

She wanted to hear the sound of those words not just think them.

16 Eggs Benedict

Jamison heard his mother shout, "Rise and shine!" He hated it. She did that every morning. He lay on the sofa a few minutes staring at the ceiling before swinging his feet around to the floor. Chores first, then breakfast, and then off to school. Same old stupid thing day after day, nothing new ever happened.

He hated school.

Paul Roberts was making his life miserable again. Thumping him on the back of the ear in history class and then lifting his desk with his feet when Mrs. Anderson wasn't looking. When he tried to get his desk straightened, she would turn around every time and fuss at *him* for making noise and not paying attention. One time she threated to send him down to the principal's office.

He imagined Paul getting eaten by a mountain lion. Blood and guts everywhere. That would be justice. And Mrs. Anderson too. Maybe the same mountain lion would come walking through town cleaning out the people he didn't like. The people like them.

Jamison pulled on his clothes, shouted, "the bathroom is all yours," and then went down the hall to the kitchen to begin helping his mother get breakfast prepared.

It was still dark outside.

He wondered what it would be like to sleep past sunrise. Other kids in town didn't have to get up this early. They were lucky.

His sister was already in the kitchen when he walked in. Her back was to him, and she was working busily at the stove while she sang some song from a movie.

He grumbled, "When did you get here?"

Cheerily she said, "About ten minutes ago."

"I didn't see you."

"You were still asleep."

While he took the plates and silverware into the dining room to set the tables, he mimicked her voice, "You were still asleep." He muttered, "You're such a goody-goody. Mother's favorite child. And singing in the morning! What was that about? How could anybody be that happy in the morning."

Mrs. Wells called out from the front desk, "Jamison. Be kind. She is a good helper. You should be more like your sister!"

"Not me! I'm fine the way I am," he shouted back. *Mother has ears like a bat. Maybe I'll run away and join the army.*

When he went back into the kitchen, his sister brushed a long lock of red hair back from her face and laughed at him. Her green eyes were almost the color of jade....

Maggie's eyes blinked wide open, and she stared at the ceiling of the rail car. She wanted to scream. *That was not ME in the kitchen. How could they not tell the difference?*

Her heart was pounding in her chest, and she had a butterfly stuck in her throat. The railcar continued its side-to-side motion, clacking and jerking along the rails to Fort Worth. She was here, not in the hotel's kitchen.

It was a dream.

It didn't feel like a dream. It felt real. It wasn't in bits and pieces like a dream. It was like I was watching them, and they couldn't see me. Like I was a ghost. Was I dead?

Maggie didn't want to close her eyes after that, although she was so sleepy she couldn't help it. In minutes, she slipped back into sleep.

***

"Ma'am, it's time to get ready." Mrs. Smith was standing on her tiptoes by the bed tugging gently on her sleeve. "Ma'am?"

Maggie opened her eyes. She was still in the rail car, but the sense of motion had stopped.

"Are we in Fort Worth?"

"No, Ma'am. We've arrived in Dallas. There's a delay before we can continue. We'll arrive in another two hours. Would you care for breakfast before we depart?"

"Sure, I'm starving. Not literally of course."

"Of course, Ma'am. The lounge area in the front of the car has been prepared. When you have dressed, you can proceed there for breakfast." And as usual, Mrs. Smith left the room as silently as she had entered. It was difficult to focus on her long enough to notice her moving in and out of a room. It was more like appearing and disappearing than entering and leaving.

Mrs. Smith had laid out a simple green and white belted gingham dress for her to wear along with a pair of white socks and plain black flats.

These didn't seem like the sort of clothes one would wear to a war with Fomoire or anyone else. Armor or some chainmail would be more reassuring.

Maggie smiled at the thought of wearing armor through the streets of Fort Worth.

On the other hand, Mrs. Smith is probably right. I'll blend in wearing clothes like the ones I used to wear in Fort Richards.

She slipped the outfit on and then went to the lounge for breakfast.

The group was already gathered when she entered. The three brothers were crowded around a table with Abarta while Niamh and Áine were sitting at a second table waiting for her.

Abarta broke the silence, "No buffet this morning."

Gee leaned back in his chair, balancing on its back legs, and said, "Eat well this morning, Princess. This will be our last meal from Avalon. At least until we have secured the Engine and can return."

Maggie wondered how the chair managed to hold together. Gee was a big guy even if he was a teenager. He looked like he could crush steel cans with his bare hands. For that matter his brothers did too.

Well, maybe not Luke.

"I'm planning on it. I'm famished." Mother always said it was impolite to say that you were starving. She should have recalled that earlier when she was talking with Mrs. Smith.

Maggie sat at the table with Áine and Niamh. After the confrontation last night about talking to the helpers, things felt a bit chilly. They were older than her, so she wasn't sure what she should do. Start a small conversation about something trivial, or just let it go?

Eventually someone will have to say something.

At that moment, the helpers entered with platters of food.

Maggie didn't recognize half of the recipes that she saw. At home they just had a basic breakfast of scrambled, fried, or maybe poached eggs if someone asked for those. There were always orders for oatmeal, grits, or cream of wheat, depending on where the guest was from, and the rest of the menu was always eggs, ham, bacon, sausage, biscuits, and toast.

This morning there were dishes that she didn't even recognize. So, she took servings of all of them.

"What is this?" Maggie pointed at one of the dishes.

Niamh replied, "That's Eggs Benedict. You might like that if you haven't tried it before. It's a soft cooked egg set on a slice of ham, which in turn is placed on a slice of toasted bread. The stack is topped by a light Hollandaise sauce."

"Sounds like an egg sandwich without a top."

"I guess it is in a way, except for the sauce."

Áine said, "The sauce is rich and can be overpowering sometimes. This morning, though, with what we have ahead, I'm in the mood for something rich."

With that the group began talking among themselves about what they were expecting to happen as they traveled to secure the Engine.

In spite of the looming struggle, the group was speaking again, and Maggie was happy. After a few minutes, Abarta started telling jokes, and then everyone was laughing.

When the railcar jerked into motion, Maggie glanced at Gee. He was staring out a window.

She asked him, "Are we on our way?"

Gee turned to her. He looked anxious, which didn't reassure her. "It won't be long now."

Abarta said, "It'll be about an hour before we pull into the terminal."

Even though she was going home, Maggie's stomach was churning, and she had the feeling that she was going to vomit.

That would be something they would talk about. About like the exploding orange!

She controlled her emotions and watched a fitful parade of small homes and scruffy trees slide by outside the windows.

The land here was quite different. Mostly scrub oaks without pines and unlike the land they had traveled through before now. There were some marshy flats where the Trinity River sometimes flooded and occasional creeks that they crossed over on steel trestles. She was attuned to the feeling of the flowing water and, when it was near, she felt her heart flutter.

Áine leaned over and asked, "Have you tried juggling any more objects?"

"Not since yesterday."

"It might be good to practice while we wait. Could come in useful later."

"Especially if you can make them explode like that orange did." Abarta was still focused on her exploding things.

Maggie snapped, "That was an accident." It was so annoying that he kept wanting her to make things explode.

Abarta smiled as though he hadn't noticed her irritation and he probably hadn't. She thought he didn't have people become annoyed with him often enough to notice. Or he simply didn't care.

He said, "Sure, but good to know how to do.

Angry at Abarta. I must be in a bad mood this morning. Must be nervous about getting home. She shrugged, said, "Sure, why not," and reached to take a pear from the bowl of fruit in the center of the table. Before her hand could reach it, the pear rose from the bowl and soared into her outstretched hand.

Áine said, "Looks like you have that control thing figured out."

"I didn't do anything." The pear sat in Maggie's palm for a moment and then shot straight up into the ceiling where it splattered, raining bits of fiber, peeling, and the gritty wet remains of the core on the group.

Áine shouted "Hey! Why'd you do that? Now I have to go wash my hair and change my clothes!"

Niamh was even more annoyed because none of the bits of pear had gotten on Maggie. "I see you were able to shield yourself, though!"

"Sorry, I didn't mean to make it do that. Make it crash into the ceiling."

Áine and Niamh immediately stormed out of the lounge to get cleaned up and change into fresh clothes.

Abarta howled with laughter. "If we can catch the Fomoire by a fruit stand, you can just pummel them to death with watermelons."

Maggie was really in a foul mood now and snapped at him, "It's not the season for watermelons. That was in the summer." Then she had to laugh and say, "It would be pumpkins now."

Gee, serious as always, asked her, "What were you imagining when it took off like that?"

"I don't know. I wasn't thinking about anything in particular. Not like yesterday when I was remembering my teacher."

Luke said, "I think Áine was correct. You should try to use this gift more frequently so that you can control it. We might need for you to use it today."

CR was nervously twisting the gold ring on his finger and added, "All newly acquired gifts require time and use before they are in control. Please, try moving the objects again, and do not worry about them exploding." Then he grinned at her. "Niamh and Áine are not here now."

Maggie had a worried expression on her face as she reached to take another fruit from the bowl. The group huddled around her watching. This time it did nothing. It just sat in the palm of her hand like bananas usually do, no spinning, no exploding.

Luke asked her, "Are you thinking of something?"

"I was thinking that I wanted it to spin on its end like a top."

"Words or images?

"Words I guess. I'm thinking, *I want you to spin like a top.*"

Gee said, "Try thinking of the image of a top spinning. Our abilities don't work by demanding or commanding. It's more of a partnership with the material."

Maggie said, "Ok. My cousin has a top that he used to spin all the time. I'll remember what that looked like."

Everyone backed up a bit just in case the banana exploded. Instead, it just sat in her hand not spinning or doing anything.

They all sighed in unison.

"I guess I'll have to practice. I'm not really sure yet how to do it."

Abarta said, "That's alright. We will secure the Engine with the tools and abilities that we have."

Gee agreed. "Quite right, Abarta. The gift is new and unexpected."

In moments, Áine and Niamh returned with new outfits and washed hair.

Áine said, "No more suicidal pears or exploding oranges, OK?"

Niamh added, "That's right. My helper says she is not going to fetch another change of clothing today!"

They were grinning and Maggie laughed, relieved that they were not angry. And Niamh said had her helper talked to her.

Was that an offer of peace? None of the others seemed to notice, so it must be.

"Don't worry." Maggie held up the banana that she had picked up. "I've been practicing and so far, nothing happens." Instantly the banana shot out of her hand and through the window. It punched a neat hole in the glass where it went through.

There was a moment of silence in the group before they all broke into loud laughter.

"Bananas!" Abarta shouted, "you never can predict what they will do!"

Luke howled with laughter. "Or know what they are thinking!"

Áine checked her dress and said, "At least we didn't have to change clothes again."

Niamh added, "Or wash our hair another time this morning!"

Gee took a close look at the broken window. "That's an impressive hole in that glass. Vivienne is not going to believe this one. Usually it's one of us that breaks out her windows! You know, this is perfectly round."

CR mumbled, "I'd have expected the banana to just make a messy smear on the window. Not punch a hole in it."

Luke stood quietly behind his brothers staring at it. Suddenly he pointed and whispered, "Look, the hole is closing. The glass is healing itself."

Áine frowned. "I don't think the glass was broken. It just opened a hole for the banana to fly through."

They were stunned into silence for several seconds before Gee finally whispered, "I've never seen that before."

At that moment, the railcar jolted and began to slow. All of them looked from the glass to each other.

Niamh quietly said, "We're here."

Abarta murmured, "Time for the fun to begin."

17   Get to the Cars!

It felt odd to Maggie to step from the railcar onto the loading platform without carrying a bag.

When she asked what she should take, Niamh had said, "The helpers take care of that. We just have to focus on getting to the cars alive and then leaving for the Engine."

So, the group walked cautiously from the loading platform into the terminal. After New Orleans, no one was taking anything for granted. There could be no fast trip from Fort Worth to Avalon if one of them was mortally wounded.

The terminal was new and enormous. It dwarfed the one in New Orleans. It had a huge open multistoried space with lots of glass to let in light and ornate decorations that covered everything.

The October morning air was chilly, and Maggie wished the she was wearing a light sweater.

Mrs. Smith nudged Maggie's elbow to get her attention. She was holding out a pale green sweater.

Maggie smiled at her and took it. It was feather light. When she slipped it on, she immediately felt the warmth on her arms.

How does she do that? And where did she get that sweater?

They moved quietly and quickly through the crowd. Maggie's eyes darted from stranger to stranger looking for any hint of an attack, any indication that they might be holding a weapon. Although, she had no idea exactly what she was looking for.

Niamh gave her a gentle shove and laughed, "You need to loosen up. The brothers and their helpers have it all under control."

Maggie managed a weak smile. *Yesterday they didn't.*

The brothers' helpers were moving on either side of their group, which made Maggie feel better.

Three giants protecting you should make anyone feel safer.

Today the helpers were dressed in work shirts and jeans. They looked like most of the ranch hands she had seen, except they were so large. Most ranch hands were skinny and a lot shorter than the helpers. There weren't many horses big enough to carry giant cowboys, at least, she had never seen any. None of that mattered, though. She was glad to see them.

As they walked, other helpers who weren't in the railcar joined them. The brothers must have had more helpers on the train than she realized.

The group made its way through the front doors and was walking to a group of cars parked at the curb when the bomb exploded. Abby couldn't stop screaming as she and the others in the group crouched on the concrete.

All around her, people were running in different directions, not sure of what had happened or where they could go to be safe. Children were crying and people were shouting. It was total chaos in front of the terminal.

Abarta was shouting at them, "Get to the cars! Get to the cars!"

There was a ringing in her ears, and Maggie wasn't able to understand him.

One of the brother's giant helpers picked her up and began running to some cars parked by the curb when a second explosion ripped across the space.

The helper bent over, covering her from the blast with his body. When he straightened up, she could see that the cars were transformed into twisted steel hulks. Flames poured from what had been doors and windows. One of the helpers, blackened and still burning, lay in a contorted pose without moving on the concrete beside a car.

The helper, who was carrying Maggie, knelt and gently placed her on the concrete. Dirt and debris, flaming bits of something, perhaps the remains of cloth, fell around them.

The rest of the group and their helpers gathered, and Mrs. Smith was standing at her elbow. She did a quick count to see if any in the group were missing. One of the brother's helpers wasn't there.

She could see that they were talking but couldn't hear them.

She pointed to her ears and shouted "I can't hear you!" Her own voice sounded like it was coming from the end of a distant tunnel. Her heart was beating so hard and fast it felt as though it was hammering its way out of her chest.

Abarta was saying something, so she put her ear near his face to hear him say, "They destroyed our cars."

She shouted, "Are you hurt? Is everyone alright?"

He shouted back, "We're ok."

Maggie let out a sigh of relief. "That's a miracle."

Abarta looked around them and told her, "I'm not sure."

That's when Maggie saw the circle of bodies strewn around them. Bodies were lying scattered on the concrete as if a storm had dropped a set of store mannequins out of the air.

Maggie gasped and cried out, "We have to help them."

Abarta shook his head and shouted, "We can't. We have to get some new cars and go to the Engine."

Maggie stood in the center of the carnage. "We can't leave them! They're hurt because of *us*."

Abarta looked at the bodies on the concrete around them. "They're hurt because of the Fomoire. Not us."

Maggie argued, "But it was *us* that they were trying to kill. These people, they just happened to be in the way."

Niamh spoke up. "To some extent, she's right. They were hit by debris intended for us. I believe the Princess was able to shield us from the blast, but these unfortunates were not spared when the metal shards were deflected."

Maggie desperately turned to Mrs. Smith and asked, "Mrs. Smith, can you help them?"

Mrs. Smith quickly moved among the bodies strewn around them. "No, Ma'am. Those that can be helped are capable of being cared for by the authorities here. The others no longer require any assistance."

Áine said, "You mean they're dead."

"Yes, Ma'am."

The sound of sirens filled the air.

Abarta gently tugged on Abby's arm and said, "Come. We must go before they arrive."

Áine agreed, "He is right. They'll detain us once they arrive. If we reach the Engine too late to defend it, worse than this will happen in the world."

"Quickly," Gee told them. "Follow me. My helpers have other vehicles waiting." He began walking quickly behind the giant helper who had carried Maggie. This time he was carrying the body of the fallen helper.

Luke saw that she was watching and told her, "We always return our own to the Otherworlds."

Maggie nodded her head in understanding, and that was all that was said while they walked. She saw that one of the other helpers was also carrying a body, which confirmed that two of their group had died in the blast.

The group followed Gee and the helpers resumed their positions around them making a small circle of protection. Mrs. Smith walked close to Maggie's side.

Maggie whispered "Mrs. Smith were those people killed because of me? Did I kill those people back there?"

At first, Mrs. Smith didn't answer. Then she said, "No Ma'am, you did not kill them. It is unfortunate that they died, but in that situation, there was nothing else that could be done. You did not intend for that."

That doesn't make me feel better. I did kill them, even if it was an accident.

They walked silently past the line of cars parked at the curb in front of the terminal. The only burning hulks behind them were the cars that they were supposed to use. Passengers and drivers from other parked cars were milling about on the sidewalk. Some were running toward the carnage to help, others were standing with shocked and blank expressions, while others remained terrified inside their cars, looks of horror frozen on their faces.

Maggie saw it all in one flash, a panorama of fear and panic. It was a memory she would always have.

Halfway down the line of parked cars, Gee and his helpers darted between the cars and ran across the street to a cluster of nine large Packard limousines and touring cars.

Gee called over his shoulder, "Vivienne had a backup plan in case we ran into trouble."

Abarta grinned and shouted, "Smart move. Remind me to throw her a party when we get back."

Niamh called out, "I have the red one!"

Áine shouted, "The blue one is mine."

There were several black cars of which Luke and CR each claimed. They didn't want any fancy colors.

Abarta said that he wanted the white car, which left the grey car for Maggie. She didn't mind. After seeing the bodies of the people killed and injured by her, the color fit her mood.

The trip back was not as happy as she had imagined when sitting in Avalon's cavern.

The remaining cars would carry the helpers. One by one they made their way past her car to those behind her.

I wish Mrs. Smith were riding with me instead of in one of the other cars.

There was a soft tapping on her window.

Mrs. Smith was standing on the running board so that she could look through the window. Standing beside the large car she was as tiny as a child.

The helper who would drive Maggie's car stepped out from the front, opened the car door, and unfolded the companion's seat for Mrs. Smith. It was odd. It swung down from the back of the front seat and didn't look very comfortable, but Mrs. Smith was so small she seemed right at home perched on it, her legs dangling over the edge.

It was also odd having Mrs. Smith face forward when they should be facing each other as they traveled. It wouldn't be easy to talk.

"I'm so glad you are here. I didn't want to travel alone. Not after the bombs."

"I know, Ma'am. You shouldn't bother about that now though. There is worse to come, and you must be ready for it."

Mrs. Smith rolled up the glass divider so that the helper who was driving could not hear them. With the divider up, the noise from the road and engine was muted.

Maggie settled into her seat. "Are you comfortable there, or would you rather sit beside me?"

"No, Ma'am. This is quite fine." She turned so that she was sitting sideways. "It's certainly better than riding with other helpers. Some of them are so large that it can be uncomfortable."

Maggie laughed and said, "I can imagine. The brothers' helpers are like giants."

"Yes, Ma'am. They are. It takes those to be of any use in the forges and workshops."

"Where do the helpers come from?"

Mrs. Smith looked puzzled and said, "From the Otherworlds."

The cars pulled away from the curb and began negotiating their way through Fort Worth traffic. After the bombs and assassins, Maggie focused on each building that they passed. The buildings were multi-storied brick structures, tall windows that could be used by any sniper to ambush them.

Mrs. Smith told her that the brothers and their helpers were on watch, so she should relax. Maggie couldn't relax, though. She had to stay alert. *Anything could happen at any time.*

Looming ahead as they came down Main Street was the courthouse. It wasn't as ornate as the one in Fort Richards, but it was ten times bigger.

I wonder if there's an Imaginærium Engine in that one? She paused a moment, *No, I would know.... somehow.*

Bombs and dead people. If the Engine wasn't real, would any of this have happened?

Main Street ended at the square surrounding the courthouse. Their driver made a right turn and followed the street around the courthouse and onto the ramp to the bridge that crossed the river, moving them down from the high bluff to the flat ground far below, heading north to the stockyards.

North Main.

After all of the trips to Fort Worth, she'd never thought that the buildings around them were ugly, industrial buildings. Now they just looked like a bunch of ordinary large brick warehouses and storefronts, and none of them were grand.

If this is what it looks like to me now, what is Fort Richards going to look like?

When they reached the stockyards, a street sign said they had entered Niles City. She couldn't tell the difference between Niles City and Ft. Worth other than the buildings were not as tall and large.

She told Mrs. Smith, "The slaughterhouses and meatpacking plants are just to the east of us. Sometimes when we come to town we have to wait on them to finish moving cows into the stockyards. Cowboys riding horses down N. Main just like it was still the old west. Real cowboys working the cows.

"I always thought it was like living in the old west, but my grandfather says it isn't wild anymore. Not like it was when he was growing up."

The driver took a left on W25th street, and Maggie saw there were no cars in front of them. She leaned forward searching for any sign of them. "Where are the others?"

"They are taking different paths, Ma'am, in case the Fomoire are following. It will confuse them."

"But what if they attack us? What can we do if it's only us?"

"Ma'am, I suppose you will defend us as you did at the terminal."

"But that was just luck... I had no idea what I was doing. Or that I had even done anything."

"Yes, Ma'am, that's true. And you should not feel badly about those who were injured. Their injuries were not your responsibility."

And, if the Fomoire attack us, how am I supposed to protect us? She didn't answer that!

The driver continued navigating the streets until they were out on the old Springtown Road.

Maggie fought the urge to beat on the divider glass. "Mrs. Smith, why is he going on this road? It's the old road."

Mrs. Smith very calmly replied, "Yes, Ma'am. The new highway has too many agents on it. They will be watching for us."

Maggie grumbled, "It's going to take forever." She looked out of the window at the passing buildings before she replied, "You're right. My grandfather says that's a bad stretch of road. He says it's called it Thunder Road because it has so many bootleggers and criminals. It's got lots of gangsters and what he calls clubs along there."

"Yes, Ma'am."

"Every time we leave their house, he always tells us to be careful and not have car trouble until we reached 9 Mile Bridge and cross Lake Worth. I laugh every time. Like we can control where we have car trouble."

Mrs. Smith nodded, "The Fomoire have recruited heavily along that section of highway, Ma'am. As your grandfather has said, we must remain especially vigilant until we can cross the lake."

Maggie was thinking now about the road that they would soon be traveling. She said in a soft voice, "On the other side of the lake, there is a giant roller coaster called The Thriller in a huge amusement park. It's called Casino Beach, but I don't believe it has much gambling.

"Sometimes we go there in the summer to swim when it's hot. There's a nice sand beach on that side of the lake. Mother said that even before the Casino and park got built, she used to go there to swim. That was when she was young.

"People from all around go there to cool off when it gets hot. And have fun, of course. They have concessions there where you can buy hot dogs and hamburgers. Since the Depression started, we still go, but we don't have much money now, so we don't go as often.

"Around here it was about the only place to meet somebody who wasn't from your own town. That's where my Mother met my father. He was…"

Maggie stopped talking in mid-sentence. It sounded trivial to her after all that had happened in the last couple of days.

Mrs. Smith looked intently at her. "It's alright, Ma'am. You are most fortunate to have two families that have loved you. Two mothers who care for you. Many of us never have that chance."

Maggie turned and stared out of the window. Her mind's eye was elsewhere. She did not see the lonesome countryside with scrub oaks, waist high prairie grass, and an occasional small farmhouse that was more shack than house. Until the new piece of highway, everyone had traveled this road. It was slow and the road was narrow. Today, with the new road, there was very little traffic on it.

She didn't see that though.

Instead, her mind was retracing the images of all she had experienced in the past few days and all that she believed about herself, examining each image and each belief.

How can I know if it's true or not?

Of course, it's true. I lived it, but this could be true too because I'm living this now.

Does that mean they are both true even if one is different from the other?

How can I know what's true or not?

She didn't know.

"Ma'am, when we reach the Casino we will meet the others in the Grand Ballroom. They believed it would be the safest place to regroup before moving on to Fort Richards."

"What if the Fomoire attack us when we get there? There could be thousands of people on the boardwalk."

Mrs. Smith replied, "It's late October, Ma'am, so the feeling of the group was that few visitors would be there. Also, the Casino is beside the lake. That is in your mother's realm. There will be protection. You will be stronger too."

They sat quietly as the driver steered the big Packard around curves and corners.

Mrs. Smith said, "Ma'am, our weakest point will be when we are most distant from these lakes and streams."

Maggie recognized some landmarks and sighed. They would arrive at Lake Worth in a few minutes, cross the bridge, and after that they would be at Casino Beach.

The string of shops and houses had ended miles back.

All these dreams shriveled and died before they could become anything.

Maggie had never had such a desolate feeling when they traveled into Fort Worth to see her grandparents. Today it all looked different to her, a poor stretch of road on the highway to town.

The driver turned onto the new divided highway that took them across Nine Mile Bridge and on to the Casino.

18 They're Probably Demons Anyway

Across the bridge, they turned left off of the main road and onto a gravel road that took them out to the Casino.

The Casino was actually a complex of giant structures that ran along the western edge of the lake. The Casino Ballroom was the main building by the highway with a swimming pavilion and a boardwalk extending several hundred feet south from that.

But the main feature of the Casino was the giant rollercoaster standing between the boardwalk and the parking area.

The Thriller, Maggie always wanted to ride it but was too afraid. Jamison told her that you could see Fort Worth from the top - if you had the guts to look. She always told him he was lying but, every time she saw the size of that thing, she suspected he was right.

Every time she did said he was lying, he threatened to tell Mother that she had called him a liar. That was when she would threaten to tell Mother about his John Carter books. They would go back and forth like that for an hour or more. Or at least until it became boring.

The driver parked the car, and they got out. It was good to be standing on the ground again.

The parking area wasn't paved. It was just cleared hard-packed sandy clay that extended in from the beach. Generally, you drove your car into an open space as near to the front gate as you could get. Today, only a few cars were parked outside, so they were able to get close to the gate.

Middle of the week in October, school day so no kids my age on the boardwalk. Too cold for swimming and only a few people in the ballroom. Wonder why they're here?

Looks like we have it to ourselves. And no sign of the others yet. I wonder if they got lost? She laughed. *After all that's happened, that would be funny.*

Mrs. Smith walked to the front gate. "Ma'am, the others are only a few minutes away. We should go inside and wait for them in the Ballroom."

"I don't have any money."

"Here, Ma'am." Mrs. Smith held out a small purse and opened it to show a roll of dollar bills. "This will be more than enough to purchase our tickets."

"I can't take your purse."

"It's not mine, Ma'am. It's yours. Take good care of it. It will provide when you are in need."

Maggie took the purse and started counting the bills but stopped when Mrs. Smith touched her on the arm.

"Ma'am, it's not good to show that you have so much money. Others will be watching. Trust me when I say that you will always have what you need. Provided of course that you keep the purse safe. If you lose it, its thread to the Otherworlds will be broken."

Maggie closed the purse and looked around her. In fact there were two men standing by the entrance who were watching her. She suddenly didn't feel as safe as she had. Instead, she felt stupid for having so quickly forgotten the danger around her.

"Are those two men by the gate Fomoire agents?"

"No, Ma'am. They appear to be workers who are on a lunch break."

"Lunch. I had forgotten about that. Now I'm starving. I mean hungry."

"Ma'am, we can purchase food when we are inside the Ballroom. As I understand it, there is some sort of vendor inside who sells hot lunches. Not as good as my own of course. Today we will just have to make do with what is available."

"I could eat a horse." Maggie laughed, "Áine and Niamh aren't around yet, so I thought I'd say it one last time."

Mrs. Smith was frowning. "They would be most upset, Ma'am, to hear you use that expression."

"I'm sure they would be."

The man at the counter said, "Two tickets. That's 50 cents, little girl." He was dressed in an outrageous orange and brown plaid suit, wearing suspenders, and smoking a nasty cigar.

Maggie fumed, but pulled out a dollar bill and handed it to him.

Little girl, who is he calling little girl? What an imbecile. He looks like an extra from a movie about New York City low life's.

The man slid her change across the counter and she and Mrs. Smith entered the park.

"Did you hear that? He called me a little girl."

"Yes, Ma'am. He is obviously poorly educated. If he knew who you were, he would have bowed instead. Perhaps we will return after this business with the Imaginærium Engine is concluded, and you can instruct him regarding his error."

"I would like that." *Maybe I'll explode his head like that orange!*

"But, Ma'am, don't make his head explode."

"Mrs. Smith!" Maggie tried to sound shocked and surprised, but she wasn't convincing. "Alright, I promise, I'll try not to."

They walked into the Grand Ballroom. Orange and black crepe paper streamers slung from the rafters in the space high above their heads. Orange and black balloons were hanging from the rafters in clusters like diseased grapes. Giant cardboard pumpkins and scarecrows were plastered on the walls around them.

"I forgot Halloween's tomorrow."

"Yes, Ma'am. For us it is Samhain, the time when the barriers holding the Fomoire from this place are weakest."

"Do you dress up in costumes?"

"No, Ma'am. It is a serious time for us. Much work must be done in a short time, as you will discover when we reach the Imagnærium Engine."

"I was just curious. We always dress up in costumes and go through the neighborhood Trick or Treating. Jamison dresses up like a skeleton. I usually dress up like a Fairy Princess."

Mrs. Smith looked puzzled. "But you are, Ma'am. I don't understand why you would pretend."

"You know with a magic wand and wings. Haven't you seen those before? My costume always has lacy wings."

"Ma'am, Fairies don't have wings. Unless they want them. It is a matter of preference."

"Talking with you is so strange. Half the time I think you're serious."

They had been standing by the entrance to the ballroom while they talked and not realized that a food vendor had opened. The smell of grilling hamburgers filled the air.

Maggie said, "Let's get some food."

"Yes, Ma'am."

They crossed the floor of the ballroom to the vendor's booth, and Maggie ordered two cheeseburgers with fries and two vanilla shakes. Mrs. Smith looked around her and seemed to be concerned.

"What's the matter?"

"Ma'am, there is no place where I can eat."

"Sure, there is. We can eat here at the counter. Or, if you prefer, we can go outside. The others should be here soon I would think."

"It's not that, Ma'am. Helpers should not be seen eating. It isn't proper. Especially at the same time as Tuatha."

"I don't understand any of that. If you would like, you can eat at the counter, and I will go outside."

"I will wait, Ma'am, until you have eaten. That will be the correct thing."

Maggie shrugged and sighed. *It's so frustrating trying to figure out the crazy rules they have. Nothing is simple with them.*

Maggie wolfed down the cheeseburger. She took her time eating the fries though. Mrs. Smith stood beside her the entire time and scanned the room for threats, while Maggie ate.

"Your burger is going to be cold. Sure, you don't want to eat it? I can look the other way."

"No, Ma'am. I will wait and eat when the others have arrived. It would be safer if you were not alone."

"The shake is fair. It's imitation vanilla though. Can you drink that if I am here, or is it the same as eating?"

"Ma'am, it would be the same. That's alright, though. I can see the rest of the group now. I will eat and drink in a moment."

Maggie turned around and saw the others standing at the entrance. She started to wave to get their attention, but they were already crossing the ballroom floor.

Maggie called out to them, "The vendor just opened. You can get something to eat if you're hungry. My treat."

The three brothers immediately headed for the serving counter and ordered barbequed brisket dinners and shakes, while their helpers milled around looking a bit lost as to what they should do. Abarta, Áine, and Niamh remained at the doorway scanning the room for signs of trouble.

Maggie turned to Mrs. Smith to ask her to advise the other helpers and was just in time to see her wiping the corners of her mouth with a paper napkin.

"You ate all of that just now?"

"Yes, Ma'am. As I said, I only required a moment."

"Isn't that going to give you heartburn or something? My grandfather always said he gets indigestion when he eats too fast."

"No, Ma'am. I will be alright. Although, the meat in the sandwich was not up to my expectations. And there was a bit too much mustard on it as well. The lettuce was…"

Maggie felt a bit disappointed, and it showed on her face with her fading smile.

Mrs. Smith resumed, "…, but we are traveling, and, on such short notice, the meal was appropriate. When we return home, I shall prepare a good beef sandwich for you."

"What about the fries were they any good?"

"Oh, yes, Ma'am. They were delightful."

Maggie smiled. *She's probably just saying that to make me feel better.*

Abarta, Áine, and Niamh gathered around Maggie as their helpers clustered in a small group to one side.

Maggie cheerfully asked them, "Did you have any trouble getting here?"

Niamh said, "What a dismal piece of road. The trashy little buildings were scattered all along the way between here and the outskirts of the city."

Abarta smiled and told Maggie, "Niamh is sensitive to that sort of thing. Ugliness! But, we had no difficulty getting past them." His smile faded. "I was concerned at first that we might encounter trouble. There wasn't any, though. What about you?"

Áine said, "Looks like she made it here ahead of us, so I'm guessing they had it easy."

Maggie told them, "No trouble. I was glad that we didn't go on the new road. My grandfather calls that part of it Thunder Road."

Abarta was puzzled. "Does it rain there more frequently than here? We didn't hear any sounds of thunder."

Maggie giggled. "It's because of the bootleggers. They have these hot rods that they use to drive bootleg whisky from the city to the towns out here. At night I guess they make a lot of noise. At least that's what I was told."

Niamh scowled and looked around the ballroom. "Sounds like Fomoire. A loud and nasty bunch of hooligans. Always looking for ways to inject chaos into the world."

Maggie tried to explain the name again. "I'm not sure about the chaos and noise part. The bootleggers make a lot of money running moonshine, that's what they call it, into the dry counties. Because, it's illegal. That's why it's expensive."

Áine said, "But the effect is to breakdown the stability of this space. That's what drives them. The more unstable and turbulent it is, the easier it is for them to take control."

Maggie decided to let it drop. They obviously had a fixation on what they already believed was true. *Daddy always says you can't argue with fanatics no matter who they are.*

So, she changed the subject, "Of course you saw the roller coaster on your way in. Isn't it huge!"

Áine said, "We should ride it before we go to the Engine. We have time and it would be a nice break from the task. Even for a few minutes."

Niamh said, "I don't like being off the ground. Air is not in my realm."

Áine said, "Oh, come on it will be fun. Besides we don't get to do this sort of thing very often. And when we get to the Engine there is going to be no fun for a long time!"

Abarta grinned and said, "I'm game. Let's go!"

Niamh countered, "First, I'm going to get something to eat. I'm famished. Then I might consider it."

Maggie's stomach felt like it had just shrunk into a small knot around the cheeseburger she'd eaten.

Why did I even mention that roller coaster! Stupid stupid stupid. I hate that thing! Should have known this bunch would want to ride it.

Oh, look at the life-ending ride! We should all go jump on this thing before we go off to fight a bunch of killer demons.

Why am I even with this bunch of lunatics?

All I want is to get home. If I can just get home, everything will be ok.

Maggie spoke up, "I'm with Niamh. Everyone should eat first and then we can decide."

Áine looked at her and said, "You're so much like your mother. Vivienne would have said the same thing. Alright then, let's get some of this Texas cuisine. Do they have barbeque? I haven't had that in ages."

While the group ordered and ate their food, Maggie wandered around the almost empty ballroom. There was a band on a stage at the far end of the ballroom playing swing music.

It's not my favorite music, but for dancing it's probably ok.

She had not been to a dance yet, so she didn't really know. It was just something that she believed. Next year was the spring dance at school, and Mother had said that she could go to that if someone asked her. Hopefully she would be asked. It would be humiliating if no one asked her. Jimmy Van Pelt had been talking to her some at school lately. She thought he might like her, but she wasn't sure if she liked him.

Just because he's friendly doesn't mean that I have to like him. Not like a boyfriend anyway. And he's just a boy. He can't actually do anything important like Abarta or the three brothers.

After all that's happened, going to a school dance doesn't seem that big a deal.

"Want to dance?" Abarta had walked up behind her.

Maggie gave a start. She had been lost in her thoughts and hadn't noticed that he was standing behind her.

"No, I don't think so." *Mother would die if she knew she had danced with a boy.* "I hate to admit it, but I don't know how. Not this kind of dancing anyway."

It was swing music, and she hadn't learned how to do that.

"I do." Áine stepped out onto the dance floor. "Let's go!"

She and Abarta danced to several songs before Niamh came up and shouted at them, "Hey, let's get on the road! We have work to do!"

The brothers were standing at the counter watching the pair dance and, when Niamh interrupted, they started walking toward the door.

Abarta shouted back, "Niamh, you always could spoil a good time!"

All of them laughed, except Maggie. For some reason, she felt the tips of her ears burning in embarrassment. She found that confusing. She shouldn't be embarrassed. It wasn't her that was dancing.

Maggie called out, "Áine, how do you know how to dance like that? You were great."

Áine was walking back from the dance floor. "I have a place in Kentucky. Horses, you know. So, I go there a lot and sometimes go out. I try to stay current. Music, fashion, things like that. Never know when you might need to blend in here."

Maggie asked, "What about you, Abarta. You dance well too. How do you know how to dance to swing music?"

He grinned. "I'm not much of a country life kind of guy. I prefer New York and Paris, so I have a couple of places there. That's where I go when I'm bored. We always go out on the town. New York City is bright lights and crazy music all night long." He grinned at her, and Maggie felt a bit uncomfortable again.

"Come on you guys! We have to get going." Niamh was impatiently hurrying them from the dance floor.

Beautiful as she was, Maggie found it hard to see Niamh dancing or doing anything that didn't involve whacking away at something or somebody with a sword.

That might be unfair though. I've only known her for a couple of days.

Right. Days that feel like years.

They stepped out into the open.

After the dim light of the ballroom, the light from the October sun blinded her. Maggie quickly shielded her eyes from the glare but was too late. They were already tearing. In the seconds while she stood with her eyes closed, waiting for them to stop hurting, she felt uneasiness in the air, a low thrumming feeling, but not a sound. Not a sound she could hear, a thrumming that she felt in her chest, uncomfortable and frightening.

"Does anyone else feel something strange, or is it just me?"

All of the helpers immediately formed a circle around the group. Mrs. Smith rushed up to stand beside Maggie.

"Ma'am, it's Fomoire agents. They are here."

In that instant, a group of long black cars sped into the parking area, skidded across the packed ground, and crashed into the fence. The fence held and prevented them from breaching the barrier. Doors on the cars swung open, and several groups of gangsters leapt out, firing pistols, rifles, and shotguns at them.

Abarta began running for The Thriller and shouted, "Follow me!" As he ran, the helpers fanned out behind them, dropped to one knee, and began to fling gold and silver knives at the gangsters. The knives glittered and sparkled as they flew through the air, covering the agents in auras of red and blue flame when they struck. Some of the gangsters fell, killed by the knives. The worst part, though, was that a few helpers also fell.

Maggie stopped running and turned. "We have to do something. We can't let them be killed."

"Yes, Ma'am. The three brothers will defeat the agents."

As Mrs. Smith said that, the brothers turned back to protect the helpers, pulling long barreled pistols from inside their jackets.

Maggie crouched behind a stack of lumber to watch.

The crack of the brother's pistols could be heard above the mix of sounds coming from the chaos.

Maggie had heard pistols fired before, only they didn't make the sounds that these did. These pistols made a cracking sound like lightning bolts. When the bullets from the brothers' guns hit their targets, they exploded in crackling electric blue arcs of electricity that engulfed the gangsters. She thought she remembered from school that a lightning bolt was hotter than the sun. She had believed that was an exaggeration until now, when she saw smoke rising from the wounds in the fallen gangsters.

One by one the Fomoire agents fell, and within seconds, the gunfire stopped.

The members of the group slowly walked back to the spot where the fight had happened.

Some of the agents' bodies were charred black by the electric bullets fired while others lay still with long thin silver and gold knives sticking out of their chests.

The helpers were retrieving their knives when the sound of sirens came from across the lake.

Áine saw a line of police cars crossing the bridge and shouted, "We have to leave. If we don't go now, they'll stop us from reaching the Engine."

Abarta replied, "She's right. Let's get to the cars, now! Delaying us might have been their only intention."

All of them ran through the gate and back to the cars. The man in the plaid suit tried to stop them, but Gee picked him up and threw him out into the parking lot.

Maggie couldn't help chuckling. *Serves him right!*

The helpers carried the injured so that no one was left behind.

Their driver already had the door of the car open and the engine racing when Maggie and Mrs. Smith jumped inside. As he drove the big Packard out onto the highway, Maggie grabbed the handle of the door and slammed it closed. She did a quick check to make sure they were headed northeast to Fort Richards.

The wildness of the attack and their escape left Maggie flushed and excited. She shouted over the road and engine noise, "I feel like Bonnie and Clyde!"

Mrs. Smith tilted her head quizzically and asked "Who, Ma'am?"

"Never mind. They're probably demons anyway."

19 Grainé's Song

"How are we going to defeat the Fomoire?"

"What do you mean, Ma'am?"

"I mean that was just a bunch of gangsters back there. Those weren't Fomoire. And even then, we almost got killed. What are we going to do when it is the real thing?"

"We will triumph then as we did now, Ma'am."

"That didn't feel like a triumph. More like successfully running away."

"Ma'am, even in escape there can be triumph. Did you not see how the three brothers returned to aid the helpers? I have never seen that before."

"I guess that was pretty cool. Those guns of theirs are amazing. Electric bullets! Jamison would love those. It's right out of John Carter. Sort of."

"I don't know of this John Carter, Ma'am. However, the brothers are the makers of weapons for the Tuatha, so they always have the most formidable weapons. Although, I have not seen *these* before."

Their conversation stopped as they drove northwest.

The Packard was not as luxurious as the Rolls, but it was more luxurious than any other car that Maggie had ridden in. Soft light brown cashmere wool upholstery, shiny chrome fittings, her head was barely above the back of the seat. Wrapped in its steel shell and nestled into its soft seats and upholstery she felt safe.

After the latest encounter with Fomoire agents, she appreciated and held onto that feeling.

Mrs. Smith looked outside of her window at the passing countryside and said softly, "Ma'am, success in any form is not easy or to be taken lightly." She then turned to Maggie and smiled as she said, "We have confidence in ourselves and we have commitment to stand together in the struggle. We shall triumph together, or we shall all die together."

Maggie frowned. "That's a cheery thought. The dying together part."

Mrs. Smith said, "It is what it is, Ma'am."

Maggie said, "I can't see the others. Are they behind us?"

"Yes, Ma'am," Mrs. Smith replied. "They are following at a discreet distance. If Fomoire agents are following, it will be more difficult for them to find us."

"Wouldn't it be better if we were altogether instead of scattered? I'd feel better if the brothers and their electric bullets were close by."

"Yes, Ma'am. I would as well. However, Abarta said that a group of Packards traveling together in such a remote region would be suspicious, so we should separate. If one of us is attacked, then the others will rush to assist them."

"Between you and me, I expected more from him back there when the agents attacked us. If it weren't for the brothers, things might have been worse."

"Ma'am. His concern was our safety not victory. He did what he believed was necessary."

"I suppose so." Maggie let the conversation drop and returned to staring out the window at the passing countryside.

Home in a couple of hours. What was that going to be like?

Hi, Mother! I'm back and by the way there are these killers from Fort Worth chasing me.

How am I going to explain that, much less everything else? I thought I'd be happier than this.

If it was just returning home, I'd be happy.

"We are nearing a town, Ma'am. Do you know which town it is?"

"It might be Springtown. It's about halfway between Fort Richards and Fort Worth. There's a creek that runs through there. That's why they named it that. Out here, any water is precious. My daddy would say that every time we drove through here on our way to Fort Worth. Marketing was what he called it. Said the world seemed like real estate speculators and developers settled it. He never cared much for them."

He probably doesn't even know I was kidnapped. Last time I saw him was a couple of months ago.

Maggie looked at Mrs. Smith who was still trying to get seated comfortably after jumping into the car. "It's not much of a creek. There's a small bridge across it, but you can't even see it from here. Mostly dry right now, too."

Mrs. Smith settled herself in the companion's seat and replied, "Yes, Ma'am. On the surface that might be true, but in the earth, it is still a conduit. Don't you sense it?"

Maggie looked through the windows on the right side of the car. *There is something over there but can't see*

anything yet. "We're too far from town to see the trees on the creek bank."

"Ma'am, I thought you could feel it. That's the flowing water."

At that moment, the windshield of the Packard exploded and the driver's head snapped back and then forward. He slumped over the steering wheel and the Packard limousine skidded off the highway and out into the prairie ground that stretched out across the right side of the road.

The bullet smashed through the divider glass before burying itself into the seat cushion next to Maggie. She screamed and slammed herself into the armrest beside her seat to move away from the bullet hole. Mrs. Smith was silent but looked terrified as she frantically grabbed for anything solid to hold on to.

The car continued out across the ground, bouncing and rocking as it lurched its way over mounds of dirt and shallow channels cut in the earth by occasional heavy rain. For several minutes it continued on its lurching course across the ground, while Maggie and Mrs. Smith regained their composure.

Over the scraping and crashing sounds coming from under the car, Mrs. Smith shouted, "Ma'am, our driver has been killed, but he still has his foot pressing on the accelerator."

"What should we do?"

"I'll cross into the front, Ma'am, and stop the car. It shouldn't take long."

Mrs. Smith knocked out the remains of the glass divider and swiftly climbed through into the driver's compartment. In a moment the car rolled to a stop.

Maggie opened the door and fell out of the car.

Fortunately, the spot where the car had left the highway was not fenced and the drainage ditch that they crossed was very shallow.

"Don't look, Ma'am." Mrs. Smith had joined her beside the car. "There's blood and other stuff everywhere."

"I'm going to have nightmares for a long time after this." She looked down at her hands and they were trembling in spite of herself. She clenched them into fists to try to control them. "How're we going to get back to the highway?"

"The others will find us, Ma'am. We haven't gone that far from the road."

"I hope so." Maggie looked across at the open land. It wasn't a place where she wanted to be stranded overnight. "It'll get dark fast now that we're into the afternoon. Dark and cold."

'Yes, Ma'am. We need the helpers to come and return the driver's body to the Otherworlds. I've sent a notice for final care."

"How do you do that? Do you have some sort of radio?"

"I don't know radio, Ma'am, just that they will join us soon. Until they arrive, we must remain to guard his body."

"Of course. Did you know him? Before this trip that is."

"Yes, Ma'am."

"I'm sorry he was killed."

"Ma'am, he was a good helper."

They stood silently beside the car until Mrs. Smith tried to break the gloom by asking, "Ma'am, which direction is the creek that you mentioned earlier?"

Without thinking, Maggie pointed to their left and said, "It's over there, a few miles."

Mrs. Smith smiled but said nothing.

"Do you think they will track us out here?"

"Yes, Ma'am. I believe they will. We should be vigilant as we wait for the others."

"How long do you think it will be before they find us?"

"The assassin will not be far away. Perhaps twenty minutes. The rest of our group will take longer. We should prepare ourselves."

Maggie's pulse raced. She murmured, "What can we do? I'm just a kid."

Mrs. Smith quickly replied, "Ma'am, you are Tuatha De. Not just a kid."

Maggie said nothing and wondered how they could prepare to meet a Fomoire agent committed to killing both of them. "Is there anything in the car that we can use?"

"I don't know, Ma'am. If you will check the boot, I will examine the driver's compartment."

"The boot?"

"Yes, Ma'am. At the back of the automobile." She pointed to the trunk attached to the rear of the car.

"Oh, right. I forgot you were British." Maggie opened the trunk and rummaged around inside. It had her luggage, which didn't seem promising. She didn't have any super pistol like the three brothers or even gold and silver throwing knives like their helpers. All she had were clothes, a toothbrush, a hairbrush, bath soap, toothpaste, and perfume. Just the essentials required for her during a short trip.

Not much here to fight off demon scum from hell.

She smiled.

Demon. Scum. Hell. Mother would not want me to use any of those words. Even if that's what it is.

I wonder, if I had one of Gee's pistols, could I actually shoot them?

As she closed her luggage, she saw a long black case nestled in behind it.

"Mrs. Smith, do you know what this is?"

"Just a moment, Ma'am."

The tiny woman was instantly at Maggie's elbow. "Yes, Ma'am?"

"I found this case with my luggage. Is it yours?"

"No, Ma'am. I do not have luggage. It would be for you."

"Can I open it?"

"Of course, Ma'am. It is yours."

For a moment the worry about Fomoire agents attacking was replaced by curiosity and a bit of excitement about opening the unknown case. It was comforting to have something exciting replace the sense of dread.

Maggie pulled the case from the trunk and set it on her luggage. It was a beautiful case, leather bound with gold hinges and clasp. She ran her fingertips along the stitched patterns in the leather. The needlework of silver and gold threads was perfect. It was a scene of forests, hunters, hounds, and stags leaping from riverbanks.

Same scene keeps repeating over and over. Maggie whispered, "This is just like the scene carved in the sideboard at home."

Mrs. Smith didn't say anything for a few seconds. "Ma'am, are you going to open it? The assassins will be here at any moment."

"Oh, right." Maggie glanced around them to see, if perhaps, they had already arrived. Then she released the clasps and opened the case. Inside the case, nestled in a bed of black silk was a wooden stick. Her heart fell.

"I was hoping it was a gun or something we could use to fight the killers."

Maggie picked the stick up and turned it in her hands. It looked like a flute, heavily carved with the same scenes that were stitched into the leather of the case.

"Ma'am, that is Grainé's Song. I have not seen it in generations."

"Oh," the disappointment in her voice was unmistakable. "What does it do?"

"I've heard that she would summon the birds of the field with its tone."

It's just a flute. She turned it in her hands. *That has no little holes in it. How does that work? How do you play a tune with this thing?*

"Who is Grainé?"

"She is Áine's sister, Ma'am. As Áine rules the summer sun, Grainé rules the winter.

"I see." *No idea what she's talking about.*

Don't think I could kill anybody, but I'd have been happier to find a big gun like **Gee's** *in there.*

Maggie stared off in the direction of the hidden river. "Shouldn't we find some place to hide?"

"No, Ma'am. We have to protect the body of the fallen helper. The Fomoire can't be allowed to take it. If they do, they will corrupt it."

Corrupt? "So where should we stand while we wait?"

"This is as a good location as any, Ma'am. When the agent arrives, we can adjust if need be. I expect them to approach from the direction of the town."

Abby held the carved wooden tube in her hands and stood in the shadow of the car. Absentmindedly her fingers traced the patterns of the carvings. "How do you play this thing? It doesn't have any finger holes."

"I'm only familiar with it, Ma'am. I know of it from stories among helpers, only not how it is used. Perhaps you should experiment with it before it is needed?"

"If it doesn't do anything, then it won't be needed."

"It wouldn't have been provided, Ma'am, if it did nothing."

"Who do you think put it in the trunk?" She knew the answer before the words were out of her mouth. *Vivienne, of course. She had provided the backup transportation.*

"Yes, Ma'am."

Maggie placed the wooden tube to her lips and carefully blew into it. Nothing happened. She took it down and looked at it as though it had done something puzzling.

"I wonder if it changes sound based on the section of carving that you touch?"

"Ma'am, I wouldn't know. Only Tuatha can use the device."

Maggie adjusted her fingers so that they were covering several characters in the carving and then blew gently on the flute. This time, a deep tone echoed from the hills surrounding them.

"That's something, except no flames or balls of lightening striking down killer Fomoire."

"Do you understand what the carvings mean, Ma'am?"

"Not yet." *Perhaps it's the combination of carvings? Objects, animals, hunters, and forests. Does it tell a story?*

Maggie selected a different combination of carvings and then tried blowing on the flute again. A different tone came from the hills around them, but still nothing dramatic.

Crazy how the sound comes out of the ground instead of the flute. Don't suppose there were any written instructions in the case?

Maggie rechecked the silk lining in the case.

Nothing. Figures.

"They're here, Ma'am."

Maggie looked up in time to see the tops of two cowboy hats emerge above the crest of the hill in front of them. The way they rose and fell she knew they were riding horses, following the trail of the car through the brush and across the ground.

"Please, Ma'am. Try to use Grainé's Song again. We only have a few minutes before the assassins arrive."

Guess I'll just try everything I can and hope something works. Whatever that is.

The faces of the agents appeared and then their horses' heads and necks.

Horses. Maybe that's a key.

Maggie placed her fingers on the carved horses, blew gently in the flute, and then covered the carvings of the forests. The tones emerged from the hills around them and the horses began leaping and galloping away from them in different crazed directions.

The two agents leaped from the horses, leaving their rifles strapped to their saddles.

"Very good, Ma'am. They are on foot now and without their long guns."

"It didn't stop them though."

"No, Ma'am. Although, they are on foot. Perhaps the others can reach us before we are caught."

Maggie took the flute down and began desperately studying the carvings.

It DID do something. Made those horses run off. What else could it do? Maybe it's like telling a story only with objects.

Maggie experimented by touching different combinations of carvings, thinking about what the combinations might mean.

After a minute of study and practicing the fingering, she put the flute back to her lips and gently blew as she tapped out a pattern on the carvings.

The two agents were walking toward them with their pistols drawn.

One of them called out across the shrinking distance, "Ya'll got nowhar to run. You try and we'll just find you. My partner here could track a mountain goat crosst bare rock."

Maggie shouted back, "Why are you doing this? Who are you?"

The agents laughed and one of them said, "We ain't letting any Nazi fascists come in our county and blow up our dam."

"Mister, we're not Nazis. Why would you even think that? I'm just a girl."

"Ma'am, what are Nazis?"

"Some sort of political group in Germany. I've seen stories about them in the newsreels, but they're in Germany. Nobody around here is worried about Nazis."

"It's a Fomoire ruse, Ma'am. They are attempting to confuse you."

"What do we do, Mrs. Smith?"

"Ma'am, we must depend on your ability to shield us from their bullets."

"You're kidding! Right?"

Mrs. Smith paused before adding, "As you protected us this morning, Ma'am, at the train station."

"I don't know how I did that!" Maggie was beginning to panic.

The two agents, pistols drawn, walked down the hill towards them.

"At least they don't have their rifles."

"Yes, Ma'am. You were successful in driving away their horses. Is there nothing more that can be done?"

"I tried something, but it didn't seem to work."

"Would you try again, Ma'am. Just to be sure?"

Maggie studied the carvings again, trying to think of any combination of objects that might help or even make sense.

"I don't suppose I could just pull a couple of guns out of my new purse, could I?"

"No, Ma'am. Those objects are not in your realm."

"I figured as much. That would be too easy."

There was a long pause as Maggie studied the carvings while the agents walked steadily towards them. Mrs. Smith positioned herself between the agents and Maggie. Maggie almost laughed when she saw her do that. There was nothing that Mrs. Smith could do to shield her, since she was so much taller, but the intention was touching.

"I believe I'll change the sequence of the objects that I used. Perhaps the dogs before the hunters and then the stricken stag."

"Yes, Ma'am. Please hurry, they are almost here. I will do what I can to shield you. The others might arrive before it is too late."

Maggie placed the flute to her lips and softly blew into it as she touched the carved objects in the new sequence.

This time, as the two agents raised their pistols to shoot them, there was a rumbling tone from the hills and a white blur flashed past and around them, moving so rapidly that the agents were blocked from sight. In moments, the white blur slowed and became a giant white dog standing over the crumpled bodies of the two agents.

The giant hound began to howl a long and mournful sound.

Mrs. Smith took Maggie by her arm and whispered, "Don't look at the dead, Ma'am. It is a bloody sight."

"Of course, it would be. That seems to be the way the day has gone." Maggie sighed, "I don't think tomorrow is going to be any better."

The giant white hound softly padded its way across the open ground between them and the mutilated agents. Maggie waited for him to growl or bite her. He just lay down at her feet and tried to clean the sticky blood from his hair.

"At least he seems friendly. To us, that is."

"Yes, Ma'am. This is Grainé's sídach."

"What's that, some sort of giant killing dog?"

"Not exactly, Ma'am." Mrs. Smith was quiet while she tried to think of a way to describe him. "A bit of a wild one but not a dog as you would know of one. That would be a cú in the old language. Those are the tamed ones and, as you can see, he is not."

"He's sure not a wolf either."

"No, Ma'am. He's not. I've heard stories of him, but never seen him before now. There's a bit of old song in the *Táin Bó Cúalnge* about him."

"No idea what that is."

"Ma'am. It's about a battle and a bit horrible. Lots about blood and slaughter. Not very romantic."

"Of course. That's pretty much what happened just now. It's not pretty."

They were silent for a while. Around them the sounds of night resumed.

"I guess we don't sing so much about killing and getting ripped apart anymore. What's his name?"

"I do not believe he has a name now, Ma'am. He is a helper from Grainé's land."

Maggie started to bend down to touch the giant hound, until he looked up at her and growled, so she stopped. "Ok, maybe he's not that friendly."

"No, Ma'am. He is a fierce hunter and warrior. I imagine he is not inclined to being touched."

The hound lay on the ground and continued to clean the blood from his coat while they waited. After several minutes Maggie asked, "Do you think we should try to bury those men?"

"No, Ma'am. When the other helpers arrive, they will make the necessary arrangements."

"That's good. I really didn't want to go out there and see any more bodies anyway."

"Ma'am, I would rather not either."

20 Howl

In the distance, several pairs of headlights bobbed their way across the prairie like giant glowing eyes. After the day they had had, Maggie wouldn't have been surprised if it turned out to be the glowing eyes of some giant night monsters.

She was sitting on the roof of the car so that she could see farther out. The giant white hound was sitting on the roof beside her. It was comforting to have him there, especially with the approaching headlights in the distance, although she hadn't tried to touch him after the first attempt. He seemed to do what he wanted and, since he'd literally ripped up the two agents, she decided that was good with her.

"It looks like some cars or trucks are headed this way. Do you think it's more Fomoire agents?"

"It's our group, Ma'am. They are trying to locate us."

"Do you have a flashlight? I could use it to signal them."

"Ma'am, just a moment and I will hand it up to you."

Maggie reached over the edge of the roof and took the flashlight from Mrs. Smith. It was a 2-foot long, chrome plated flashlight packed with batteries.

"This thing weighs a ton. Where did it come from?"

"I had it with the emergency supplies."

"You think of everything." *That seemed too convenient to have just happened. To be on hand as we needed it. Wonder how she does that.*

"Yes, Ma'am."

Maggie switched the light on and flashed it in the direction of the bouncing headlights. They immediately headed for her.

"They've seen your light, Ma'am, and should be here in a few minutes."

Maggie turned the flashlight off. "Ok, sídach. We can get down now. The others are coming."

She carefully slid down from the roof of the car and handed the flashlight back to Mrs. Smith. She watched closely as Mrs. Smith placed the flashlight back in the driver's compartment.

Maybe she really did put emergency supplies in the car.

The sídach landed softly beside her and stood looking in the direction of the headlights.

"Is he going to stay with us?"

"I believe he will, Ma'am. You summoned him and, until you release him, I expect he will remain to protect you."

"That's good. I feel better having him here."

"As do I, Ma'am."

Within minutes Maggie could hear the sound of the engines and the scratching crunch of scrub brush passing under the cars. Headlights flooded the area around their Packard with warm yellow light as car doors opened and voices filled the night with sounds other than crickets and locusts.

Niamh called out, "We were afraid you were dead."

Abarta ran up to her. "Are you alright? What happened?"

The sídach growled at him but did not attack.

Abarta laughed, "I see you have a new traveling companion. That explains the two dead guys we saw driving in. You know," Abarta pointed finger at the hound, "he never has liked me. Can't imagine why."

Maggie was surprised, "You know this dog?"

Áine said, "He's my sister's sídach. The best that she has. How did he find you?"

Maggie asked, "He came when I blew on the flute. What's his name?"

Áine said, "He doesn't have a name. He's a helper. Why do you have to name everything? And how did you get your hands on Grainé's flute?"

"It was packed in the trunk. The flute." *Don't want to go down that naming road again.* "And I was just curious if the dog had a name. People around here usually give their dogs names."

Gee interrupted, "Tell us, how did you defeat the two Fomoire agents?" Which was enough of a chance for Maggie to change the direction of the conversation.

While Maggie told them the story of the agents and finding Grainé's Song in the trunk, their helpers quickly went to work cleaning the car and the countryside, erasing all evidence of their having been there.

Periodically, one of the members of the group would interrupt her with a comment explaining something or asking a question. By the time Maggie finished the story, the helpers had finished cleaning and were standing around them waiting.

Abarta said, "All we have to do now is drive back to the highway. How far are we from the Engine?"

Maggie said, "About 30 miles or more from Fort Richards. At night, it could take us an hour to get there."

Niamh said, "So, we are close. I can't wait to get this day over. I'm so tired of traveling like this."

Maggie pointed and complained, "I don't want to ride in that car."

Gee looked at her with an odd expression. "Of course not. It is damaged. The helpers will change cars with you. Theirs is not as nice as the one you had, though it is in good repair and should get you safely to our destination."

Abarta looked out on the hills around them. "Somebody's going to be looking for these two dead guys. We need to get rolling before they get here."

Everyone got back into their cars while Maggie, Mrs. Smith, and the giant hound climbed into the car that the helpers had been traveling in.

As they pulled out of the dip in the ground and headed slowly across open land to the road, Maggie saw that the helpers had managed to replace the broken windshield. Even though the car didn't look damaged, she was still glad to not be riding in it, damage or no damage.

The driver who had been killed was wrapped in a large white cloth, a bed sheet perhaps, and had been placed on the floor in the back of the car.

I wonder who he was. All day long I hardly noticed him. He was just the driver. I should have paid more attention.

"Don't worry about the helper, Ma'am. He was trying to save us and the Otherworlds."

"Of course." *I'm not sure about me, though. This can't be real. What if it's only a nightmare? Would I be willing to die for them?*

The hound lifted his head, looked at her, and then placed it in her lap. When they had gotten into the car, he had curled up on top of her feet. Now she felt his black eyes looking into her face for a sign that she knew what she was doing. Deep eyes and so sorrowful.

She wanted to cry.

Tears rolled down her cheeks and her breath came in short gasps, while the hound waited with his head in her lap as though he understood. After a long time, her tears stopped and her sobbing ended.

She was glad that it was dark in the car and she was not where the others in the group could see her.

Mrs. Smith was silent, politely looking out of the window as if the dark Texas night held something that fascinated her.

Maggie stroked the hound's head.

His hair was so soft and gentle, unlike anything in his character that she had seen when he killed the two agents. And then there was his long and low mournful howl after they were dead. A sound of deepest sorrow at having to do some terrible deed, which is what it was. His curse. A gentle soul, he was born a hunter, defender, and killer in one being.

After today, I think I know how you feel.

Maggie stared out of the window as she stroked the hound's soft hair, long and fine as cashmere. He was a paradox like all of the things that her life had become in the last two days. Ever since the strange woman and little boy arrived at the hotel.

I got my wish. My life is no longer boring or predictable. Don't know if I really want it though. I wonder who I really am.

The hound, satisfied that she was finally alright, put his head back on the floor of the car and seemed to go back to sleep. Maggie knew he was only waiting.

"I'm going to call you Howl. Is that alright?"

21 No! That's *My* Job!

The drivers parked the group of Packard limos in front of the hotel.

The town square was empty. It was almost 8PM and the town looked deserted. That's the way it always was once the sun went down.

Maggie had hoped they would arrive during the day so that all of her friends could see the fancy cars. No one in town could afford cars like these. And to see so many new Packards arriving at one time would have been something that they would talk about for years.

"The day that Maggie came home." I'd be famous! Didn't happen though. Not surprised.

The car doors were opened and the members of the group stepped out on the street.

Áine said, "Quaint."

Niamh whispered, "Now I see why your mother chose this place for the Engine."

Maggie didn't say anything. It was just one of the loose threads she was trying to piece together. If she were really Vivienne's daughter, why would she have been placed here?

The helpers formed a loose circle around them as they moved from the cars to the front door of the hotel. Out of the corner of her eye, Maggie saw that the Packard carrying the dead driver continued down the street.

"Where is the car going?"

Abarta turned to watch the car. "The helpers are taking the body of the driver and the other dead back to the Otherworlds, so the Fomoire can't corrupt them."

"How do they know where it is?"

The members of the group chuckled.

"Oh, they know," Luke told her. "It's their responsibility to care for the Engine. Vivienne always has helpers here that care for it. They will visit them for assistance."

"You mean Mr. Munroe?"

"I cannot say. I have never met them and would not know what they are called in this place."

"Of course." Maggie was silent. Bits and pieces of the past were whirling through her thoughts like puzzle pieces looking for the places where they fit.

Mr. Munroe. He said he grew up in Oklahoma. He was a cowboy. But he's really a helper. Must have been lying about everything he told us.

Áine led them up on the porch and opened the door to the hotel just as Maggie was saying, "That's probably locked."

Abarta said, "Don't worry. They are expecting us. Reservations have been made." And followed Áine into the hotel.

"Go ahead, Marguerite." Niamh was standing behind her. "I want to get off this street."

Maggie glanced over her shoulder. Until tonight, she had never thought that Fort Richards might be dangerous. She shrugged and went inside. She didn't believe there was anything out there yet that was hunting them.

"hey," Áine shouted as the giant sídach shoved his way past her to follow close on Maggie's heels. "I'm going to tell Grainé."

He looked back at Áine for just a moment but continued inside.

Áine muttered, "Be that way." As she entered the lobby, she told Maggie, "I guess he's with you now. Be sure to take care of him or Grainé will hate you forever when we get back. Really…

"…And he likes to eat chicken."

Abarta and the brothers were behind Niamh with the helpers trailing behind them. Maggie wondered if there was some sort of hierarchy as to who was allowed to enter before the other. She didn't know them well enough yet to see any pattern.

Suddenly, her attention focused on her mother who was standing at the front desk.

Maggie gasped and took a step to race across the room to her mother before she spotted the red-haired girl standing beside the front desk.

*She's the one in my vision, the **new Maggie.***

Maggie stopped short, her blood turned to ice in her veins, and watched her mother turn to the **new Maggie** while she told them, "Welcome to Ft. Richards. After you've registered," she vaguely waved her hand in the direction of the red-haired girl, "my daughter will show you to your rooms."

Maggie blurted out, "No! That's my job!" The words tumbled out of her mouth before she realized she had shouted them out loud.

Everyone in the lobby turned and stared at her.

Part III

Home...

22 Drafty Old Place

Maggie ran to the front desk and frantically asked Mrs. Wells, "Don't you recognize me?"

"No, sweetie." Mrs. Wells smiled condescendingly. "Should I?"

In the corner, sitting at the table where they always played cards while killing time, Jamison laughed.

The giant white hound had followed Maggie into the lobby and growled at him.

Mrs. Wells looked at the hound from across the counter and said, "I'm afraid we can't have your dog in the hotel sweetie. It will have to stay outside. You can tie it up out back."

Maggie looked at the giant hound standing beside her. He was as tall as she was and his eyes, level with hers, were fixed on her, waiting for her to decide what she wanted to do. He had dark eyes, jet black.

This isn't the way I imagined it at all. She's so mean. I don't remember her being like this. Not to me.

Mrs. Wells added, "I'm sure it will be just fine out there tonight." And then gave her that expression of the adult knows best.

She has no idea what's really going on. She thinks she does. Only she doesn't. Maggie told her, "He stays with me."

"I'm sorry dear, but he can't be in the…"

Maggie shouted, "He stays with me!" *I can't believe I just yelled like that at my mother.*

Quickly Abarta stepped forward with his smiling face and said, "The Princess always travels with her hound. He's special. A sídach, actually."

Mrs. Wells paused. "Never heard of that kind of dog before. Princess you said?"

Maggie glanced at Abarta who was beaming his most charming smile.

She doesn't know who these people are or who I am. No idea that a bunch of crazy killers are headed here.

"Of course, madam." He winked at Maggie. "Who would you expect to be traveling in company with the Queens and Princes of Tir na nÓg?"

"Where?"

"Tir na nÓg. It's a distant country. I doubt that you've heard of it."

Mrs. Wells stared at him, "When I was growing up, my grandfather told us fairy tales about Tir na nÓg."

"I can assure you the place is real even though the stories might be fanciful."

Mrs. Wells hesitated a moment before saying, "All of you are from Tir na nÓg?"

Abarta continued his charming sales pitch, "Actually we are, but, as you can see, we are real not imaginary. We are traveling from New Orleans and of course," he motioned to the helpers, "we have our attendants with us. And you will be compensated."

Mrs. Wells didn't appear to be convinced. "Well..."

Abarta slid a wad of cash across the counter and signed the register for all of them.

Mrs. Wells picked up the money and examined it. "Alright, the dog can stay with the girl. The princes." She turned to the red-haired girl standing by the front desk. "Lorenda, show them to their rooms." Then she turned back to Abarta and said, "Once you are settled, y'all come back down, and I'll have supper ready for you."

The group followed Lorenda down the hallway and up the stairs to their rooms. Each member of the group had private rooms with a single room reserved for the helpers.

Maggie whispered to Luke, "Can all of the helpers stay in that one room? It's going to be crowded in there."

"Don't worry. They will be patrolling the town tonight while we rest. Some will rest while others are on watch. How they arrange it is up to them."

"I see." Maggie glanced at Mrs. Smith who shook her head to stop her from asking more questions. Maggie quickly glanced around her and realized that most of the helpers had not followed them.

CR added, "You may relax here. There will be no attacks from the evil ones this evening."

Inside the room, Howl took up his position at the foot of the bed, while Mrs. Smith quickly opened the suitcases that the other helpers had placed in the room.

"Did you want to change clothes for dinner, Ma'am?"

"I probably should. These have been through a lot today."

"Yes, Ma'am. I thought so. I'll set out a fresh dress while you freshen up."

"Do you think there's time for a bath? I feel pretty grubby."

"Of course, Ma'am. Dinner will wait until you are present."

"I don't remember my mother being so cold."

"Of course not, Ma'am. That it is the way things happen when we have a different perspective."

"At least I was able to keep Howl with me."

"Ma'am, you should probably have him remain here during dinner. I doubt that these people would understand."

"You're right. They wouldn't. Mother used to have a fit about having animals in the hotel. Not even cats."

Maggie stepped into the bathroom. *It's odd being here as a guest and not just to clean.* "I'm surprised she agreed to let me bring him inside with me. Even for the extra money."

***

With a few exceptions, dinner went as Maggie recalled how all dinners went at the hotel. The biggest exception was that instead of working in the kitchen, Maggie was sitting at a table eating while Jamison served and helped the girl named Lorenda.

Mrs. Wells sat at her table as usual, even though the normally scheduled dinner had already been served and she had already eaten. Instead of dining with the guests, she sat at her table while drinking a late-night cup of coffee.

She had closed the hotel's books for the day and, with the helpers standing watch outside, there was no need for her to lock up for the evening.

Maggie was uncomfortable sitting in familiar surroundings without familiar work to do. She drummed her fingers on the tabletop while she waited for a chance to get back to the room.

What's Howl doing? Is he sleeping? Tearing up something? Mrs. Smith can handle him though.

Except she's so tiny.

Don't hear any screams. They must be doing ok.

Need to get some food for him. Chicken.

And Water. Need a bowl for water.

The conversations around her were a blur of sound. She smiled at times when they were talking to her. But, when they weren't, she didn't follow half of what was being said. Most of it was talk about places or things she didn't know anything about.

Suddenly, Luke stood and crossed the room to the carved sideboard where Jamison was standing. Jamison cautiously backed away from him, but Luke's attention was fixed on the piece of furniture.

"I recognize this piece. I haven't seen it in ages."

Mrs. Wells said, "That's unlikely, young man. It's been in my family for generations. My grandfather brought it here when he settled in this area."

Luke turned to her and with a thin smile asked, "What was your grandfather's name?"

"Connor MacLear." Mrs. Wells sat straight and stiff when she said the name. "When I was growing up, he was the one who told us the fairy tales."

Luke, smiling, turned to the rest of the group and said, "Well, that makes an interesting twist to things."

Mrs. Wells leaned toward him and eagerly asked, "Have you heard of him?"

Luke frowned for a moment before resuming his bland smile. "It's possible. Then again it might be another Connor. You have an interesting piece here. Very nice craftsmanship."

"It is a beauty." Mrs. Wells beamed. "My family is very proud of it."

"As they should be." Luke returned to his chair and there was some murmuring among the group, but not so that Maggie could understand.

She tried to listen but couldn't concentrate on the hushed whispers. She was tired anyway and decided not to complain about being left out of the conversation. After the main course dishes were cleared and before dessert was served, Maggie's head began to droop in spite of every effort to keep her eyes open.

Gee pointed to Maggie then made a motion to everyone to be quiet. He stood up and carefully lifted her from the chair and carried her up the stairs to her room. Outside her door, he set her feet on the floor. She wobbled a bit but managed to stand.

"Thank you, Gee. I'm so tired. I don't think I could have climbed those stairs on my own."

"It was the least I could do. You were quite brave today. Very impressive." And with that he turned and returned to the dining room where the others were beginning to eat their dessert.

Maggie opened the door and stumbled her way into the room. Mrs. Smith quickly steadied her.

"You are exhausted, Ma'am."

Howl lifted his head and looked at her for a moment before dropping back into his own deep sleep.

"I think we are all exhausted, Mrs. Smith. I don't know how you do it."

"I do my best, Ma'am," and then helped Maggie change into her nightgown. It was soft flannel, a pale yellow floral print.

Every night a new nightgown. What happens to them? My suitcase isn't that big.

Mrs. Smith helped Maggie climb into bed and then covered her with blankets.

"It's going to be cold tonight, Ma'am, and this hotel is drafty…"

Maggie was asleep before Mrs. Smith could finish her sentence.

The tiny woman turned the light off and took her station in the corner of the room. "Yes, it's always been that way. A drafty old place."

***

Two black snakes slipped through the gap under the door of the apartment and worked their way across the floor to the couch where Jamison was sleeping.

The largest of the pair lifted its head high enough to gaze at Jamison's face while the smaller snake slid its way into the short hallway that contained the doors to the two rooms where Mrs. Wells and Lorenda were sleeping. It paused in the hall as if it was unsure of which door to choose.

In the parlor, a billowing ink black cloud spread from the large snake and covered Jamison's face.

Maggie sat up in bed screaming out, "No!"

Mrs. Smith and Howl were instantly beside her.

"What is it Ma'am. What have you seen?"

"I'm not sure. It was two black snakes. They were in the apartment. One covered Jamison in a black cloud. Like the ink cloud a squid makes. And the other was trying to decide which room to enter, my mother's or that Lorenda's room."

Immediately Howl was at the door. Mrs. Smith opened it while shouting to the other helpers, "Demons are in the house. Follow the hound."

From around the hotel came the sound of running feet heavy on the floorboards as they raced after the hound who had already leapt from the stairs to the ground floor and was racing to the apartment in back.

Maggie climbed out of bed and stood by the open door. "How do you know it was demons?"

Mrs. Smith shook her head and said, "It's one of their favorite guises, Ma'am. Normally a harmless reptile capable of climbing walls, trees, anything. Unnoticed by most, and yet in this form, conveying their wickedness."

They heard Mrs. Wells shouting downstairs, "What are you doing in my apartment? I'm going to call the sheriff. And get this dog out of here. I knew I shouldn't have let that girl keep it in the hotel."

After a few minutes, Howl returned and took up his station at the foot of Maggie's bed, but he no longer slept or pretended to sleep.

A few minutes after the hound returned, Abarta and the three brothers arrived. In seconds, Niamh and Áine joined them.

Abarta was laughing. "That didn't go well!"

Gee and his brothers who were not laughing frowned at him. They were worried and it showed on their faces.

Gee asked Maggie, "What was it that you saw?"

Maggie described the scene that woke her and, as she retold it, each one of the group became silent and exchanged worried glances.

After Maggie finished describing the snakes and the ink cloud that closed over Jamison. Áine was the first to say anything. "It seems they may have already been here."

Abarta countered hopefully with, "Or it could be that they will arrive later."

Gee said thoughtfully, "We should keep watch tonight. We know the form of their attack and can prevent it. If it has already happened, then we must be on watch for betrayal by this woman and her children."

Niamh countered, "We do not know if the woman and the girl were corrupted. The boy certainly seems to be or might be. We must certainly guard against any evil he might do."

Luke added, "If these have been discovered by the Fomoire, there will now be other agents in the town."

CR murmured, "Tomorrow promises to be a difficult day."

Not laughing now, Abarta said, "Agreed. We must rest until morning arrives."

Abarta and the brothers quickly left the room, while Áine and Niamh lingered.

"From this moment on," Áine added, "there will be no peace here."

They briefly hugged Maggie before they left.

Maggie climbed back into bed with the giant hound keeping watch at her feet.

"I feel so sad, Mrs. Smith."

"Yes, Ma'am. It is a sad time in which we live."

23 Keeper of the Engine

I'm home, but it's not what I imagined. It's hard to describe. There really is another girl here who has taken my place. She's not as good a cook as I am though. Of course, Gee and I are probably the best cooks anyway so that might not be fair.

Even so...

Her meal last night was bland. Very bland. No seasoning. Just meat and potatoes with some collard greens that weren't seasoned well either. Disappointing.

The biscuits were alright. Mother probably cooked those.

And Mother's different too. She doesn't recognize me. It's like I've ended up in some crazy world that looks like home yet isn't. Something from one of Jamison's books. He likes those kinds of novels.

And he's a jerk too. He wasn't like that before. I don't know what's happened here. I feel so lost.

I have a big white hound now. He's a big as me only that's when he's on all fours so he would be a giant if he stood up.

He showed up last night when we were out on the prairie. Long story about that. Someday I'll have to write more about it. It was terrifying.

I named him Howl. He saved us from some men that tried to kill us. Mrs. Smith wouldn't let me see them after Howl killed them, but he sounded so sad afterwards. It must have been horrible. That's why I named him Howl. He is a helper, so he didn't already have a name, and I think he likes having Howl as a name.

Today the Fomoire are going to try to take the courthouse. That's what Abarta and the group say. They say that we have to stop them. More crazy talk, but ever since they kidnapped me, everything has been crazy. I keep trying to figure out what's real and what's not. I wonder if I will wake up in bed and this will all have been a dream.

I used to be so bored. Now, I'm mostly afraid.

"It's time to go downstairs, Ma'am." Mrs. Smith was standing quietly, waiting for Maggie to finish writing in her journal.

Today, instead of a soft pretty dress, Mrs. Smith had set out a basic blue dress like the one she had been wearing when she was taken by Vivienne. Her shoes today were different as well. Mrs. Smith had set out a simple pair of black flats with a pair of thin white socks. They were so light that when she put them on it felt like she wasn't even wearing shoes and socks.

Maggie looked in the dressing mirror and she looked very much the same as when she had been taken. No fancy clothes or shoes. No fancy hairstyle today, just a simple pony tail.

"Should Howl go with us?"

"No, Ma'am. Mrs. Wells would be very difficult if he were to follow us this morning. Besides he will need to rest. He has been on watch all evening and we will need him when the attack begins."

Maggie cautiously reached out to touch him and he lifted his head while she stroked his hair.

"He has the softest hair. And so warm. It's just like cashmere."

"Yes, Ma'am. He is well suited for hunting leopards in the snow of the high mountains. That is where his joy is. Running in the mountains and hunting the leopard."

"No mountains and snow here. I hope he isn't sad."

Mrs. Smith looked at the hound and murmured, "He is here to help you, Ma'am."

"Another helper. Has he eaten? Does he have water?" While he was watching over her, she had forgotten to care for him. There was no longer any trace of blood in his snowy coat.

"Yes, Ma'am. He has been groomed and has eaten. We should go down now for breakfast. The others will be waiting."

"I suppose they are." Maggie sighed and closed her journal.

"What's wrong, Ma'am?" Mrs. Smith opened the door for her.

Maggie walked out of the room as she said, "It's just that this is not what I was wanting. Expecting."

"Of course, Ma'am. Things seldom turn out the way we expect or want."

Mrs. Smith closed the door behind her and the giant white hound lay his head back down and was asleep before they had reached the stairs.

***

Mrs. Smith stopped outside the doorway to the dining room and stood with the other helpers. Maggie glanced at her, reluctant to enter without her. Mrs. Smith gave her a small brief smile and then made a discrete motion for her to continue.

Maggie took a deep breath and entered what used to be one of her favorite rooms in the hotel.

Halloween decorations were everywhere. Cardboard pumpkins and ghosts were dangling from the ceiling.

Maggie remembered the hours that they spent making those and then hanging them every year. Scarecrows were parked in each corner of the room. They had always frightened her when she was growing up. And, they still did, especially after everything that had happened and what she had seen lately.

Jamison was in his customary place by the sideboard, ready to serve guests their coffee, tea, or juice. The tea and coffee cups were stacked on the marble top along with pitchers of apple and grape juice.

The sight of the apple juice instantly brought Avalon and Vivienne to mind.

Maggie was startled to realize that she missed her bizarre sleeping area in that cavernous space. The feeling of being free, without walls that defined where she could or could not be.

She bit her lower lip and refocused on the task of getting through breakfast in a place that had suddenly become so uncomfortable and unfriendly. She looked around the dining room. The members of their group were the only ones' present.

Still, I'd feel safer if Howl were here. Look at that smirk on Jamison's face. I think the Fomoire have changed him. He never smirked before. That I noticed.

Or did he and I just never did notice?

Áine called from across the room, "Princess **Marguerite**, come sit with us. There's plenty of room."

Maggie frowned. She didn't like the joking about her being a princess. But, since Abarta had started it, she had to go along. She couldn't shout back, I'm not a princess. She didn't want Howl to be tied up at the back of the hotel.

When Maggie reached the table, Niamh and Áine stood and pretended to kiss her on each cheek just like she had seen in movies about France. Maggie stood there, shocked, with her eyes the size of saucers.

Áine couldn't help giggling and whispered, "Sit down, silly. That boy is staring."

Maggie sat and angrily whispered, "I bet he is! What was that about? Are you out of your minds? People here don't act like that."

Niamh replied, "Good thing you don't live in France."

Maggie fumed, "It's not funny. This is not France and that was gross."

Abarta, Niamh, and Áine laughed while the three brothers quietly sat at their tables and watched them.

Niamh whispered, "Relax. It's just a custom. And when we take you to Europe it'll happen all the time. Better get used to it."

Áine said, "Serves you right, too. We've been waiting for you for hours. And we're starving. Let's get some breakfast. What do they have here that's good?"

Without thinking, Maggie rattled off the menu that she had helped prepare for years.

Áine and Niamh agreed, "Huevos rancheros sounds good." Niamh added, "But with a side order of ham."

Áine said, "I'd like a side order of sausage. Do they have good sausage?"

Maggie reassured her that the sausage would be good and, with that, they motioned for Jamison to come take their orders.

Maggie had never seen him working in the dining room before.

He does look like a stick. How embarrassing.

I can't believe I just thought that.

Before they could say anything, Niamh told him, "We want three huevos rancheros with side orders of sausage and ham and a plate of biscuits with butter and jelly. Or orange marmalade, if you have it."

"No marmalade, but we do have apple jelly and some strawberry jam. What would you like?"

"Bring both. I expect Princess Marguerite wants the apple jelly, however we would prefer the strawberry."

Áine said, "I don't believe I care for biscuits. I'd rather have two slices of toast, lightly buttered. And no jelly or jam."

"Yes, Ma'am." Jamison hurried to the kitchen with their order.

Áine muttered, "I bet he gets it wrong."

Áine really doesn't like Jamieson.

Abarta and the brothers were already eating. One look at their plates and Maggie realized the she could have guessed they would be eating steaks and eggs without even looking.

Áine said, "So what do we do today while we wait for the attack?"

Maggie told them, "I want to talk to Mr. Munroe."

Niamh wrinkled her nose. "Who's that?"

"He's the one that brought me to Avalon."

Áine said, "Oh, he's the guardian. Yes, we have to see him."

Maggie asked, "What's a guardian?"

Áine replied, "He's the keeper of the Engine. He knows all of its secrets."

Maggie quietly said, "oh," and stared into her cup of tea. *I have more questions for him than that.*

Before the conversation could go any farther, Jamison appeared from the kitchen with their plates.

He took a platter of biscuits from the sideboard and placed them on the table along with bowls of apple jelly and strawberry preserves. "My mother put up these preserves this spring."

Maggie frowned and said, "I don't remember that."

Jamison gave her an odd look as he returned to his station at the sideboard.

As she stirred her tea, Niamh asked, "Remember what?"

"Making these preserves. I was here until last week. This is where I lived. I would know."

Áine said, "Maybe that boy is not telling the truth."

Maggie looked at him, standing by the sideboard. He was watching the brothers eat their steaks and eggs. "Why would he do that?"

"Maybe he wanted to impress us. Who knows." Áine was fidgeting with her spoon. "I wonder if he is going to bring my toast. Boy," she called across the room, "are you going to bring my toast?"

Jamison gave her a dark look and quickly ducked into the kitchen.

Áine grumbled, "I knew he was going to mess up my order."

"Evil little snit isn't he." Niamh was staring at the closing doors to the kitchen.

Maggie tried to defend him, "I don't remember him being like this."

Áine added, "It's what you saw. He's been corrupted."

Niamh put her fork down and looked at Maggie. "The question now is for how long."

Niamh had only said out loud what the others in the group had been worrying about all morning.

Áine added their other concern, "And what role does he play."

Niamh murmured, "Perhaps Abarta and the brothers should keep an eye on him today?"

Áine said, "Or one of their helpers can. Discretely of course."

Niamh thought a moment and then said, "Agreed."

She slipped across to Abarta's table and whispered something that Maggie couldn't hear. After a short, inaudible conversation, Niamh returned to her seat at the table while Abarta talked to the three brothers.

All of it was done quickly and in hushed tones so that Maggie wasn't able to hear what was said. After a moment, Luke left the dining room.

By the time Jamison returned from the kitchen with the toast, everyone, except Luke, was sitting in their places eating their breakfasts. Jamison carried a small plate of buttered toast that he placed beside Áine's plate and then returned to his station at the sideboard.

"It's not his fault, you know." Maggie watched Jamison standing there, looking awkward and lost.

Niamh tried to look puzzled and asked, "Who?"

And Áine asked, "What's not?"

Maggie scowled at them, "You know exactly who and what."

Áine chuckled. "Yes, of course we do."

Niamh said grimly, "But it is who he is. The Fomoire don't change you into something that you aren't. They only recruit those who are already inclined to be like them."

Áine turned serious for a moment and told her, "If he has become an agent or worse, corrupted, it is because he was theirs from the beginning."

Maggie protested, "No, that's not true. He's my brother."

Áine and Niamh exchanged knowing glances before Áine replied, "Perhaps you're right. We shall see what happens and then decide. Ok?"

Maggie pushed her eggs around on the plate a bit before saying, "Of course, but even if he is, we have to save him."

Áine paused and then said, "If we can, we will."

Maggie sighed and settled back in her chair.

They are just pretending. I can see their faces. They don't believe he can be saved.

She looked around the dining room at the things that had been her life for as long as she could remember. The last few years, while she lived in the hotel, she had been in this room almost every day of every week.

Everything is so different. It's the same stuff, although behind it is another layer, like something's been hidden from me, behind a curtain, for years.

And I don't like it.

When Luke entered the dining room, all of them glanced at him. He subtly nodded to the group before he quietly resumed eating his breakfast.

After a few minutes, Áine whispered, "It's going to be a difficult day."

24 Dark and Twisted

Maggie and the rest of the group walked out of the dining room with their helpers following at a polite distance. Jamison was lurking on the edge of the lobby watching them. Mrs. Wells spotted him from the front desk and called out, "Jamison! You need to get ready for school."

"Yes, Ma'am," Jamison grumbled under his breath as he left the lobby to collect his schoolbooks from the apartment.

The group walked out of the hotel and stood on the front porch.

Niamh pointed back over her shoulder. "That boy is really creepy. Did you see him watching us in there?"

Áine didn't look back as she said, "I believe he's been corrupted."

Maggie decided to change the subject before they said anymore. "I'm going to see Mr. Munroe. You guys coming?"

"I'll walk with you." Áine stepped down onto the street. "He's the keeper. He'll know how we can defend the Engine."

Niamh nodded her head. "He knows all of its secrets."

"Just where does the Guardian keeper guy live?" Áine was looking at the buildings around the square. "The only things I see around here are some stores."

Maggie pointed in the direction of the river. "He lives over there. It's just a few blocks away."

Niamh looked up at the cloudless sky and said, "Let's leave the cars and walk. I'd like to get a sense of the town. You can't do that while riding in a car."

Áine agreed. "Plus, it's a nice morning. After riding for so long to get here, I'd rather not sit in a car today. If I can help it, that is."

Maggie was looking at the empty streets around the courthouse. "Perhaps only a couple of us should go. No one here is used to seeing so many people out walking around in a group."

Gee looked around and agreed with her. "True. So many in a group here would cause alarm. The rest of us should just become familiar with the town and plan the defense."

Maggie started to say that it wouldn't take long to see the town but stopped herself. It wasn't large, but it was her home.

The three brothers all said they wanted to visit a machine shop they spotted last night on the way into town.

Gee laughed. "It's not just because we love metal shaping."

"Don't believe it." Luke smiled at Maggie and added, "They can't pass up a chance to bend some metal, but me, I'm just going to tag along with my brothers. Wood is my element you know. I'm not much interested in metal."

"Be careful, you three." Abarta reminded them, "There could be agents in town."

Gee kicked at a small rock in the street while he considered Abarta's comment. "True. The attack should not come before evening. However, it's possible a rogue agent might strike."

Maggie wondered if she felt some tension between them now that she hadn't noticed before.

Niamh quickly interrupted them with, "I'm going to investigate the stores. I have no interest in the Guardian or forges and metal shaping."

Abarta immediately told them he'd accompany Niamh.

Maggie frowned. *What's this about? Why's he tagging along with her!* "Don't you want to go with us to Mr. Munroe's?"

Abarta shrugged. "We need at least two in each group. In case of rogue agents."

Maggie started to protest but stopped. "Oh, right." *What's wrong with me! Why should I care about who he goes with?*

Áine gave her a puzzled look but said nothing.

Maggie was glad Áine let it drop. It was embarrassing enough that she had said anything without having to keep talking about it. Besides, she didn't understand why it bothered her anyway.

With that settled, the group divided up and went in different directions on their separate missions.

***

As Maggie and Áine started across the town square, Howl joined them. He walked soundlessly beside Maggie. He reminded her of a polar bear, only when she focused on the details, he obviously wasn't. Mrs. Smith and Áine's helper followed quietly behind the three of them.

To the people of Fort Richards, they just looked like a pair of teenagers with two grammar school children trailing along behind them. Except that they had a giant white hound with them, which was unusual if they had thought about it, but apparently no one did. It wasn't quite 8:00 AM yet, so school hadn't started. Except for the hound, they could easily have been neighborhood kids on their way to school.

Maggie saw a few people that she recognized, and yet they didn't seem to notice her. Yesterday she'd have run across the street and begged them for help, told them that she'd been kidnapped, but today, she just watched them and said nothing.

Mrs. DePrym was just opening her shop when they walked in front of it.

"Hello, Mrs. DePrym." Maggie wasn't expecting her to reply. No one in town seemed to remember who she was.

"Princess Marguerite!" Mrs. DePrym's face beamed and Maggie was stunned. "I've got some special apple ice cream that I'm making for you today!" She gave Maggie a knowing wink and said, "It'll be ready for your lunch, Ma'am."

"Thank you, Mrs. DePrym. I don't know what to say."

"It's my pleasure, Ma'am. So wonderful to see you." And the short little woman curtsied, which Maggie was surprised to see. In the years she had known Mrs. DePrym, she had never considered that she might be anyone other than a tiny Belgian woman who made pastries and ice cream.

Áine gently guided Maggie down the street so that Mrs. DePrym could enter her store without drawing any more attention to them.

"Is she one of Vivienne's helpers?"

Áine absentmindedly replied, "It appears so. Vivienne placed a number of helpers here to watch over you.

"By the way, did you enjoy anything about living here?"

Maggie glanced at her but didn't say anything for a few steps. "I had… I have some good friends here. We grew up together and go to school together. Have fun doing stuff. You know."

"Not really. Although, I have my friends as well. I suppose I understand. But this place is so bleak. It has no trees."

"They're here. It's almost winter, so the leaves have fallen. In the spring, they get green and the grass comes back. At least until summer." Maggie looked around her as they walked down the street.

It wasn't a flashy place like a city, but it was a good place. Compared to the pines and oaks that they had just traveled through, the trees here were small and few. They weren't lush like those in Avalon. They were tough and hard. Each year they survived drought, hot summer, and freezing winter.

Every winter, Dad used to say the only thing standing between us and the North Pole was a fence post in Oklahoma.

The air was clean and the sky was deep blue. At night the sky filled with billions of stars that you couldn't see in the city. After he moved to Fort Worth, her grandfather complained that he missed the night sky. In some ways, town was drab and dusty, but it was open space surrounding them and she didn't feel trapped here.

Perhaps that's why Vivienne chose this place for the Engine.

The houses were scattered and small compared to those in Fort Worth. They were small wood frame houses. Most just had two bedrooms, a kitchen, and a parlor. She had some friends that lived a few blocks away and they all had to share their bedrooms with brothers and sisters.

She was lucky. Even though the apartment was small, she had a room to herself. Until now, she'd never thought about it like that. Her room was barely large enough for her bed, and yet she had the hotel too, so it never had been something that she thought about.

She told Áine, "We go to the clock tower every day after school and chores. That's fun. From the tower you can see for miles around. That's the most fun. But, only me and Jamison go up there. The other kids are afraid. Plus, there's a secret door you have to go through and Mr. Munroe wouldn't have let them go up there anyway. He made us promise not to ever tell anyone about the door before he took us up."

"So, you have actually been in the Engine?"

"Well, I've been up to the observation room under the clockworks. I'm not sure where the Engine is."

"That's it."

***

A couple of blocks from the courthouse they reached an old white farmhouse. It didn't look any different from the other houses on the street, other than being in good repair. Most of the houses needed to be painted or had broken steps, windows, or trim.

"My Dad told me that before the depression hit, these homes were all fine places. People can't afford to keep them up now."

Áine wrinkled her nose in disgust and said, "No trees, brown grass, and decaying houses. I'll be happy when we can return home."

Maggie pointed to the farmhouse, "That's where Mr. Munroe lives." They walked up the dirt path that led to the front steps and knocked on the door. "He should be here. I don't think he goes over to the courthouse until after lunch."

The door was made of oak and finished in a dark almost black stain. Maggie noticed the ring of carvings around its edge. They were similar to the carvings on Grainé's flute. She carried it with her in her purse now and reflexively touched it.

I wonder if Luke carved these, too.

The door opened before they could knock and Mrs. Munroe was standing there.

"Yes?" When she saw their faces, she immediately gasped, "Oh my," bowed her head and then said "Please forgive me, Ma'am."

Áine glanced at Maggie before turning back to Mrs. Munroe, "There's nothing to forgive. And don't bother with formality here."

"Yes, Ma'am."

Mrs. Munroe stepped aside so that they could enter the house.

Howl followed Maggie as though it was normal for him to be there. Mrs. Munroe said nothing, which surprised Maggie. Country people never let dogs come in the house. At least none that she knew.

Standing together in the parlor, Maggie realized that Mrs. Munroe and Mrs. Smith were the same size and even looked alike. Both were helpers working for Vivienne. On a whim she asked, "Mrs. Smith, do you know Mrs. Munroe?"

"Yes, Ma'am. She is my sister."

Maggie exclaimed, "Oh, I didn't know."

"Of course, Ma'am. You weren't intended to know."

More secrets.

Mrs. Munroe motioned toward the two armchairs that she had in the parlor, "Please be comfortable, Ma'am, while I bring Mr. Munroe. Would you want any tea while you wait?"

Áine told her, "That would be nice," and Mrs. Munroe slipped away to the kitchen. Howl settled in at Maggie's feet while Áine's helper stood silently beside her chair.

Mrs. Smith hesitated a moment and then asked Maggie, "Ma'am, would it be permissible for me to help my sister prepare the tea?"

Maggie smiled at her. "I would be happy if you did."

"Thank you, Ma'am," and she disappeared into the kitchen.

Maggie whispered, "I never thought about Mrs. Munroe having a sister somewhere. I feel so terrible."

Áine frowned, "Why would you feel terrible about that?"

"That I never thought about her. All this time I lived here and never even thought about who she was."

Áine shrugged. "You know, you worry about a lot of things. She's a helper. That's the way it is."

At that moment, Mr. Munroe entered the parlor.

Maggie glared at him and blurted out angrily, "You kidnapped me!"

"Please, Ma'am. I didn't. I only returned you to your home." The old man looked bewildered.

337

"I can't believe I ever trusted you!"

"But, Ma'am, all the years you were here I protected you."

Maggie sneered, "I suppose that makes you one of Vivienne's helpers?"

"Yes, Ma'am. I'm your protector and Guardian of the Imaginærium Engine."

"Of course," Maggie said sarcastically. "Is there anyone in this town that isn't a helper?" Maggie couldn't keep the bitter edge out of her voice.

"I don't understand, Ma'am. Those of us who are here were sent to protect and provide for you."

"That's crazy." *I'm living a nightmare of lies.*

"Yes, Ma'am. I can understand how you might believe that, but you can be certain that in all these years we have only been concerned for your protection. Nothing else."

"And the Imaginærium Engine."

He tilted his head in a quizzical way and said, "You and the Engine are inseparable, Ma'am. To protect you is to protect the Engine."

"That makes no sense to me."

He wrung his big old hands in distress and complained, "But it's the truth."

"Well, I don't understand any of it." Maggie scowled. "None of this makes any sense. And," she shouted at Mr. Munroe, "I am so *MAD* at you!" Then she looked at Áine and added, "At *all* of you!"

Áine sighed and told her, "Just accept it and move on. You're alive so you know he's not lying about protecting you. If he hadn't been, you'd have been dead a long time ago. Believe me.

"You've already seen them try to kill Vivienne and yourself. That's what you know. So, let's just get on with it. You'll figure the rest out later.

"Life is never what you're told it is. Usually it turns out to be something completely different from what you thought. That's what makes it confusing. And, if it's not confusing, it's usually false."

Maggie sat in the chair fuming. *She's probably right, but I'm still mad at them.*

I don't have to like it though, even if it is true.

They sat in an uncomfortable silence while Maggie slowly cooled off. It took a long time before Áine finally asked her, "Are you going to be alright?"

Maggie sighed. *I feel so tired. So empty.* "Yes, I guess I'm ok."

"Good," Áine looked in the direction of the kitchen and shouted, "because, I'm still waiting for my tea!"

Immediately, Mrs. Smith and Mrs. Munroe bustled out from the kitchen carrying trays of teacups and scones.

Maggie managed to smile. "Just like the ones at Avalon?"

Mrs. Smith nodded her head slightly and smiled.

Maggie turned back to Mr. Munroe as she sipped her tea. "So, all these years you really were more than just the janitor at the courthouse."

Mr. Munroe laughed, which made her feel good for the first time in days. He always had the warmest laugh and the sound of it brightened her mood. Even if she was still mad at him.

At least something from the past was real.

Áine became impatient and interrupted them. "That's all well and good, but as you know we have a horde of Fomoire agents and demons on their way to capture the Engine."

A worried look crossed Mr. Munroe's face. "Yes, Ma'am. There have been scouts in the area for two days now. And there was a twisted spirit here the night that we returned Princess Marguerite to the Otherworlds. A panther spirit."

Áine looked at Maggie and mumbled, "Perhaps that's when they corrupted that boy at the hotel." She quickly turned back to Mr. Munroe and asked, "Do you know if they've turned any of the townspeople?"

He looked down at Mrs. Munroe, "I don't think so. Mrs. Munroe, you get around more than I do. Have you detected anyone being turned?"

Mrs. Munroe looked up at him and said, "I don't believe they have. At least not in any one I've met in town."

I always thought they were an odd pair. He is so giant and she is so tiny. She looked closer at Mr. Munroe. *Wonder if he's related to the brothers' helpers?*

Áine sighed. "That's good to know. I was afraid that they might have turned others in town. One or two we can deal with, but not an entire town."

Mr. Munroe scratched the stubble on his cheek and asked, "How many are expected, Ma'am?"

Áine told him, "A large number of agents with a core group of Fomoire demons and monsters. Ten agents attacked us on the way here, but they were killed. Then two assassins tried to kill Princess Marguerite, but Grainé's sidach interceded and those were eliminated."

Áine sipped some tea before saying, "Princess Marguerite saw two demons in a vision corrupt the boy at the hotel."

Mr. Munroe groaned softly. "That would be Jamison. Sad news." He looked down at his hands as though they might have something on them. Without looking up he said, "A vision, Ma'am? You have foresight?"

"Yes," Maggie said, "but we're going to try to help him. He's not really one of them."

Áine and Mr. Munroe exchanged glances and Áine said, "Of course we are. That's the plan."

Mr. Munroe asked, "The agents on the road, do you have any idea who they were?"

Áine said, "Gangsters out of Fort Worth."

Maggie added, "It was at the Casino."

Mr. Munroe stared at the floor and mumbled, "Probably bootleggers and gamblers from down there on Thunder Road." He rubbed the stubble on his cheek the way he always did when he was thinking. "I heard the Chicago crowd's been down here organizing them a bit. I suspected it was Fomoire agents, but I don't get down that way to know for certain."

Áine shrugged. "They weren't that difficult to handle."

"There will be more coming up the road though." Mr. Munroe closed his eyes and sighed heavily. "These days were bound to come. They always have."

Áine ignored his comment. "So, as the Guardian, what secrets do you have in this place that we can use to defend the Engine?"

Mr. Munroe leaned back in his chair. "The structure is protected by wards. So long as the entries are protected, they will hold the twisted spirits out. If the entries are breached, then they will have access to the tower and the Engine."

Maggie interrupted him, "What are twisted spirits?"

Áine leaned back in her seat and said, "The ones you call demons. We also call them broken or dark spirits. Dark demons sometimes…" Áine swirled the tea in her cup and watched the tea leaves race each other at the bottom, "…but it's all the same thing.

Áine asked Mr. Munroe, "How many entries are there?"

"The four doors on the compass points, those must be protected. The wards will have no effect on the agents though since they're human."

Áine nodded, "Sounds like work for Abarta and the brothers."

Mr. Munroe agreed, "Yes, Ma'am. They should be able to handle the agents. But, if the doors fall, they will take all of us."

Maggie interrupted again, "What's a ward exactly?"

Áine looked at her and slowly said, "A ward. Hmm… hard to describe. Do you have my sister's flute with you?"

"Sure." Maggie took the flute out of her shoulder bag and reluctantly handed it to Áine.

"Don't worry I'm just going to show you what they are. I'll give it back in a second." Áine held up the flute and pointed to one of the carvings. "This is a ward. See? It's linked to the Otherworlds and draws some of its force into this space when *you*, a Tuatha, touch it.

"Each of these wards," Áine pointed to several other carvings on the flute, "is tuned to a different force. You combine them in this space for different purposes. It's like harmonics.

"All forces move at different rates. When you change their harmonics, you can alter the nature of matter."

Maggie had a cynical look. "Ok, so what about the wards on the doors? Nobody touches those. Why do they work?"

Áine paused before saying, "When they are crafted, they're designed to be constantly active. Luke's a master at that. Those wards only do a single thing – in the case of those at the Engine they block the Fomoire, the twisted spirits, from passing them. The ones you call demons. You can combine a group of individual wards to do something. Their purpose is fixed once it is formed. Like writing a sentence.

"Kitchen wards work the same way, except for doing good cooking or something like that. I bet the hotel kitchen has a few of those wards in it."

Maggie scowled. "I never noticed any." *Maybe that's why I had a so-called gift for cooking? Maybe I don't have a gift at all.*

Áine ignored her scowl and continued, "The wards on the flute are only active when a Tuatha enables them. If somebody found this on the street," she held up the flute, "it wouldn't do anything except act like a stick of carved wood. Just like the sideboard at the hotel. It's only a piece of carved furniture unless a Tuatha enables it."

Mr. Munroe interrupted her, "Ma'am, how could the dark ones get past the hotel's wards?"

Áine returned the flute to Maggie and then turned to Mr. Munroe, "I'm not sure. The wards must have been removed or damaged."

345

She stopped and stared at a statue of a horse on the mantle. "Perhaps an agent was able to tamper with them. They would not be affected. Damaged just enough for the demons to be able to enter the place where the boy was sleeping. Yes, that's possible."

Quickly she turned to Mrs. Munroe. "You must go to the courthouse now and check the wards in place there. It's possible they have been damaged. If they are, they must be restored immediately."

Mrs. Munroe lowered her head and softly said, "Of course, Ma'am."

Mr. Munroe slowly stood up and said, "I better go with her. Some of them are placed a bit high."

Áine set her teacup and saucer on the tray. "I imagine so." She stood. "Maggie, we need to return to the hotel now and speak with the others. Mr. Munroe, meet us at the tower when the attack begins. I think it will be best if we join you inside the Engine itself. We will form the last line of defense should the dark ones gain entry."

"Yes, Ma'am. That sounds prudent." Mr. and Mrs. Munroe bowed their heads to the two girls.

As Áine was leaving the house, she paused and told Mrs. Munroe, "Thank you for your hospitality. I

appreciate what you've been able to do here with so little."
Then she smiled. "And the statue of the chestnut mare on
the mantle is *much* appreciated."

Mrs. Munroe bowed her head. "You are kind to
notice, Ma'am. We have been honored by your presence."

Áine paused a moment on the front porch and
breathed deeply. "The air is clean here. Like the
Otherworlds and much better than in the cities."

Maggie nodded. "October air is the best. The winds
shift out of the north. Dry and cold."

With that, they left the Munroe's house and began the
short walk back to the hotel. Howl trotted silently in front
of them.

***

Áine said, "Did you notice that this street is named
Archer? I find that ironic."

Maggie replied, "Why would that be ironic?"

Áine, "An archer is one who shoots arrows. Tonight,
there will be no bows and no arrows. No archers. Guns,
knives, daggers, or worse."

Or worse, like demons. Howl killing people, tearing them into pieces to save us. Yes, much worse.

Áine laughed. "And yet here we are walking on Archer back to the hotel to plan the defense of the Engine. I just think it's ironic that's all."

Maggie replied, "I see. I think."

Howl glanced back at them, while he continued walking toward the hotel.

Áine said, "It's good that you were able to summon Grainé's sídach. He is a fierce defender. The twisted demons have no power over him and he cannot be corrupted."

Maggie asked, "What do they look like? The demons. I thought they were monsters or devils but the ones I saw looked like giant black snakes."

Áine shrugged. "They can manifest in any form they choose. Snakes, bats, panthers, shadows, or monsters, it's their personal preference, really."

Maggie sighed. "So, they could look like anything."

"Pretty much."

"That's just great. So, there's no way of knowing what they look like."

"Don't worry." Áine laughed. "You'll know them when you see them."

Maggie rolled her eyes in exasperation. *More nonsense. Time to change the subject.* "So, how long have the Munroe's been watching over the Engine?"

"Since it was constructed. They've been living quietly here all that time."

Maggie's eyes widened in surprise. "How old are they? The courthouse was built ages ago."

Áine shrugged and said, "They are not my helpers, so I don't know the answer to that. I imagine they are quite ancient."

"What's ancient mean?"

Áine glanced at Maggie. "It's a relative term don't you think? Let's just say that they are very old and let it go at that. It's not polite to discuss people's ages."

Maggie sighed. *Feels like another secret nobody wants to talk about.* "Sure, that's what Grams always tells me when I ask her how old she is.

"How old are you?"

For a moment, Áine looked surprised and then asked, "How old do you think I am?" Then she posed with her head turned in profile.

Maggie studied her. "You could be 16 or maybe 17."

Áine said, "That sounds good. Right, I'm almost 17."

Howl snorted and shook his head.

Áine scowled at him and said, "Must be pollen or something in the wind. Grainé's hounds all have sensitive noses."

Maggie looked at Howl who was smiling. "I think he's laughing."

Áine glanced at the giant hound and frowned. "I think he's just thirsty. Looks like he's panting. When we get back to the hotel, he needs some water. Perhaps he should have gotten some when we were at the Keeper's house."

"He might be hungry too." Maggie looked confused for a second. "I never had a dog or cat before. How often do you feed them?"

"Whenever they ask. Don't worry, your helper will take care of that for you."

Maggie looked back at Mrs. Smith who was following behind her. Mrs. Smith just gave a small nod and a grin.

THANK YOU, MRS. SMITH! I didn't even think about that! He would have starved to death if he was depending on me.

Neither one of them said anything after that. They simply walked down the street to the hotel.

It was quiet in town. Maggie had always wanted something exciting to happen, but, knowing how this day would end, she enjoyed the peace of the moment - while it lasted.

When they reached the town square, Áine said, "Well, that was a nice outing. And it's a beautiful day. Not quite my summer sun, but not yet winter's either.

"I'm glad we didn't spend the morning sitting around in the hotel."

Maggie nodded and agreed, "It was good to get out. Thanks for going with me."

Áine stared at the ornate courthouse with its clock tower. "It was important. We will be prepared to defend the Engine tonight." She paused a moment before saying, "I hadn't heard there was a panther spirt here the night you returned to the Otherworlds.

"How did that happen?"

Maggie admitted, "I didn't see it. Mr. Munroe did."

"Yes. Of course, he would have seen it."

Maggie frowned. *She sounded disappointed.* "He said it was coming down the middle of the street," she pointed in the direction of the old Overland stage coach building, "here. That's why he had to take me to the cavern instead of the hotel."

"If a panther spirit was tracking you, then you were fortunate to escape. The Keeper did well protecting you. I know of only one other who was found by a panther spirit and survived."

"I wouldn't know anything about that."

"That would be one of Bres' high demons. They are relentless killers. They have been in this space for ages. Bres is always trying to destroy us. Revenge, you know." Áine paused a moment before finishing, "Revenge is a powerful force."

"Who's Bres?"

"Just an old has-been Fomoire. A wicked king, he lost to us in a battle. Never got over it."

25 We Look Like a Bunch of Gangsters

Abarta and the others were standing on the porch of the hotel when Maggie and Áine walked up. There was a mix of cars and trucks wandering around town. No one was traveling fast.

Abarta scanned the street and told them, "This is a sleepy little town. I can see why Vivienne placed the Engine..."

Niamh interrupted him, "What did you find out from the Guardian?"

Áine pointed at the courthouse. "There are wards on the entry points. As long as we hold the entries, the Fomoire can't enter. It also means that their agents will attack those points first."

Abarta asked, "The entry points are the doorways?"

Áine gave him an exasperated look and said, "Yes, Abarta. That usually means the doors." She pointed at the courthouse. "There are four of them here, on the compass points."

Maggie told them, "Vivienne says there are five points on a compass."

Only Gee seemed to notice her comment. "What is the fifth point, Princess?"

"The center. She says it's the key point on the compass. The one that makes everything else relevant. And why does everyone keep calling me Princess!"

Gee looked up at the clock tower. "Interesting. The Engine itself is the fifth point. Makes sense, it's the focal point of everyone's efforts today."

Áine ignored the side conversation between Maggie and Gee. "The Guardian is checking the wards now to ensure they have not been compromised. He believes the Fomoire that Maggie saw in her vision corrupted the boy earlier this week. Apparently, the wards at the hotel were damaged in some manner before that. A guest perhaps."

Gee immediately responded, "We should check those. Maggie, why don't you have your helper go with mine to inspect them."

Maggie turned to tell Mrs. Smith, except she was already walking into the hotel with Gee's helper. Maggie shrugged, turned back to Gee, and asked, "How many wards would there be in the hotel?"

"There must be a series of wards on every entry point to the hotel. How many doors are there?"

"Front door, back door, and two side doors."

"I expect that the compromised wards are on one of the side doors. Those are easily missed when the check is done at night."

Niamh asked him, "What did you find at the machine shop?"

"Ah, that was the most fun we've had in days. Made me homesick. An old man named José was there and we talked to him. He remembered the old days, when we shaped metal with hammer and tongs."

Niamh put her hands on her hips and said in an annoyed tone, "But were you able to make anything!"

"Oh sure. We have a few special weapons for tonight. The old man, José, will bring them around this afternoon. He had a good supply of steel."

Abarta looked surprised. "You've already made them?"

"We got them started, but José and his helper will have to complete them. They learn quickly, though."

Áine couldn't contain her curiosity. "What are they exactly? These new weapons."

"Bows and arrows." Gee and the other two brothers were laughing.

Áine and Maggie looked at one another in surprise. Áine couldn't help shouting at Gee, "You're joking!"

Gee grinned broadly. "Not at all! A bit different from what you're imagining, though."

Abarta sneered. "Better be, or this will be a short battle. For us."

The three brothers laughed and slapped each other on the back.

After a minute of laughing, Gee was able to catch his breath long enough to tell him, "It'll be fine, Abarta. Don't worry."

Áine tried to change the topic and asked Abarta, "What did you and Niamh find out in town?"

Niamh said, "Wasn't much of a store, but the clerk was talkative. Told us all about a big night last week when they turned on the new floodlights at the courthouse. Turned the square from dark to day."

Gee said, "That was one of Vivienne's ideas."

Abarta looked startled. "What?"

Nonchalantly, Gee told him, "Installing the floodlights."

Abarta was caught by surprise. "I didn't know about that."

Gee smirked. He seemed to enjoy the moment of knowing about something that Abarta didn't. "It's a new thing. It's not just any light. It's got lots of blue wavelength in it."

Maggie stared at Gee. *It's really weird hearing him talk about wavelengths of light.*

Niamh was puzzled as well. "What's so special about that?"

Gee looked around the little group. It wasn't often that they didn't know something and he did. "The blue wavelength messes with Fomoire ability to focus energy, or elemental forces, if you prefer. The demons and their monsters of course, not the agents. That's why you never see them out during the day. Werewolves, vampires, that lot, and the dark spirits. It's something one of her helpers in Germany discovered. I made the housings for the energy pod."

Áine quietly laughed. "Good for you, Gee! A modern weapon. That helps level out the odds a bit. The agents are the ones we have to be careful of now. The wards don't affect them either."

Gee beamed, "Which is why we made the new weapons today. I don't believe the agents will be any trouble once we get those."

Maggie hadn't seen him so happy before. "I hope they won't be trouble. It's all scary to me."

Abarta said, "Fomoire love terrifying. It's also their greatest weakness, at least in the long run. They'd rather terrify than anything."

Niamh crossed her arms and impatiently tapped her toe on the sidewalk. "I'm getting hungry. Let's go inside and eat lunch."

Maggie asked, "What time is it?"

Áine said, "It's almost noon. Why?"

Maggie said, "She won't have the food ready to serve until noon."

"That's alright," Niamh said. "We'll just sit in the lobby and wait. It can't be much longer."

And, at that, the group left the front porch of the hotel and took up places in the hotel lobby.

As Maggie expected, the helpers remained outside either standing beside the front door or sitting inside the cars. Maggie looked at them. *We aren't dressed in black, but we look like a bunch of gangsters. The sheriff will be over here asking questions before long.*

As she was sitting in one of the armchairs, Mrs. Smith discreetly arrived at her elbow and whispered, "The wards on the side doors have been removed."

Maggie turned to ask her a question, but she had already gone. Instead of asking Mrs. Smith, she told the group about the missing wards and then asked, "How did the wards get there in the first place."

Luke was the wood worker in the group so all of them looked at him. When he saw everyone looking at him, he blushed and told Maggie, "They were placed when the hotel was built. Why do you ask?"

"My great-grandfather built this hotel. How would he know to place wards in the door frames against demons?"

Luke quietly said, "I believe he knew more of the Otherworlds than the fairy tales he passed down to Mrs. Wells. Perhaps she also knows more of the Otherworlds than she has told us."

At that moment, Mrs. Wells opened the door to the dining room and invited the guests inside for dinner.

The members of the group stood to enter the dining room, while Áine pestered Luke with questions about what he meant when he said Maggie's great-grandfather knew about the Otherworlds. It wasn't like Luke to be so mysterious and that piqued everyone's curiosity.

Luke insisted, "Later, when we have time to speculate. Not now."

And that was that.

26 This is Magnus Igne

Maggie and the others in the group were just finishing afternoon tea when Gee's helper arrived with news that the gangsters from Fort Worth had been seen on the highway driving into town. Immediately everyone left the lounge and rushed across the square to the courthouse.

When they reached the courthouse, they found that the helpers had set up large interlocking steel panels across the front of each door and positioned the bundles of new weapons behind them.

Niamh took a look at the preparations and remarked, "Steel walls. Seems like someone was doing more this morning than just making a few new weapons."

Gee sounded serious when he replied, "If it's going to be a long night, we have to live through today."

This time there was no snappy comeback from Niamh.

As agreed, Abarta and his helper took the eastern door while the three brothers with their helpers moved to positions at the other doors.

Earlier in the afternoon, when they planned how to set up the defense, they decided that, since the courthouse was perfectly square, they would be able to cover all sides of it from where they stood at the doors - provided of course that they were able to keep from being killed.

Maggie listened without participating in that discussion. The idea that one or more of them might be killed was upsetting.

Mrs. Smith held the door open for Maggie, Niamh, and Áine to enter the courthouse lobby. Maggie immediately noticed the emptiness and silence of the courthouse. "Where is everyone?"

Mrs. Smith told her, "They are sleeping, Ma'am. Safer for them if they are unaware of what happens now. The other helpers are removing them from the building. It wouldn't do to have any of them injured."

"Thank you, Mrs. Smith." *I know almost everyone that works here.*

"Yes, Ma'am."

Maggie was just getting ready to ask where Mr. Munroe was when the secret door to the clock tower opened and he stepped out.

"It's going to be a tight squeeze in the tower, Ma'am, so you oughta have your helpers wait somewheres else till this is over."

Maggie looked around their little circle and realized he was right. She knew the room was small, large enough for only four or five, certainly not large enough for the helpers, too.

"Mrs. Smith, would you join the other helpers and take them over to the hotel to wait for this to end?"

"Ma'am? Are you sending me away? I can help!"

"I know you can, but Mr. Munroe is right. The room up there is too small for all of us to fit inside, so it would be a bigger help if you could gather the others and have them ready for when this is over. I expect we will especially need your help then."

Mrs. Smith's head drooped and her shoulders sagged.

Maggie impulsively reached out and hugged her for a second. "I know that's probably the wrong thing to do, but I want you to know how much I appreciate you helping me."

"Yes, Ma'am." Mrs. Smith turned and was gone.

Áine and Niamh looked at Maggie as though she had lost her mind and then turned to their helpers. Each one was holding ornately carved wooden boxes.

Áine's was of ebony, and, when she opened its lid, Maggie saw a long-curved dagger inside, nestled in a bed of red silk. Beside it was an ornate necklace with a lapis lazuli stone set in its pendant.

Áine glimpsed her looking at the dagger and, as she lifted it from the silk, told her, "This is *Magnus Igne*. Gee made it for me ages ago. I've also added a few of my own touches to it. It cuts with fire as well as steel."

Maggie automatically stepped back from her. "That's a wicked looking blade."

Áine whirled it around her head and then made a series of high speed slashing moves. "Yes, it has a perfect balance for slashing." Then she took a jewel-covered scabbard from the box and buckled it around her waist. Next, she lifted the necklace from its place in the box and placed it around her neck. Maggie felt as though she was watching a ceremonial preparation. She wanted to ask but didn't. That would have broken the aura of calm that seemed to have wrapped them.

After Áine had buckled the scabbard and placed the necklace around her neck, Niamh opened her mahogany box and withdrew a hunting bow and a quiver of arrows.

Áine rolled her eyes. "A bow and arrows? Why not just use rocks and a slingshot!"

Niamh laughed and told Maggie, "She's just jealous. Luke made this for me a long time ago. This is *Pleiades*. He's one of my favorites. Silent and deadly at ranges

364

farther than this battle will be. I can take them down before Áine ever gets a chance to slice them."

Maggie only counted ten or twelve arrows in the quiver. "What are you going to do when you run out of arrows?"

"What?" For a moment Niamh seemed confused.

"You only have a few arrows. What are you going to do when you've used them up?"

"Oh, I understand now. Actually, they return to the quiver when they come to rest. I don't believe I've ever lost any."

Áine slid *Magnus Igne* into its scabbard and made a discrete motion to the helpers for them to leave. "Let's go. We have to catch up with the Keeper."

As they ran up the stairs, Maggie shouted, "I thought the bad guys were supposed to attack tonight. Not now."

Niamh was at the front of their little group and shouted back, "Yes, this is a surprise."

In between breaths, Áine managed to say, "They probably want to seize the Engine before we can finish preparing to defend it."

Maggie shouted, "There wasn't much to prepare though, since it's only us."

Áine reassured them, "Others are coming to help. They will arrive at dusk."

Maggie was surprised. "Who?"

"Friends, but they are traveling from far away." That was the only thing that Áine would say about them.

Mr. Munroe pushed open the door at the top of the stairs and they stumbled into the observation room under the clock mechanism.

From the tower windows they could see different clouds of dust as groups of cars drove into Ft Richards.

Maggie peered over the edge of the window in time to see the first group of cars arrive, skidding sideways on the clay and caliche road to stop on each side of the courthouse. Before the cars stopped completely, Fomoire agents leapt out and ran towards the courthouse doors while firing pistols, automatic rifles, and submachine guns. The sound of the guns was deafening.

Maggie gripped the edge of the windowsill and crouched.

"That's not going to help, you know." Niamh was standing beside the window next to Maggie shooting arrows at agents who were trying to cross the courthouse lawn. "You can't fight them if you can't see them."

Slowly, Maggie stood. *Maybe they won't shoot up here.*

She looked down where Abarta and the brothers were firing their crossbows at the agents. A few agents were able to take a couple of steps from the cars before steel bolts shot from the brothers' crossbows dropped them. Those who weren't hit by the bolts broke and ran back to the cars. Some tried to use the car doors as shields while they shot at Abarta and the brothers, but the bolts punched through the doors and pinned them to whatever was behind them.

Agent's bullets that missed the steel panels punched holes in the stones around the courthouse doors and those that did hit the panels couldn't punch through them. They only flattened themselves on the steel and rang out like the tower bell.

The noise was deafening.

Maggie watched the chaos below. The bodies of the dead lay scattered around the courthouse grounds. Some were dressed in the black suits that she expected gangsters to wear. Others were wearing rough work shirts and jeans like most of the cowboys around wore. One of the dead was dressed in a ridiculous orange and brown plaid suit. He had to be the man from the Casino. She wasn't sure if she was happy or sad to seeing him lying on the ground below.

Suddenly two Buicks left the carnage.

Maybe they are giving up.

Mr. Munroe was standing by her when they drove away. "Don't get too hopeful just yet, Ma'am. I expect they're just going for more help. They have to take the Engine tonight."

When not masked by the sound of the agents' guns, the bows made an eerie whining sound when they launched their steel bolts. The bolts were made from huge nails the brothers had found at **Murray's Hardware&Feed** and then modified at the machine shop to work with the crossbows.

Nothing the agents had was able to stop them.

The bolts punched holes in their cars and, when a car or an agent didn't stop them, they stuck themselves into the walls of the buildings around the square.

***

The Buicks that left when the first attack failed now returned. Driving fast and stopping short, the cars skidded on the street. The gangsters had gotten their own steel panels and placed those in front of their cars. The brothers' crossbows could not penetrate the gangsters' panels. For a short time, unless there was an opportunity to hit someone, both sides stopped shooting at the other.

Mr. Munroe rubbed the stubble on his cheek the way he always did. "Looks like they figured out how to handle the brothers' new weapons....

"If we are defeated tonight, we must destroy the Engine. You can't let them Fomoire get at it." He looked down at Maggie. "Ma'am, if something happened and I can't, you ought to be the one to do that. Since it belongs to your mother and all."

Maggie was going to protest, "But, I'm just a kid," when Mr. Munroe raised his hand to stop her from saying any more.

"Ma'am, there's more to you than you know. Now let me show you the mechanism that will kill the Engine. Of course, once you kill it, the power for the passageways into the Otherworlds will collapse. You understand?"

Niamh and Áine nodded their heads but said nothing. Maggie glanced from them to Mr. Munroe before saying, "I'm new here. You'll have to explain it to me."

He looked down at her with the saddest expression and said, "You will not be able to return to any of the Otherworlds."

"Ever?"

"That's how I understand it, Ma'am."

Maggie looked out the window at the mob of gangsters gathered below.

Funny to think that I could feel "trapped" in the place where I grew up.

That being trapped here was a bad thing.

That going back to Avalon would be better than living here, with my family. It does seem that way though.

Mr. Munroe interrupted her thoughts, "Here, Ma'am. Let me show you the mechanism before it's too late."

He stepped over to the wall opposite the entrance to the stairs and opened a hidden panel. She had noticed it before as an odd pattern on the wall but had never had a desire to investigate what it was.

People don't see what they aren't interested in finding. One of Vivienne's protections I suppose.

Behind the panel door was a brass lever and beside it a handle.

"It's pretty simple, Ma'am. All you have to do is pull this locking lever down and then pull on the handle to remove the Engine's heart. It's in a glass and brass bound cylinder inside here. Without that, it can't work. And then, once you do that, the Engine mechanism will explode into a million pieces. This whole tower will blast out across town, and what bits of the Engine that are left will be scattered for miles around."

Maggie looked out the window at the open country around them. "If we are here when I destroy the engine, how will we live through that?"

"Well, Ma'am. The only thing you can do is not be up here when that happens. I was told that it takes a moment to explode after you remove its heart."

"I see." *Dying wasn't one of the things I had in mind to do today.*

"Of course, Ma'am. That is only if all else fails. And even then, you will only need to destroy it yourself if I can't. I am the Keeper of the Engine, so it is my duty to protect it and, at the end, to destroy it. The rest of you will need to leave the tower before I remove its heart."

The sound of machine gun fire pulled their attention back to the street below them.

Niamh was watching the crowd below. "It looks like they are trying to rush the doors again. I'll take this side. The three of you help the others."

Áine complained, "She always has to sound like she's the boss. Just because she's the oldest, she thinks she can tell everybody what to do."

Maggie grinned at the sound of their bickering, just as though it was a normal day. Somehow it made her heart feel a bit lighter.

But only a bit.

27 The Engine's Heart

Abarta and the brothers held the gangsters from taking the doors through the afternoon, but in October, dark comes early and fast. By 5PM, dusk set in and the gangsters began to edge their steel walls forward.

Mr. Munroe was watching the change in tactics and pointed it out to the three. "They're coming. The sun is almost gone now and the demons will be loose."

Niamh agreed. "It's going to get really bad now." Then she laughed and said, "As Gee called them, 'That lot'."

Maggie and Áine laughed too. After the long afternoon, it felt good to be able to laugh at something.

Mr. Munroe reached over to a switch mounted on the wall and flipped it. The night outside turned into shades of blue. "That'll help hold them off for a time."

Niamh looked out over the edge of the window at the ground flooded now in pale blue light. "Impressive. I had forgotten about those."

Scattered around them at the edge of the blue light were the bright orange yellow flashes from the guns that the agents were firing.

This would be pretty if it wasn't real.

Suddenly there was a flash of blue and lightning struck one of the agents behind a steel panel.

"Wow! What was that!" Maggie was blinded for a second and she could hear that the gunfire had stopped.

Áine was standing beside a window holding an orb of blue lightning in her left hand. She said, "That was my contribution. It took a few hours for the clouds to arrive."

There was a second strike that hit one of the agent's panels, knocking several of them back beyond the edge of the light.

Surprised, Maggie asked, "Do you control lightening?"

Áine shrugged. "I wouldn't say control. More like I can influence it a bit. In this case, it was easy to persuade the clouds to help us, since these are agents of dark."

"I'm impressed. That stopped the fighting." Maggie leaned over the edge of the window to get a better view.

Mr. Munroe placed one of his giant hands on her arm. "Ma'am don't lean so far out of the window. One of them scum might take a shot at you."

"You're right. I forgot for a second."

"It ain't over yet, Ma'am."

"I know, and yet I'm beginning to believe we can hold the tower."

No sooner had she said that than the door into the clock tower room burst open and Jamison stumbled inside followed by the panther spirit and the two shadow demons that had now transformed from harmless black snakes into large, billowing black cobras.

"Jamison," Maggie screamed, "what are you doing?" She saw him raise their father's shotgun and point it at her.

Jamison didn't say a word as he squeezed the trigger. In the same instant, Mr. Munroe stepped in front of Maggie and the blast from the gun caught him full in the chest, knocked him out of the window, and onto the roof below.

The recoil from the shotgun slammed Jamison back into the wall and he lay stunned on the floor.

In a flurry of red flame and blue electric fire, Áine slashed the shadow demons with *Magnus Igne*. From out of the dark, hawks suddenly flew through the open windows into the tower room and also attacked the shadow demons, ripping at their heads, trying to tear out their eyes. The demons hissed and swirled, striking into the air trying to catch the hawks. It was so crowded in the room that the demons only managed to strike one another, while the hawks flew untouched in and out through the open windows.

While Áine and the hawks attacked the shadow demons, the panther spirit turned on Maggie, slashing at her with its giant claws extended like knives. Maggie immediately slammed the panther with a force that knocked it into the wall next to Jamison. The panther lunged for her again, this time ripping its claws across her right shoulder.

When the tower door first opened to let the demons into the room, Niamh managed to slip behind them and now slammed it closed. The rest of the demon horde, shrieking and screaming, was temporarily trapped on the staircase.

Downstairs, Abarta and the three brothers were fighting the agents, who were now advancing across the courthouse grounds, and the demons that were now behind them inside the courthouse.

Niamh, who was trying to dodge poisoned spikes being shoved by demons through the tower door, shouted down to them, "We need some help up there!"

Downstairs Abarta shouted back, "Sorry, I'm a little busy down here. How are the rest of you guys doing?"

Gee yelled, "We have Fomoire behind us now. Wasn't planning on that!"

Luke shouted out, "My helper is injured."

After a tense moment, CR yelled, "No better over here."

The tower room was a mad house of action. Niamh was fighting to keep the horde trapped in the staircase by holding the door. Áine was slashing the shadows with *Magnus Igne* while her hawks continued ripping at their heads. By now the shadow demons were ripped and covered in their own black blood. The hawks had blinded one of them, so it was simply thrashing about the room hoping to kill something by luck.

Maggie, who was now covered in blood flowing from her arm, blasted the panther again, knocking it into the wall. Jamison was trying to stand and raise the shotgun when the panther fell on top of him.

The demons blocked in the stairway splintered the door with the poisoned spikes and managed to stab Niamh several times. The shadow demons were still striking at Áine and, even though she was unhurt, she was tired. The hawks were unable to tear away the second demon's eyes and it was closing in on her.

Niamh and Áine looked at each other and nodded in silent agreement before shouting at Maggie, "That's it. We're done. Remove the Engine's heart while we hold the demons."

Before the panther could rise again, Maggie opened the panel to pull the lever, but couldn't raise her right arm. The panther had managed to rip the muscles in it when it slashed her. Instead, she lifted her left arm and used it to pull the lever that Mr. Munroe had shown her.

She yelled, "Áine and Niamh! You have to leave before I remove the heart."

Niamh shouted back, "You will die!"

Tears began to run down Maggie's cheeks. She shouted back, "There's nothing else we can do."

Áine yelled, "Alright then. On two!"

Niamh shouted, "One" and Áine shouted "Two!"

Niamh released what was left of the door and jumped with Áine through the window into the dark.

As they leaped from the windows, Maggie sent out a blast of power across the tower room that knocked the panther and the snakes to the floor. Without Niamh to secure it, the shattered door to the secret stairway burst open. Tentacles, claws, and long bone fingers from the different demons crowed behind it scrambled to grab the edge of the doorframe and pull themselves inside. Their shrieks and groans came up from the stairway in a rolling wave of horror.

Maggie pulled the handle and slipped the brass and glass canister out of its socket in the engine. In that moment, as the first rumble ripped through the engine, Howl bounded up out of the stairway, over the heads of the demons, faster than they could react, grabbed the collar of Maggie's coat and then leaped with her out of the window and away from the tower.

As the first giant ball of fire tore the tower apart, Howl landed on the roof below with Maggie dangling from his jaws. He quickly made a second great leap from the roof to the ground and pulled her across the street to shelter behind one of the gangster's Buicks.

A second blast ripped the Engine into flaming shreds of brass shrapnel. Some of the shrapnel peppered the surrounding buildings in the square while the rest of it arced out over the rooftops in flaming tracers, like fireworks, to land in the countryside for miles around.

The fire from the tower spread down onto the roof and in minutes the courthouse was a flaming mass so hot that the stone blocks forming its walls cracked and then crumbled, unable to hold weight.

Shrieks and screams from the demons trapped inside the Engine's inferno filled the night. Trapped in the narrow space of the stairway, there was no escape.

Maggie staggered to her feet, still clutching the canister that held the heart of the Engine. She lifted the canister up to get a better look at it in the light from the flames. The rubies inside it still pulsed in glowing light.

*It **is** like a heart. And it's still alive.*

Howl nuzzled her under the chin to make sure that she was alright and she hugged his neck. "I hope that was ok." He didn't seem to mind. "That's twice in two days you saved my life."

As the demons died and the courthouse began to collapse, the remaining gangsters ran to their cars, dragging their dead with them. As soon as they could get their cars started, they raced out of town as quickly as they had raced into it.

As Maggie watched the escaping agents, she spotted the panther spirit loping across the burning courthouse lawn to slip away into the dark. It was dragging something with it.

Jamison. He's still alive.

***

Flames from the courthouse soared into the sky. They could be seen for miles around.

One by one the members of the group and their helpers drifted across the burning ground to stand beside Maggie and the giant hound. All of them were exhausted and wounded. Mr. Munroe and one of Luke's helpers were dying and lay on the ground, while Mrs. Smith tried to tend to them.

Abarta and the three brothers were wounded, but no broken bones, punctured organs, or severed arteries. They would live.

Niamh was walking with a limp. "I sprained my ankle when we jumped off of the roof."

Áine explained, "We were too heavy for the hawks to carry so we sort of fell. Luckily I landed on Niamh!"

Maggie stood beside the white hound, one hand lightly on his neck. It was reassuring to have him close. Her other arm dangled uselessly beside her, with the muscles in it torn by the panther spirit's claws.

Niamh, doubled over in pain from the demons' poison, whispered, "Maggie, how did the demons get inside the courthouse?"

Maggie glanced at her and then quickly looked away. "Jamison guided them through a secret passage into the basement. From there they were able to reach the stairs into the tower."

Niamh looked surprised. "How do you know that?"

"I saw it when I hit the panther with that blast. It just came to me, like one of those dreams. With everything happening so fast, I didn't have time to think about it. It makes sense now, though. He knew how to open the hidden door."

Niamh nodded her head. "Yep, makes sense. Say, what about that blast you sent out. Did you know you could do that?"

Áine grinned. "And *how* were you able to do that?"

"I had no idea what I was doing. I was so terrified. I think my brain just went a little crazy or something."

Áine sighed. "Glad it did. Are you feeling ok?"

"A little queasy. Kind of shaky." Maggie paused. Howl remained standing beside her while they talked but was still watching the dark for threats. She looked at him and said, "Howl saved me again. That's twice now."

Áine watched Maggie and Howl with a strange expression. "Looks like you're a team now. My sister will be pleased to know."

Maggie wasn't sure what she meant by team, and was going to ask her what she meant, when Mr. Munroe groaned and her attention quickly shifted to him.

"Mr. Munroe!" Maggie knelt on the ground beside him. "Thank you." She held his big old hand and he gave hers a gentle squeeze.

"Ma'am. Sorry I wasn't able to stay 'til the end. Afraid I missed your big show."

"Just rest, Mr. Munroe." Maggie smiled down at him and said, "Thank you for watching over me all these years."

He closed his eyes and she wasn't sure if he had heard her or not. He was still alive, but only barely. His breathing was fast and shallow. Mrs. Smith looked at her with a worried expression.

"What can we do for him, Mrs. Smith?"

"Ma'am, if we were able, we would return him to Avalon. In this place though, I don't know what we can do. He's a tough one. Maybe he will survive."

Maggie stared at the Engines heart she still carried. It continued to pulse. "Can we make another Engine? The heart is still working."

Áine walked up in time to hear Maggie ask about making a new Engine. "The helper could. The one you call Mr. Munroe. He helped build this one."

"He said somebody named William Williams built it."

"That was just the building."

"So, we might be able to…"

"If the helper survives."

Maggie glanced at Mrs. Smith who was cleaning and bandaging his wounds. "If anyone can save him, she will."

The group had collected around Mr. Munroe when Mrs. Wells ran out into the street from the hotel shaking her fists at them and screaming hysterically over and over, "What have you done! What have you done!"

Gee and CR's helpers quickly caught Mrs. Wells before she could hurt anyone.

She screamed at them, "You destroyed our town!"

Even though the giants had a firm grip on her, Maggie was worried that she might slip away.

Áine smirked. "Kind of freaked out isn't she." Then she paused and looked at the burning building. "Maggie, why don't you put out the fire now? All of the demons are dead."

Maggie turned to her. "What do you mean?"

"Your mother's realm is water and I have a huge set of clouds gathered here." She pointed up above them.

Maggie looked into the dark at the thundercloud shapes silhouetted by flashes of lightning that still crackled across the sky. "But *you* brought the clouds."

"Yes, but I don't do rain remember? Summer goddess, you know. That's sun not rain." She held up her hand so that the ball of blue energy in it lit the area around them. "See?"

"Oh, yeah. Right." Maggie stared at one of the clouds above the courthouse fire and frowned.

That one feels like it could burst.

And raindrops began to fall from it. Slowly at first and then in a flood of heavy sheets of rain until it drowned the flames in the courthouse and returned night to the town square.

Mrs. Wells was standing beside Maggie still shouting that they were criminals, they should be arrested, and other things that Maggie found absolutely embarrassing to hear her saying.

When Mrs. Wells began accusing them of being Nazi spies, Maggie couldn't take it any more…

"You are not my mother."

What a horrible thing to say. That just slipped out.

But it's true.

And, with that, Marguerite turned her back on the shouting woman and walked inside the hotel. As she walked away, Marguerite called over her shoulder, "Mrs. Wells, in case you want to know, it was Jamison that helped the demons. Not us. He's been corrupted."

The giant hound, Howl, walked silently beside her, inspecting the faces of everyone around her, looking for any sign of threat.

The rest of the group followed Marguerite into the hotel, leaving Mrs. Wells standing alone in the street.

28 Don't Stop for Anything!

The sound of sirens was coming from all roads around them.

Maggie stood with the others in the hotel lobby, blood dripping from her dangling right arm onto the floor. "What are we going to do now?"

Áine motioned to the helpers to load the cars. "We're going to get out of here before we get arrested." She motioned to the helpers to load the cars. "We can go to my place. It's in Kentucky and safe. Once we get there we can decide."

Abarta agreed. "That's a plan. For now, that's a start. Later I'll go on to New York from there."

Luke's helper carried the sideboard from the hotel dining room to a pickup truck parked in the street.

Maggie started to protest, but Luke raised his hand and interrupted her. "This is one of Vivienne's pieces. I made it for her ages ago. It belongs to you now and we need it if we are to save your injured helper."

Maggie waved her left hand towards the truck. "By all means. Let's take it." In spite of everything, she felt happy for the first time in days.

Gee and CRs helpers carried Mr. Munroe to the pickup truck and carefully placed him in the back on a mattress that they had taken from the hotel. He was so large, it was difficult getting him wedged in beside the sideboard. Somehow, they managed.

Mrs. Munroe climbed in beside him and the other helpers covered them with blankets.

Their breath made fog in the cold night air.

Mrs. Smith climbed into the Packard with Maggie and Howl and the Packard's started their engines. Mrs. Smith had started cleaning and bandaging Maggie's injured shoulder when suddenly Maggie stuck her head out of the window and shouted, "Áine, do we know how to get there?"

Áine laughed and shouted back, "Just take the road heading east and don't stop for anything!"

***

Mrs. Wells and Lorenda stood on the front porch of the hotel and watched the Packards and the stolen pickup truck leave the town square on the highway headed east.

Mrs. Wells hugged Lorenda to her and kissed the top of her head. Tears were in her eyes when she said, "That was the hardest thing I've ever had to do."

Lorenda looked up into her mother's face and asked, "What's happened to Jamison?"

"The shadow demons claimed him." She breathed heavily for a moment and closed her eyes before saying, "After all of the generations keeping watch, and, in the end, it was one of us who betrayed the trust...

"You and I will have to make this right."

"Yes, Ma'am."

"At least Maggie is safe, and these years were not wasted. I was so proud of her today."

The taillights of the cars disappeared into the dark.

Mrs. Wells let out a long, tired sigh and said, "Let's go inside now and decide what can be done to save this mess.

I think I need a good cup of tea and a nice scone. Would you like one too?"

"Yes, Ma'am."

Mrs. Wells hugged her daughter one more time and then they went inside.......

Epilogue

6AM ... before I left for NY

Next thing I knew somebody was shaking my shoulder saying, "It's time to go. You'll have to wait till next time you're here to read more."

My head was on the open book and I was drooling a little. That was embarrassing. I sat up really quick and wiped my mouth on my sleeve. I must have dropped off. That was the first time I ever did that reading a book. Of course, up to that point I didn't read books much if I could help it.

It took a minute for my eyes to focus, and I didn't actually remember where I was until I saw Grandmother looking at me. Then it all came back.

"We have to go now, or you'll miss your flight."

"Who wrote the book? Is it about you? Us? What happened to…," I was trying to ask a bunch of questions about the book all at once when she stopped me.

"If I told you, then that'd ruin it."

"What about being in danger? What kind of danger? Is this real or make-believe?"

"You've started reading the book. You'll know when you sense it, but I suspect you already know if it's real or make-believe. Now come on. I got to get you to the airport. I already have your bags in the truck."

"What about breakfast?"

"I packed something for you. You can eat while I drive."

And that was the end of my visit this summer.

I had a million questions, but she wouldn't answer any of them, so we just rode to the airport in silence. My mind was going crazy thinking about Fomoire. It couldn't be real. If it was, and I now knew about them, then what would they do?

Grandmother parked her truck at the airport lot and walked with me inside the terminal. All the time I kept looking around me just in case something might happen like to Vivienne at the train station. Everything seemed normal and nothing happened.

Grandmother kept her hand on my shoulder the entire time we were walking. Normally I would hate that, but this morning I didn't mind.

"Grandmother, you have to tell me. Am I really in danger?"

She looked down at me, her old face frowned a moment and then she had a thin smile when she said, "Yes, dear there is always danger, and yet we go about our work every day knowing that there is risk and preparing for what might come."

"Preparing? How? I don't know anything. I'm just a kid."

"Maggie said that too. That's why you must learn if you are to survive. Learn everything you can."

"There's a kungfu place in a strip-mall down the street."

That's when she laughed out loud. It seemed like everyone in the terminal turned around to look at the old woman who'd lost her mind. I could have melted into the floor.

"That's not going to stop Fomoire, boy. You have to learn how to use the forces of the universe to battle those demons."

That really freaked me out because there's no place you can go to learn that kind of stuff.

She patted me on the arm about that time. I guess I didn't look so good.

"Don't worry, boy. You always have to start with the basics. Everybody starts out at Level 1, where you are now.

They don't teach you this in school. They're focused on stuff like making government objectives or achieving administrative goals…"

She got real mad for a bit and stopped talking. I'd never seen her look like that before, but it didn't last long.

"So, you have to start on your own. This is life or death. It's not a pretty game that *you* are going to have to play. Here's a book that will get you started."

She handed me a book called *Deviate*, by a guy named Beau Lotto. That sounded cool.

"And, when you've read this one, I'll send you the next one. You learn what's in these, and I mean *learn* not just seen the words. You have to understand what it means first and then I'll teach you more. You only have a couple of years to master the lore, so don't play around thinking it's make-believe. It's real." She touched the scar across her throat. "Trust me, grandson."

And then she hugged me before I went through the security checkpoint and she was left behind.

I was nervous all the way back to JFK. But I finished the first chapter of *Deviate* before we landed.

Notes from the Characters

Abarta

I have to admit that I'm a bit of a trickster, and sometimes stories about me are confused as to which side I'm on, Fomoire or Tuatha. I prefer to party and tell jokes so the confusion about me is perfect from my point of view. After all, these are only stories that people make up about us and all of them have errors. I'm not a deity like Goibniu or a king or prince. I'm a bit of a sorcerer, but the important thing to me is that people like to hang with me and I know how to have fun. I'm not looking for fame, just a good time

Áine (pronounced Ah-nah)

I'm the Irish goddess of summer and wealth. As the deity of midsummer and the sun, I can influence the growth of crops and the animals. Sometimes I choose to appear as a red mare.

Bres

My father was Elatha, a Fomoire prince, but my mother was Eriu, a Tuatha De goddess of war. After Nuada's hand was cut off, I became the king of the

Tuatha. I had some trouble with them. They said I was
cruel, almost evil to hear it from some of them. After seven
years, that weasel Creidhne crafted a silver hand for Nuada
so that they could restore him as king and exile me. I asked
my father to help me become king again but he wouldn't
help me. I've been fighting to regain control ever since that
time. I will not give up!

Clíodhna (pronounced Klee–oh-na)

I'm a Queen of the Banshees or fairy women and I'm
noted for being beautiful – quite different from the usual
image of banshees that are popular now. The banshees are
noted primarily for announcing the coming death of
someone in the family that they watch over. Banshees are
the guardian spirits for them. But I'm also a goddess of
love and beauty. I don't dress in rags and wander around
the fairy mounds wailing in the night! I have three
exotically colored birds that love to eat the apples from
Vivienne's realm. Their songs can heal sick.

Creidhne (pronounced Crey-nya)

I'm a goldsmith of the Tuatha Dé, but in the old times
also worked with bronze and brass.

One of the things I did that made me famous was help
craft the silver hand for King Nuada. His hand was cut off

during a battle and, according to the rules of the Tuatha, he could not remain the king without it. So it was important that he had it replaced. I made him a bionic hand and really cool, but later it was replaced by a regenerated biological hand. That's a story by itself. Old man Bres hates me because of that.

Goibniu (pronounced Gov-nuh)

I'm a smith and I also help with the Tuatha's feasts. CR, Luke, and I make the weapons for the Tuatha Dé. I'm also the brewmaster for the Tuatha and drinking my mead restores health and immortality. My feasts protect the Tuatha Dé from sickness and old age. That's about it. I don't talk much. Not like Abarta.

Luchtaine

I'm the carpenter or wright of the Tuatha Dé. I don't get a lot of press like my brothers but my work is important too. It's hard to top making a hand for the king like Creidhne did or brewing the drink that makes us immortal like Goibniu does. But everyone that works with wood knows me. Along with my three brothers, we are called the three gods of art. Except, art for us is more like crafts.

Niamh (pronounced Nee-af)

I'm one of the Queens of Tir na nÓg. The thing about me that most people know is that I'm an equestrian. My horse, Embarr, is able to cross between this world and the Otherworlds. While I'm not considered to be a deity like Áine, I am respected for my influence among the Tuatha. After all, I am a Queen of Tir na nÓg.

Tuatha Dé

Tuatha is an Old Irish word. It means people, tribe, or nation. The word Dé means god, gods, goddess, or supernatural beings.

The Tuath Dé live in the Otherworlds but enter the human world and interact with humans. Each member of the Tuath Dé is associated with one or more specific aspects of existence or nature. Their eternal, mortal opponents are the Fomoire.

Vivienne

I am also known as The Lady of the Lake and referred to by different spellings of the names Nimue or Vivienne. My name Nimue is related to Mneme and is a shortened form of Mnemosyne. I was one of the nine water-nymph Muses of Roman and Greek Mythology who gave weapons to Perseus. I do that over the eons. I gave Arthur his sword and others wer given weapons as well to fight the broken ones.,. Vivienne is the Celtic form of my name. It's a version of Co-Vianna, which was itself a variation of Coventina. That's my Celtic name. I've had many names.

Notes from the author

When I began reworking the original piece, I discovered
(thanks to my workshop with Marissa) that the mother and her
son were not the poor grieving widow and child that I had first
imagined. Instead, they were sinister characters, possibly even ...
vampires. They were certainly creepy enough.

That was an important change to the original storyline. I'd
never told Hannah bedtime stories about vampires.

Months later, when I discovered that Maggie was a changeling,
the pieces of the narrative began to fall into place. I began to
understand that the characters in the piece were
connected to Irish mythology.

I grew up hearing stories of brownies and fairies ... Aunt
Peggy always told us stories at night of the brownies who would
come and clean the kitchen while we were asleep. Wishful
thinking on her part, perhaps. But for me they were real -
a gift from my small fraction of Irish DNA, I guess.

* * *

If you are familiar with Greek mythology, you'll find that Irish
mythology is very different. For one thing, there is no ancient, original
written or historical record of Irish mythology. What does exist
are several collections of ancient stories and poems compiled by
Catholic monks in the middle ages. There are no surviving written
records of stories and poems prior to these collections.
The question that I ask myself is, without written records, who

were the sources for the collections? Compared to ancient Greece, the middle ages was not very long ago.

(Annála Rioghachta Éireann. Annals of the Kingdom of Ireland by the Four Masters, from the earliest period to the year 1616 1856), (Lebor Gabála Érenn n.d.)

What complicates things for the written Irish mythology is that it is essentially a record of a prehistoric oral tradition that was told from one person to another, one family to the next, and one village to the next. It did not have a single cohesive structure until it was collected by the monks. The arrangement and shadings of the stores were determined by the scribes and can't be relied on as genuine expressions of the original tellers beliefs. There is a difference between telling a story and writing it down.

In ancient Ireland, there were no city-states such as Athens or capital cities such as Rome to bind the belief system into a coherent unified structure. The life of each ancient village and town was unique and unto itself.

Consequently, in writing about Irish gods and goddesses it's not really clear how ancient Irish peoples viewed them. We know the monks' views from their writing but not the ancient people's views. For instance, how do we view the Tuatha? Are they deities or are they just super people? It is not clear in the collections what role they serve. Part of the inconsistency might come from the layering of similar myths from one group of invaders over the top of the previous group's. The mashup of oral traditions from separate cultural groups could have produced a much less structured and often contradictory mythology than that of Greece and Rome.

To my delight, I found that this less prescriptive mythology allowed me to take a fresh view of the Tuatha, the Fomoire, and their relationship to humans.

The questions in this cosmology (thanks to workshop) that I had were:

- Are they Gods in the sense that we think of gods -powerful omnipotent beings?

- Are they Super humans or heroes?

- Are they Supernatural forces?

I won't tell you what I've come to believe. That be a spoiler for rest of the books!

In the mythology, the structure of the Otherworlds and how it relates to the world that we live in is murky. The Otherworlds are portrayed in the stories as foreign lands either across the water or to the north and are reached by vessels or magical horses. The fairies, when they are defeated are driven underground and live somewhere under the surface of this world.

When viewing the ancient narratives from a 21st century perspective, it's best to understand them as narratives of reality told in the conceptual language of teller's time - the only language available to the prehistoric tellers.

That's my entry point for this work...

403

This is not a reimagining of the mythology; it's a re-expression of the ancient reality through the conceptual language of today.

* * *

At the end, in the closing piece, the grandmother tells her grandson that he needs to learn how to control the forces of the universe. Even though this might sound like fantasy, the forces of the universe are real. They are around us all of the time – unless we happen to be living in some alternate space!

Gravity is a force of the universe that we are aware of - but generally we accept it without understanding what it is. The other three forces are labeled as weak forces, electromagnetic forces, and strong forces. Sounds simple? But to control them!

The Grandmother is right - the objective of learning science concepts is to understand how the forces of the universe work!

So, while this is a work of fiction, it's fundamentally grounded in the reality that we experience each day. Grounding fantasy and myth in our daily reality was one of the challenges in creating this work.

The books referenced in this piece are real and the ideas presented here are drawn from the following bibliography. You can use it to begin your own quest to seeing the past and to learning how to control the forces of the universe - our future depends on it[1]

Bibliography

Annála Rioghachta Éireann. Annals of the Kingdom of Ireland by the Four Masters, from the earliest period to the year 1616. 7 vols. Dublin: Royal Irish Academy, 1856.

Burroughs, Edgar Rice. *John Carter of Mars: A Princess of Mars, The Gods of Mars, The Warlord of Mars (Library of Wonder).* Sterling, 2009.

Hawking, Stephen. *A Brief History of Time.* Bantam, 1998.

Lebor Gabála Érenn. n.d.

Lebor Laignech. n.d.

Lotto, Beau. *Deviate: The Science of Seeing Differently.* Hachette Books, 2017.

The Ancient Irish Epic Tale Táin Bó Cúalnge. Gutenburg Press, 2005.

Woolf, Virginia. *To the Lighthouse.* Mariner Books, 2005.

Brief bio of the author...

Clifford Wayne received his MFA in writing from the University of San Francisco. Born in Canton, Mississippi, he grew up in La Place, Louisiana. He has lived most of his adult life in Texas and California. He now resides in Alabama with his wife Theresa and their Afghan Hounds, Howl and Niki.

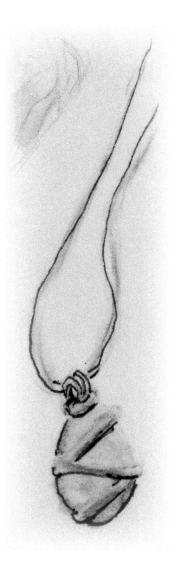

Lightning Source UK Ltd.
Milton Keynes UK
UKHW03f1957240518
323178UK00001B/6/P